KU-594-288

DEDICATION

If I were hanged on the highest hill,
  Mother o' mine, O mother o' mine!
I know whose love would follow me still,
  Mother o' mine, O mother o' mine!

If I were drowned in the deepest sea,
  Mother o' mine, O mother o' mine!
I know whose tears would come down to me,
  Mother o' mine, O mother o' mine!

If I were damned of body and soul,
I know whose prayers would make me whole,
  Mother o' mine, O mother o' mine!

PREFACE

THIS is the story of *The Light that Failed* as it was originally conceived by the Writer.

RUDYARD KIPLING

CHAPTER I

So we settled it all when the storm was done
    As comfy as comfy could be ;
And I was to wait in the barn, my dears,
    Because I was only three,
And Teddy would run to the rainbow's foot,
    Because he was five and a man—
And that's how it all began, my dears,
    And that's how it all began !

Big Barn Stories.

'WHAT do you think she'd do if she caught us? We oughtn't to have it, you know,' said Maisie.

'Beat me, and lock you up in your bedroom,' Dick answered, without hesitation. ' Have you got the cartridges ? '

'Yes ; they're in my pocket, but they're joggling horribly. Do pin-fire cartridges go off of their own accord ? '

'Don't know. Take the revolver, if you are afraid, and let me carry them.'

'I'm *not* afraid.' Maisie strode forward swiftly, a hand in her pocket and her chin in the air. Dick followed with a small pin-fire revolver.

The children had discovered that their lives would be unendurable without pistol-practice. After much forethought and self-denial, Dick had

1

saved seven shillings and sixpence, the price of a badly constructed Belgian revolver. Maisie could only contribute half a crown to the syndicate for the purchase of a hundred cartridges. 'You can save better than I can, Dick,' she explained; 'I like nice things to eat, and it doesn't matter to you. Besides, boys ought to do these things.'

Dick grumbled a little at the arrangement, but went out and made the purchases, which the children were then on their way to test. Revolvers did not lie in the scheme of their daily life as decreed for them by the guardian who was incorrectly supposed to stand in the place of a mother to these two orphans. Dick had been under her care for six years, during which time she had made her profit of the allowances supposed to be expended on his clothes, and, partly through thoughtlessness, partly through a natural desire to pain,—she was a widow of some years anxious to marry again,—had made his days burdensome on his young shoulders. Where he had looked for love, she gave him first aversion and then hate. Where he growing older had sought a little sympathy, she gave him ridicule. The many hours that she could spare from the ordering of her small house she devoted to what she called the home-training of Dick Heldar. Her religion, manufactured in the main by her own intelligence and a keen study of the Scriptures, was an aid to her in this matter. At such times as she herself was not personally displeased with Dick, she left him to understand that he had a heavy account to settle with his Creator; wherefore Dick learned to loathe his God as intensely as he loathed Mrs. Jennett; and this is not a wholesome frame of mind for the young. Since she chose to regard him as a hopeless liar, when dread of pain drove him to his first untruth, he naturally developed into a liar, but an economical and self-contained one, never throwing away the least unnecessary fib, and never hesitating at the blackest, were it only plausible, that might make his life a little easier. The treatment taught him at least the power of living alone,— a power that was of service to him when he went to a public school and the boys laughed at his clothes, which were poor in quality and much mended. In the holidays he returned to the teachings of Mrs. Jennett, and, that the chain of discipline might not be weakened by association with the world, was generally beaten, on one count or another, before he had been twelve hours under her roof.

The autumn of one year brought him a companion in bondage, a long-haired, grey-eyed little atom, as self-contained as himself, who moved about the house silently, and for the first few weeks spoke only to the goat that was her chiefest friend on earth and lived in the back-garden. Mrs. Jennett objected to the goat on the grounds that he was un-Christian,—which he certainly was. 'Then,' said the atom, choosing her words very deliberately, 'I shall write to my lawyer-peoples and tell them that you are a very bad woman. Amomma is mine, mine, mine!' Mrs.

Jennett made a movement to the hall, where certain umbrellas and canes stood in a rack. The atom understood as clearly as Dick what this meant. ' I have been beaten before,' she said, still in the same passionless voice ; ' I have been beaten worse than you can ever beat me. If you beat me I shall write to my lawyer-peoples and tell them that you do not give me enough to eat. I am not afraid of you.' Mrs. Jennett did not go into the hall, and the atom, after a pause to assure herself that all danger of war was past, went out, to weep bitterly on Amomma's neck.

Dick learned to know her as Maisie, and at first mistrusted her profoundly, for he feared that she might interfere with the small liberty of action left to him. She did not, however ; and she volunteered no friendliness until Dick had taken the first steps. Long before the holidays were over, the stress of punishment shared in common drove the children together, if it were only to play into each other's hands as they prepared lies for Mrs. Jennett's use. When Dick returned to school, Maisie whispered, ' Now I shall be all alone to take care of myself; but,' and she nodded her head bravely, ' I can do it. You promised to send Amomma a grass collar. Send it soon.' A week later she asked for that collar by return of post, and was not pleased when she learned that it took time to make. When at last Dick forwarded the gift she forgot to thank him for it.

Many holidays had come and gone since that day, and Dick had grown into a lanky hobbledehoy more than ever conscious of his bad clothes. Not for a moment had Mrs. Jennett relaxed her tender care of him, but the average canings of a public school—Dick fell under punishment about three times a month—filled him with contempt for her powers. ' She doesn't hurt,' he explained to Maisie, who urged him to rebellion, ' and she is kinder to you after she has whacked me.' Dick shambled through the days unkept in body and savage in soul, as the smaller boys of the school learned to know, for when the spirit moved him he would hit them, cunningly and with science. The same spirit made him more than once try to tease Maisie, but the girl refused to be made unhappy. ' We are both miserable as it is,' said she. ' What is the use of trying to make things worse? Let's find things to do, and forget things.'

The pistol was the outcome of that search. It could only be used on the muddiest foreshore of the beach, far away from bathing-machines and pier-heads, below the grassy slopes of Fort Keeling. The tide ran out nearly two miles on that coast, and the many-coloured mud-banks, touched by the sun, sent up a lamentable smell of dead weed. It was late in the afternoon when Dick and Maisie arrived on their ground, Amomma trotting patiently behind them.

' Mf! ' said Maisie, sniffing the air. ' I wonder what makes the sea so smelly. I don't like it.'

' You never like anything that isn't made just for you,' said Dick bluntly. ' Give me the cart-

ridges, and I'll try first shot. How far does one
of these little revolvers carry?'

'Oh, half a mile,' said Maisie promptly. 'At
least it makes an awful noise. Be careful with
the cartridges; I don't like those jagged stick-up
things on the rim. Dick, do be careful.'

'All right. I know how to load. I'll fire at
the breakwater out there.'

He fired, and Amomma ran away bleating.
The bullet threw up a spurt of mud to the right
of the weed-wreathed piles.

'Throws high and to the right. You try,
Maisie. Mind, it's loaded all round.'

Maisie took the pistol and stepped delicately
to the verge of the mud, her hand firmly closed
on the butt, her mouth and left eye screwed up.
Dick sat down on a tuft of bank and laughed.
Amomma returned very cautiously. He was
accustomed to strange experiences in his afternoon
walks, and, finding the cartridge-box unguarded,
made investigations with his nose. Maisie fired,
but could not see where the bullet went.

'I think it hit the post,' she said, shading her
eyes and looking out across the sailless sea.

'I know it has gone out to the Marazion bell-
buoy,' said Dick, with a chuckle. 'Fire low and
to the left; then perhaps you'll get it. Oh,
look at Amomma!—He's eating the cartridges!'

Maisie turned, the revolver in her hand, just
in time to see Amomma scampering away from
the pebbles Dick threw after him. Nothing is
sacred to a billy-goat. Being well fed and the
adored of his mistress, Amomma had naturally

swallowed two loaded pin-fire cartridges. Maisie hurried up to assure herself that Dick had not miscounted the tale.

'Yes, he's eaten two.'

'Horrid little beast! Then they'll joggle about inside him and blow up, and serve him right. . . . Oh, Dick! have I killed you?'

Revolvers are tricky things for young hands to deal with. Maisie could not explain how it had happened, but a veil of reeking smoke separated her from Dick, and she was quite certain that the pistol had gone off in his face. Then she heard him sputter, and dropped on her knees beside him, crying, 'Dick, you aren't hurt, are you? I didn't mean it.'

'Of course you didn't,' said Dick, coming out of the smoke and wiping his cheek. 'But you nearly blinded me. That powder stuff stings awfully.' A neat little splash of grey lead on a stone showed where the bullet had gone. Maisie began to whimper.

'Don't,' said Dick, jumping to his feet and shaking himself. 'I'm not a bit hurt.'

'No, but I might have killed you,' protested Maisie, the corners of her mouth drooping. 'What should I have done then?'

'Gone home and told Mrs. Jennett.' Dick grinned at the thought; then, softening, 'Please don't worry about it. Besides, we are wasting time. We've got to get back to tea. I'll take the revolver for a bit.'

Maisie would have wept on the least encouragement, but Dick's indifference, albeit his hand was shaking as he picked up the pistol, restrained her. She lay panting on the beach while Dick methodically bombarded the break-water. ' Got it at last ! ' he exclaimed, as a lock of weed flew from the wood.

' Let me try,' said Maisie imperiously. ' I'm all right now.'

They fired in turns till the rickety little re-volver nearly shook itself to pieces, and Amomma the outcast—because he might blow up at any moment—browsed in the background and won-dered why stones were thrown at him. Then they found a balk of timber floating in a pool which was commanded by the seaward slope of Fort Keeling, and they sat down together before this new target.

' Next holidays,' said Dick, as the now thor-oughly fouled revolver kicked wildly in his hand, ' we'll get another pistol, — central fire, — that will carry farther.'

' There won't be any next holidays for me,' said Maisie. ' I'm going away.'

' Where to ? '

' I don't know. My lawyers have written to Mrs. Jennett, and I've got to be educated some-where, — in France, perhaps, — I don't know where ; but I shall be glad to go away.'

' I shan't like it a bit. I suppose I shall be left. Look here, Maisie, is it really true you're going? Then these holidays will be the last I shall see anything of you ; and I go back to school next week. I wish——'

The young blood turned his cheeks scarlet.

Maisie was picking grass-tufts and throwing them down the slope at a yellow sea-poppy nodding all by itself to the illimitable levels of the mud-flats and the milk-white sea beyond.

' I wish,' she said, after a pause, ' that I could see you again some time. You wish that too? '

' Yes, but it would have been better if—if— you had—shot straight over there—down by the breakwater.'

Maisie looked with large eyes for a moment. And this was the boy who only ten days before had decorated Amomma's horns with cut-paper ham-frills and turned him out, a bearded derision, among the public ways ! Then she dropped her eyes : this was not the boy.

' Don't be stupid,' she said reprovingly, and with swift instinct attacked the side-issue. ' How selfish you are ! Just think what I should have felt if that horrid thing had killed you ! I'm quite miserable enough already.'

' Why? Because you're going away from Mrs. Jennett? '

' No.'

' From me, then? '

No answer for a long time. Dick dared not look at her. He felt, though he did not know, all that the past four years had been to him, and this the more acutely since he had no knowledge to put his feelings in words.

' I don't know,' she said. ' I suppose it is.'

' Maisie, you must know. *I*'m not supposing.'

' Let's go home,' said Maisie weakly.

But Dick was not minded to retreat.

'I can't say things,' he pleaded, 'and I'm awfully sorry for teasing you about Amomma the other day. It's all different now, Maisie, can't you see? And you might have told me that you were going, instead of leaving me to find out.'

'You didn't. I did tell. Oh, Dick, what's the use of worrying?'

'There isn't any; but we've been together years and years, and I didn't know how much I cared.'

'I don't believe you ever did care.'

'No, I didn't; but I do,—I care awfully now. Maisie,' he gulped,—'Maisie, darling, say you care too, please.'

'I do; indeed I do; but it won't be any use.'

'Why?'

'Because I am going away.'

'Yes, but if you promise before you go. Only say—will you?' A second 'darling' came to his lips more easily than the first. There were few endearments in Dick's home or school life; he had to find them by instinct. Dick caught the little hand blackened with the escaped gas of the revolver.

'I promise,' she said solemnly; 'but if I care, there is no need for promising?'

'And you do care?' For the first time in the past few minutes their eyes met and spoke for them who had no skill in speech. . . .

'Oh, Dick, don't! please don't! It was all right when we said good-morning; but now it's all different!' Amomma looked on from afar. He had seen his property quarrel frequently, but he had never seen kisses exchanged before. The yellow sea-poppy was wiser, and nodded its head approvingly. Considered as a kiss, that was a failure, but since it was the first, other than those demanded by duty, in all the world that either had ever given or taken, it opened to them new worlds, and every one of them glorious, so that they were lifted above the consideration of any worlds at all, especially those in which tea is necessary, and sat still, holding each other's hands and saying not a word.

' You can't forget now,' said Dick at last. There was that on his cheek that stung more than gunpowder.

' I shouldn't have forgotten anyhow,' said Maisie, and they looked at each other and saw that each was changed from the companion of an hour ago to a wonder and a mystery they could not understand. The sun began to set, and a night-wind thrashed along the bents of the fore-shore.

' We shall be awfully late for tea,' said Maisie. ' Let's go home.'

' Let's use the rest of the cartridges first,' said Dick; and he helped Maisie down the slope of the fort to the sea, — a descent that she was quite capable of covering at full speed. Equally gravely Maisie took the grimy hand. Dick bent forward clumsily; Maisie drew the hand away, and Dick blushed.

' It's very pretty,' he said.

' Pooh ! ' said Maisie, with a little laugh of gratified vanity. She stood close to Dick as he loaded the revolver for the last time and fired over the sea, with a vague notion at the back of his head that he was protecting Maisie from all the evils in the world. A puddle far across the mud caught the last rays of the sun and turned into a wrathful red disc. The light held Dick's attention for a moment, and as he raised his revolver there fell upon him a renewed sense of the miraculous, in that he was standing by Maisie who had promised to care for him for an indefinite length of time till such date as—— A gust of the growing wind drove the girl's long black hair across his face as she stood with her hand on his shoulder calling Amomma 'a little beast,' and for a moment he was in the dark,—a darkness that stung. The bullet went singing out to the empty sea.

'Spoilt my aim,' said he, shaking his head. 'There aren't any more cartridges; we shall have to run home.' But they did not run. They walked very slowly, arm in arm. And it was a matter of indifference to them whether the neglected Amomma with two pin-fire cartridges in his inside blew up or trotted beside them; for they had come into a golden heritage and were disposing of it with all the wisdom of all their years.

'And I shall be——' quoth Dick valiantly. Then he checked himself: 'I don't know what I shall be. I don't seem to be able to pass any exams., but I can make awful caricatures of the masters. Ho! ho!'

'Be an artist, then,' said Maisie. 'You're

always laughing at my trying to draw; and it will do you good.'

'I'll never laugh at anything you do,' he answered. 'I'll be an artist, and I'll do things.'

'Artists always want money, don't they?'

'I've got a hundred and twenty pounds a year of my own. My guardians tell me I'm to have it when I come of age. That will be enough to begin with.'

'Ah, I'm rich,' said Maisie. 'I've got three hundred a year all my own when I'm twenty-one. That's why Mrs. Jennett is kinder to me than she is to you. I wish, though, that I had somebody that belonged to me,—just a father or a mother.'

'You belong to me,' said Dick, 'for ever and ever.'

'Yes, we belong—for ever. It's very nice.' She squeezed his arm. The kindly darkness hid them both, and, emboldened because he could only just see the profile of Maisie's cheek with the long lashes veiling the grey eyes, Dick at the front door delivered himself of the words he had been boggling over for the last two hours.

'And I—love you, Maisie,' he said, in a whisper that seemed to him to ring across the world,—the world that he would to-morrow or the next day set out to conquer.

There was a scene, not, for the sake of discipline, to be reported, when Mrs. Jennett would have fallen upon him, first for disgraceful unpunctuality, and secondly, for nearly killing himself with a forbidden weapon.

' I was playing with it, and it went off by itself,'
said Dick, when the powder-pocked cheek could
no longer be hidden, ' but if you think you're
going to lick me you're wrong. You are never
going to touch me again. Sit down and give me
my tea. You can't cheat us out of that, anyhow.'

Mrs. Jennett gasped and became livid. Maisie
said nothing, but encouraged Dick with her eyes,
and he behaved abominably all that evening.
Mrs. Jennett prophesied an immediate judgment
of Providence and a descent into Tophet later,
but Dick walked in Paradise and would not hear.
Only when he was going to bed Mrs. Jennett
recovered and asserted herself. He had bidden
Maisie good-night with down-dropped eyes and
from a distance.

' If you aren't a gentleman you might try to
behave like one,' said Mrs. Jennett spitefully.
' You've been quarrelling with Maisie again.'

This meant that the usual good-night kiss had
been omitted. Maisie, white to the lips, thrust
her cheek forward with a fine air of indifference,
and was duly pecked by Dick, who tramped out
of the room red as fire. That night he dreamed
a wild dream. He had won all the world and
brought it to Maisie in a cartridge-box, but she
turned it over with her foot, and, instead of
saying, ' Thank you,' cried :—

' Where is the grass collar you promised for
Amomma ? Oh, how selfish you are ! '

CHAPTER II

Then we brought the lances down, then the bugles blew,
When we went to Kandahar, ridin' two an' two,
   Ridin', ridin', ridin', two an' two,
    Ta-ra-ra-ra-ra-ra-ra,
All the way to Kandahar, ridin' two an' two.
              Barrack-Room Ballad.

' I'm not angry with the British public, but I wish we had a few thousand of them scattered among these rocks. They wouldn't be in such a hurry to get at their morning papers then. Can't you imagine the regulation householder— Lover of Justice, Constant Reader, Paterfamilias, and all that lot—frizzling on hot gravel?'

' With a blue veil over his head, and his clothes in strips. Has any man here a needle? I've got a bit of sugar-sack.'

' I'll lend you a packing-needle for six square inches of it then. Both my knees are worn through.'

' Why not six square acres, while you're about it? But lend me the needle, and I'll see what I can do with the selvage. I don't think there's enough to protect my royal body from the cold blast as it is. What are you doing with that everlasting sketch-book of yours, Dick?'

'Study of our Special Correspondent repairing his wardrobe,' said Dick gravely, as the other man kicked off a pair of sorely worn riding-breeches and began to fit a square of coarse canvas over the most obvious open space. He grunted disconsolately as the vastness of the void developed itself.

'Sugar-bags, indeed! Hi! you pilot-man there! Lend me all the sails of that whale-boat.'

A fez-crowned head bobbed up in the stern-sheets, divided itself into exactly halves with one flashing grin, and bobbed down again. The man of the tattered breeches, clad only in a Norfolk jacket and a grey flannel shirt, went on with his clumsy sewing, while Dick chuckled over the sketch.

Some twenty whale-boats were nuzzling a sandbank which was dotted with English soldiery of half-a-dozen corps, bathing or washing their clothes. A heap of boat-rollers, commissariat-boxes, sugar-bags, and flour- and small-arm-ammunition-cases showed where one of the whale-boats had been compelled to unload hastily; and a regimental carpenter was swearing aloud as he tried, on a wholly insufficient allowance of white lead, to plaster up the sun-parched gaping seams of the boat herself.

'First the bloomin' rudder snaps,' said he to the world in general; 'then the mast goes; an' then, s' 'elp me, when she can't do nothin' else, she opens 'erself out like a cock-eyed Chinese lotus.'

'Exactly the case with my breeches, whoever you are,' said the tailor, without looking up. 'Dick, I wonder when I shall see a decent shop again.'

There was no answer, save the incessant angry murmur of the Nile as it raced round a basalt-walled bend and foamed across a rock-ridge half a mile up-stream. It was as though the brown weight of the river would drive the white men back to their own country. The indescribable scent of Nile mud in the air told that the stream was falling and that the next few miles would be no light thing for the whale-boats to overpass. The desert ran down almost to the banks, where, among grey, red, and black hillocks, a camel-corps was encamped. No man dared even for a day lose touch of the slow-moving boats; there had been no fighting for weeks past, and throughout all that time the Nile had never spared them. Rapid had followed rapid, rock rock, and island-group island-group, till the rank and file had long since lost all count of direction and very nearly of time. They were moving somewhere, they did not know why, to do something, they did not know what. Before them lay the Nile, and at the other end of it was one Gordon, fighting for the dear life, in a town called Khartoum. There were columns of British troops in the desert, or in one of the many deserts; there were columns on the river; there were yet more columns waiting to embark on the river;

there were fresh drafts waiting at Assiut and
Assuan; there were lies and rumours running
over the face of the hopeless land from Suakin to
the Sixth Cataract, and men supposed generally
that there must be some one in authority to
direct the general scheme of the many move-
ments. The duty of that particular river-column
was to keep the whale-boats afloat in the water,
to avoid trampling on the villagers' crops when
the gangs 'tracked' the boats with lines thrown
from midstream, to get as much sleep and food
as was possible, and, above all, to press on without delay in the teeth of the churning Nile.

With the soldiers sweated and toiled the correspondents of the newspapers, and they were
almost as ignorant as their companions. But it
was above all things necessary that England at
breakfast should be amused and thrilled and
interested, whether Gordon lived or died, or half
the British army went to pieces in the sands.
The Sudan campaign was a picturesque one, and
lent itself to vivid word-painting. Now and again
a 'Special' managed to get slain,—which was
not altogether a disadvantage to the paper that
employed him,—and more often the hand-to-
hand nature of the fighting allowed of miraculous
escapes which were worth telegraphing home at
eighteenpence the word. There were many correspondents with many corps and columns,—
from the veterans who had followed on the heels
of the cavalry that occupied Cairo in '82, what
time Arabi Pasha called himself king, who had
seen the first miserable work round Suakin when

the sentries were cut up nightly and the scrub swarmed with spears, to youngsters jerked into the business at the end of a telegraph-wire to take the place of their betters killed or invalided.

Among the seniors—those who knew every shift and change in the perplexing postal arrangements, the value of the seediest, weediest Egyptian garron offered for sale in Cairo or Alexandria, who could talk a telegraph-clerk into amiability and soothe the ruffled vanity of a newly appointed Staff-officer when Press regulations became burdensome—was the man in the flannel shirt, the black-browed Torpenhow. He represented the Central Southern Syndicate in the campaign, as he had represented it in the Egyptian war, and elsewhere. The syndicate did not concern itself greatly with criticisms of attack and the like. It supplied the masses, and all it demanded was picturesqueness and abundance of detail; for there is more joy in England over a soldier who insubordinately steps out of square to rescue a comrade than over twenty generals slaving even to baldness at the gross details of transport and commissariat.

He had met at Suakin a young man, sitting on the edge of a recently abandoned redoubt about the size of a hat-box, sketching a clump of shell-torn bodies on the gravel plain.

' What are you for? ' said Torpenhow. The greeting of the correspondent is that of the commercial traveller on the road.

' My own hand,' said the young man, without looking up. ' Have you any tobacco? '

Torpenhow waited till the sketch was finished, and when he had looked at it said, ' What's your business here?'

' Nothing. There was a row, so I came. I'm supposed to be doing something down at the painting-slips among the boats, or else I'm in charge of the condenser on one of the water-ships. I've forgotten which.'

' You've cheek enough to build a redoubt with,' said Torpenhow, and took stock of the new acquaintance. ' Do you always draw like that?'

The young man produced more sketches. ' Row on a Chinese pig-boat,' said he sententiously, showing them one after another.—' Chief mate dirked by a comprador.—Junk ashore off Hakodate.—Somali muleteer being flogged.— Star-shell bursting over camp at Berbera.—Slavedhow being chased round Tajurrah Bay.—Soldier lying dead in the moonlight outside Suakin,— throat cut by Fuzzies.'

' H'm!' said Torpenhow, ' can't say I care for Verestchagin-and-water myself, but there's no accounting for tastes. Doing anything now, are you?'

' No. I'm amusing myself here.'

Torpenhow looked at the aching desolation of the place. ' Faith, you've queer notions of amusement. Got any money?'

' Enough to go on with. Look here: do you want me to do war work?'

' *I* don't. My syndicate may, though. You can draw more than a little, and I don't suppose you care much what you get, do you?'

' Not this time. I want my chance first.'

Torpenhow looked at the sketches again, and nodded. ' Yes, you're right to take your first chance when you can get it.'

He rode away swiftly through the Gate of the Two War-Ships, rattled across the causeway into the town, and wired to his syndicate, ' Got man here, picture-work. Good and cheap. Shall I arrange? Can do letterpress with sketches.'

The man on the redoubt sat swinging his legs and murmuring, ' I knew the chance would come, sooner or later. By Gad, they'll have to sweat for it if I come through this business alive ! '

In the evening Torpenhow was able to announce to his friend that the Central Southern Agency was willing to take him on trial, paying expenses for three months. ' And, by the way, what's your name?' said Torpenhow.

' Heldar. Do they give me a free hand?'

' They've taken you on chance. You must justify the choice. You'd better stick to me. I'm going up-country with a column, and I'll do what I can for you. Give me some of your sketches taken here, and I'll send 'em along.' To himself he said, ' That's the best bargain the Central Southern has ever made ; and they got *me* cheaply enough.'

So it came to pass that, after some purchase of horse-flesh and arrangements financial and political, Dick was made free of the New and Honourable Fraternity of war-correspondents, who all possess the inalienable right of doing as much work as they can and getting as much for it as Providence and their owners shall please. To these things are added in time, if the brother be worthy, the power of glib speech that neither man nor woman can resist when a meal or a bed is in question, the eye of a horse-coper, the skill of a cook, the constitution of a bullock, the digestion of an ostrich, and an infinite adaptability to all circumstances. But many die before they attain to this degree, and the past-masters in the craft appear for the most part in dress-clothes when they are in England, and thus their glory is hidden from the multitude.

Dick followed Torpenhow wherever the latter's fancy chose to lead him, and between the two they managed to accomplish some work that almost satisfied themselves. It was not an easy life in any way, and under its influence the two were drawn very closely together, for they ate from the same dish, they shared the same water-bottle, and, most binding tie of all, their mails went off together. It was Dick who managed to make gloriously drunk a telegraph-clerk in a palm hut far beyond the Second Cataract, and, while the man lay in bliss on the floor, possessed himself of some laboriously acquired exclusive information, forwarded by a confiding correspondent of an opposition syndicate, made a careful duplicate of the matter, and brought the result to Torpenhow, who said that all was fair in love or war - correspondence, and built an excellent descriptive article from his rival's riotous waste of words. It was Torpenhow who—

but the tale of their adventures, together and apart, from Philae to the waste wilderness of Herawi and Muella, would fill many books. They had been penned into a square side by side, in deadly fear of being shot by over-excited soldiers; they had fought with baggage-camels in the chill dawn; they had jogged along in silence under blinding sun on indefatigable little Egyptian horses; and they had floundered on the shallows of the Nile when the whale-boat in which they had found a berth chose to hit a hidden rock and rip out half her bottom-planks.

Now they were sitting on the sand-bank, and the whale-boats were bringing up the remainder of the column.

'Yes,' said Torpenhow, as he put the last rude stitches into his over-long-neglected gear, 'it has been a beautiful business.'

'The patch or the campaign?' said Dick. 'Don't think much of either, myself.'

'You want the *Eurylas* brought up above the Third Cataract, don't you? and eighty-one-ton guns at Jakdul? Now, *I*'m quite satisfied with my breeches.' He turned round gravely to exhibit himself, after the manner of a clown.

'It's very pretty. Specially the lettering on the sack. G. B. T.—Government Bullock Train. That's a sack from India.'

'It's my initials,—Gilbert Belling Torpenhow. I stole the cloth on purpose. What the mischief are the camel-corps doing yonder?' Torpenhow shaded his eyes and looked across the scrub-strewn gravel.

A bugle blew furiously, and the men on the bank hurried to their arms and accoutrements.

' "Pisan soldiery surprised while bathing," ' remarked Dick calmly. ' D'you remember the picture? It's by Michael Angelo. All beginners copy it. That scrub's alive with enemy.'

The camel-corps on the bank yelled to the infantry to come to them, and a hoarse shouting down the river showed that the remainder of the column had wind of the trouble and was hastening to take share in it. As swiftly as a reach of still water is crisped by the wind, the rock-strewn ridges and scrub-topped hills were troubled and alive with armed men. Mercifully, it occurred to these to stand far off for a time, to shout and gesticulate joyously. One man even delivered himself of a long story. The camel-corps did not fire. They were only too glad of a little breathing-space, until some sort of square could be formed. The men on the sand-bank ran to their side; and the whale-boats, as they toiled up within shouting distance, were thrust into the nearest bank and emptied of all save the sick and a few men to guard them. The Arab orator ceased his outcries, and his friends howled.

' They look like the Mahdi's men,' said Torpenhow, elbowing himself into the crush of the square. ' But what thousands of 'em there are! The tribes hereabout aren't against us, I know.'

' Then the Mahdi's taken another town,' said Dick, ' and set all these yelping devils free to chaw us up. Lend us your glass.'

' Our scouts should have told us of this.

We've been trapped,' said a subaltern. ' Aren't the camel-guns ever going to begin? Hurry up, you men ! '

There was no need for any order. The men flung themselves panting against the sides of the square, for they had good reason to know that whoso was left outside when the fighting began would very probably die in an extremely unpleasant fashion. The little hundred-and-fifty-pound camel-guns posted at one corner of the square opened the ball as the square moved forward by its right to get possession of a knoll of rising ground. All had fought in this manner many times before, and there was no novelty in the entertainment: always the same hot and stifling formation, the smell of dust and leather, the same boltlike rush of the enemy, the same pressure on the weakest side of the square, the few minutes of desperate hand-to-hand scuffle, and then the silence of the desert, broken only by the yells of those whom the handful of cavalry attempted to pursue. They had grown careless. The camel-guns spoke at intervals, and the square slouched forward amid the protests of the camels. Then came the attack of three thousand men who had not learned from books that it is impossible for troops in close order to attack against breech-loading fire. A few dropping shots heralded their approach, and a few horsemen led, but the bulk of the force was naked humanity, mad with rage, and armed with the spear and the sword. The instinct of the desert, where there is always much war, told them that the right flank of the square was the weakest, for they swung clear of the front. The camel-guns shelled them as they passed, and opened for an instant lanes through their midst, most like those quick-closing vistas in a Kentish hop-garden seen when the train races by at full speed ; and the infantry fire, held till the opportune moment, dropped them in close-packed hundreds. No civilised troops in the world could have endured the hell through which they came, the living leaping high to avoid the dying who clutched at their heels, the wounded cursing and staggering forward, till they fell— a torrent black as the sliding water above a mill-dam—full on the right flank of the square. Then the line of the dusty troops and the faint blue desert sky overhead went out in rolling smoke, and the little stones on the heated ground and the tinder-dry clumps of scrub became matters of surpassing interest, for men measured their agonised retreat and recovery by these things, counting mechanically and hewing their way back to chosen pebble and branch. There was no semblance of any concerted fighting. For aught the men knew, the enemy might be attempting all four sides of the square at once. Their business was to destroy what lay in front of them, to bayonet in the back those who passed over them, and, dying, to drag down the slayer till he could be knocked on the head by some avenging gun-butt. Dick waited quietly with Torpenhow and a young doctor till the stress became unendurable. There was no hope of attending to the wounded till the attack was repulsed, so the three moved forward gingerly towards the weakest side. There was a rush from without, the short *hough-hough* of the stabbing spears, and a man on a horse, followed by thirty or forty others, dashed through, yelling and hacking. The right flank of the square sucked in after them, and the other sides sent help. The wounded, who knew that they had but a few hours more to live, caught at the enemy's feet and brought them down, or, staggering to a discarded rifle, fired blindly into the scuffle that raged in the centre of the square. Dick was conscious that somebody had cut him violently across his helmet, that he had fired his revolver into a black, foam-flecked face which forthwith ceased to bear any resemblance to a face, and that Torpenhow had gone down under an Arab whom he had tried to 'collar low,' and was turning over and over with his captive, feeling for the man's eyes. The doctor was jabbing at a venture with a bayonet, and a helmet-less soldier was firing over Dick's shoulder. The flying grains of powder stung his cheek. It was to Torpenhow that Dick turned by instinct. The representative of the Central Southern Syndicate had shaken himself clear of his enemy, and rose, wiping his thumb on his trousers. The Arab, both hands to his forehead, screamed aloud, then snatched up his spear and rushed at Torpenhow, who was panting under shelter of Dick's revolver. Dick fired twice, and the man dropped limply. His upturned face lacked one eye. The musketry-fire redoubled, but cheers mingled with it. The rush had failed and, the

enemy were flying. If the heart of the square
were a shambles, the ground beyond was a
butcher's shop. Dick thrust his way forward
between the maddened men. The remnant of
the enemy were retiring, as the few—the very
few—English cavalry rode down the laggards.

Beyond the lines of the dead, a broad blood-
stained Arab spear cast aside in the retreat lay
across a stump of scrub, and beyond this again
the illimitable dark levels of the desert. The sun
caught the steel and turned it into a savage red
disc. Some one behind him was saying, ' Ah,
get away, you brute ! ' Dick raised his revolver
and pointed towards the desert. His eye was
held by the red splash in the distance, and the
clamour about him seemed to die down to a very
far-away whisper, like the whisper of a level sea.
There was the revolver and the red light, . . .
and the voice of some one scaring something
away, exactly as had fallen somewhere before,—
probably in a past life. Dick waited for what
should happen afterwards. Something seemed to
crack inside his head, and for an instant he stood
in the dark,—a darkness that stung. He fired
at random, and the bullet went out across the
desert as he muttered, ' Spoilt my aim. There
aren't any more cartridges. We shall have to
run home.' He put his hand to his head and
brought it away covered with blood.

' Old man, you're cut rather badly,' said Torpenhow. ' I owe you something for this business.
Thanks. Stand up ! I say, you can't be sick
here ! '

Dick had fallen stiffly on Torpenhow's shoulder, and was muttering something about aiming low and to the left. Then he sank to the ground and was silent. Torpenhow dragged him off to a doctor, and sat down to work out an account of what he was pleased to call 'a sanguinary battle, in which our arms had acquitted themselves,' etc.

All that night, when the troops were encamped by the whale-boats, a black figure danced in the strong moonlight on the sand-bar and shouted that Gordon the accursed one was dead,—was dead,—was dead,—that two steamers were rock-staked on the Nile outside the city, and that of all their crews there remained not one; and Gordon was dead,—was dead,—was dead!

But Torpenhow took no heed. He was watching Dick, who was calling aloud to the restless Nile for Maisie,—and again Maisie!

'Behold a phenomenon,' said Torpenhow, rearranging the blanket. 'Here is a man, presumably human, who mentions the name of one woman only. And I've seen a good deal of delirium, too.—Dick, here's some fizzy drink.'

'Thank you, Maisie,' said Dick.

CHAPTER III

So he thinks he shall take to the sea again
For one more cruise with his buccaneers,
To singe the beard of the King of Spain,
And capture another Dean of Jaen
And sell him in Algiers.

LONGFELLOW.

THE Sudan campaign and Dick's broken head
had been some months ended and mended, and
the Central Southern Syndicate had paid Dick a
certain sum on account for work done, which
work they were careful to assure him was not
altogether up to their standard. Dick heaved the
letter into the Nile at Cairo, cashed the draft in
the same town, and bade a warm farewell to
Torpenhow at the station.

'I am going to lie up for a while and rest,'
said Torpenhow. 'I don't know where I shall
live in London, but if God brings us to meet,
we shall meet. Are you staying here on the off-
chance of another row? There will be none till
the Southern Sudan is reoccupied by our troops.
Mark that. Good-bye; bless you. Come back
when your money's spent; and give me your
address.'

Dick loitered in Cairo, Alexandria, Ismailia, and Port Said,—especially Port Said. There is iniquity in many parts of the world, and vice in all, but the concentrated essence of all the iniquities and all the vices in all the continents finds itself at Port Said. And through the heart of that sand-bordered hell, where the mirage flickers day long above the Bitter Lakes, move, if you will only wait, most of the men and women you have known in this life. Dick established himself in quarters more riotous than respectable. He spent his evenings on the quay, and boarded many ships, and saw very many friends, — gracious Englishwomen with whom he had talked not too wisely in the veranda of Shepheard's Hotel, hurrying war-correspondents, skippers of the contract troop-ships employed in the campaign, Army officers by the score, and others of less reputable trades. He had choice of all the races of the East and West for studies, and the advantage of seeing his subjects under the influence of strong excitement at the gaming-tables, saloons, dancing-hells, and elsewhere. For recreation there was the straight vista of the Canal, the blazing sands, the procession of shipping, and the white hospitals where the English soldiers lay. He strove to set down in black and white and colour all that Providence sent him, and when that supply was ended sought about for fresh material. It was a fascinating employment, but it ran away with his money, and he had drawn in advance the hundred and twenty pounds to which he was entitled yearly. ' Now I shall have

to work and starve!' thought he, and was addressing himself to this new fate when a mysterious
telegram arrived from Torpenhow in England,
which said, 'Come back quick. You have
caught on. Come.'

A large smile overspread his face. ' So soon!
that's good hearing,' said he to himself. ' There
will be an orgy to-night. I'll stand or fall by
my luck. Faith, it's time it came!' He de-
posited half of his funds in the hands of his well-
known friends Monsieur and Madame Binat, and
ordered himself a Zanzibar dance of the finest.
Monsieur Binat was shaking with drink, but
Madame smiled sympathetically :—

' Monsieur needs a chair, of course, and of
course Monsieur will sketch : Monsieur amuses
himself strangely.'

Binat raised a blue-white face from a cot in the
inner room. ' I understand,' he quavered. ' We
all know Monsieur. Monsieur is an artist, as I
have been.' Dick nodded. ' In the end,' said
Binat, with gravity, ' Monsieur will descend alive
into Hell, as I have descended.' And he
laughed.

' You must come to the dance, too,' said Dick ;
' I shall want you.'

' For my face? I knew it would be so. For
my face? My God! And for my degradation
so tremendous! I will not. Take him away.
He is a devil. Or at least do thou, Céleste,
demand of him more.' The excellent Binat began
to kick and scream.

' All things are for sale in Port Said,' said

Madame. ' If my husband comes it will be so much more. Eh, 'ow you call—'alf a sovereign.'

The money was paid, and the mad dance was held at night in a walled courtyard at the back of Madame Binat's house. The lady herself, in faded mauve silk always about to slide from her yellow shoulders, played the piano, and to the tin-pot music of a Western waltz the naked Zanzibari girls danced furiously by the light of kerosene lamps. Binat sat upon a chair and stared with eyes that saw nothing, till the whirl of the dance and the clang of the rattling piano stole into the drink that took the place of blood in his veins, and his face glistened. Dick took him by the chin brutally and turned that face to the light. Madame Binat looked over her shoulder and smiled with many teeth. Dick leaned against the wall and sketched for an hour, till the kerosene lamps began to smell, and the girls threw themselves panting on the hard-beaten ground. Then he shut his book with a snap and moved away, Binat plucking feebly at his elbow. ' Show me,' he whimpered. ' I too was once an artist, even I ! ' Dick showed him the rough sketch. ' Am I that ? ' he screamed. ' Will you take that away with you and show all the world that it is I,—Binat ? ' He moaned and wept.

' Monsieur has paid for all,' said Madame. ' To the pleasure of seeing Monsieur again.'

The courtyard gate shut, and Dick hurried up the sandy street to the nearest gambling-hell, where he was well known. ' If the luck holds, it's an omen ; if I lose, I must stay here.' He placed his money picturesquely about the board, hardly daring to look at what he did. The luck held. Three turns of the wheel left him richer by twenty pounds, and he went down to the shipping to make friends with the captain of a decayed cargo-steamer, who landed him in London with fewer pounds in his pocket than he cared to think about.

A thin grey fog hung over the city, and the streets were very cold; for summer was in England.

' It's a cheerful wilderness, and it hasn't the knack of altering much,' Dick thought, as he tramped from the Docks westward. ' Now, what must I do? '

The packed houses gave no answer. Dick looked down the long lightless streets and at the appalling rush of traffic. ' Oh, you rabbit-hutches ! ' said he, addressing a row of highly respectable semi-detached residences. ' Do you know what you've got to do later on? You have to supply me with men-servants and maid-servants,'—here he smacked -his lips,—' and the peculiar treasure of kings. Meantime I'll get clothes and boots, and presently I will return and trample on you.' He stepped forward energetic-ally ; he saw that one of his shoes was burst at the side. As he stooped to make investigations, a man jostled him into the gutter. ' All right,' he said. ' That's another nick in the score. I'll jostle you later on.'

Good clothes and boots are not cheap, and

Dick left his last shop with the certainty that he would be respectably arrayed for a time, but with only fifty shillings in his pocket. He returned to streets by the Docks, and lodged himself in one room, where the sheets on the bed were almost audibly marked in case of theft, and where nobody seemed to go to bed at all. When his clothes arrived he sought the Central Southern Syndicate for Torpenhow's address, and got it, with the intimation that there was still some money owing to him.

'How much?' said Dick, as one who habitually dealt in millions.

'Between thirty and forty pounds. If it would be any convenience to you, of course we could let you have it at once; but we usually settle accounts monthly.'

'If I show that I want anything now, I'm lost,' he said to himself. 'All I need I'll take later on.' Then, aloud, 'It's hardly worth while; and I'm going into the country for a month, too. Wait till I come back, and I'll see about it.'

'But we trust, Mr. Heldar, that you do not intend to sever your connection with us?'

Dick's business in life was the study of faces, and he watched the speaker keenly. 'That man means something,' he said. 'I'll do no business till I've seen Torpenhow. There's a big deal coming.' So he departed, making no promises, to his one little room by the Docks. And that day was the seventh of the month, and that month, he reckoned with awful distinctness, had thirty-one days in it!

It is not easy for a man of catholic tastes and healthy appetites to exist for twenty-four days on fifty shillings. Nor is it cheering to begin the experiment alone in all the loneliness of London. Dick paid seven shillings a week for his lodging, which left him rather less than a shilling a day for food and drink. Naturally, his first purchase was of the materials of his craft; he had been without them too long. Half a day's investigation and comparison brought him to the conclusion that sausages and mashed potatoes, two-pence a plate, were the best food. Now sausages once or twice a week for breakfast are not unpleasant. As lunch, even, with mashed potatoes, they become monotonous. As dinner they are impertinent. At the end of three days Dick loathed sausages, and, going forth, pawned his watch to revel on sheep's head, which is not as cheap as it looks, owing to the bones and the gravy. Then he returned to sausages and mashed potatoes. Then he confined himself entirely to mashed potatoes for a day, and was unhappy because of pains in his inside. Then he pawned his waistcoat and his tie, and thought regretfully of money thrown away in times past. There are few things more edifying unto Art than the actual belly-pinch of hunger, and Dick in his rare walks abroad—he did not care for exercise, it raised desires that could not be satisfied—found himself dividing mankind into two classes,—those who looked as if they might give him something to eat, and those who looked otherwise. ' I never knew what I had to learn about the human face before,' he thought; and, as a reward for his humility, Providence caused a cab-driver at a sausage-shop where Dick fed that night to leave half eaten a great chunk of bread. Dick took it,—would have fought all the world for its possession,—and it cheered him.

The month dragged through at last, and, nearly prancing with impatience, he went to draw his money. Then he hastened to Torpenhow's address and smelt the smell of cooking meats all along the corridors of the chambers. Torpenhow was on the top floor, and Dick burst into his room, to be received with a hug which nearly cracked his ribs, as Torpenhow dragged him to the light and spoke of twenty different things in the same breath.

' But you're looking tucked up,' he concluded.

' Got anything to eat?' said Dick, his eye roaming round the room.

' I shall be having breakfast in a minute. What do you say to sausages?'

' No, anything but sausages! Torp, I've been starving on that accursed horseflesh for thirty days and thirty nights.'

' Now what lunacy has been your latest?'

Dick spoke of the last few weeks with unbridled speech. Then he opened his coat; there was no waistcoat below. ' I ran it fine, awfully fine, but I've just scraped through.'

' You haven't much sense, but you've got a backbone, anyhow. Eat, and talk afterwards.' Dick fell upon eggs and bacon and gorged till he could gorge no more. Torpenhow handed him a

filled pipe, and he smoked as men smoke who for
three weeks have been deprived of good tobacco.

'Ouf!' said he. 'That's heavenly! Well?'

'Why in the world didn't you come to me?'

'Couldn't; I owe you too much already, old
man. Besides, I had a sort of superstition that
this temporary starvation—that's what it was, and
it hurt—would bring me more luck later. It's
over and done with now, and none of the syndicate know how hard up I was. Fire away. What's
the exact state of affairs as regards myself?'

'You had my wire? You've caught on here.
People like your work immensely. I don't know
why, but they do. They say you have a fresh
touch and a new way of drawing things. And,
because they're chiefly home-bred English, they
say you have insight. You're wanted by half-a-
dozen papers. You're wanted to illustrate books.'

Dick grunted scornfully.

'You're wanted to work up your smaller
sketches and sell them to the dealers. They seem
to think the money sunk in you is a good investment. Good Lord! who can account for the
fathomless folly of the public?'

'They're a remarkably sensible people.'

'They are subject to fits, if that's what you
mean; and you happen to be the object of the
latest fit among those who are interested in what
they call Art. Just now you're a fashion, a
phenomenon, or whatever you please. I appeared
to be the only person who knew anything about
you here, and I have been showing the most
useful men a few of the sketches you gave me

from time to time. Those coming after your work on the Central Southern Syndicate appear to have done your business. You're in luck.'

' Huh! call it luck! Do call it luck, when a man has been kicking about the world like a dog, waiting for it to come! I'll luck 'em later on. I want a place to work in first.'

' Come here,' said Torpenhow, crossing the landing. ' This place is a big box-room really, but it will do for you. There's your skylight, or your north light, or whatever window you call it, and plenty of room to thrash about in, and a bedroom beyond. What more do you need? '

' Good enough,' said Dick, looking round the large room that took up a third of a top storey in the rickety chambers overlooking the Thames. A pale yellow sun shone through the skylight and showed the much dirt of the place. Three steps led from the door to the landing, and three more to Torpenhow's room. The well of the staircase disappeared into darkness, pricked by tiny gas-jets, and there were sounds of men talking and doors slamming seven flights below, in the warm gloom.

' Do they give you a free hand here? ' said Dick cautiously. He was Ishmael enough to know the value of liberty.

' Anything you like: latchkeys and licence unlimited. We are permanent tenants for the most part here. 'Tisn't a place I would recommend for a Young Men's Christian Association, but it will serve. I took these rooms for you when I wired.'

' You're a great deal too kind, old man.'

' You didn't suppose you were going away from me, did you?' Torpenhow put his hand on Dick's shoulder, and the two walked up and down the room, henceforward to be called the studio, in sweet and silent communion. They heard rapping at Torpenhow's door. ' That's some ruffian come up for a drink,' said Torpenhow; and he raised his voice cheerily. There entered no one more ruffianly than a portly middle-aged gentleman in a satin-faced frock-coat. His lips were parted and pale, and there were deep pouches under the eyes.

' Weak heart,' said Dick to himself, and, as he shook hands, ' very weak heart. His pulse is shaking his fingers.'

The man introduced himself as the head of the Central Southern Syndicate and ' one of the most ardent admirers of your work, Mr. Heldar. I assure you, in the name of the syndicate, that we are immensely indebted to you; and I trust, Mr. Heldar, you won't forget that we were largely instrumental in bringing you before the public.' He panted because of the seven flights of stairs.

Dick glanced at Torpenhow, whose left eyelid lay for a moment dead on his cheek.

' I shan't forget,' said Dick, every instinct of defence roused in him. ' You've paid me so well that I couldn't, you know. By the way, when I am settled in this place I should like to send and get my sketches. There must be nearly a hundred and fifty of them with you.'

' That is—er—is what I came to speak about. I fear we can't allow it exactly, Mr. Heldar. In the absence of any specified agreement the sketches are our property, of course.'

' Do you mean to say that you are going to keep them? '

' Yes ; and we hope to have your help, on your own terms, Mr. Heldar, to assist us in arranging a little exhibition, which, backed by our name and the influence we naturally command among the Press, should be of material service to you. Sketches such as yours——'

' Belong to me. You engaged me by wire, you paid me the lowest rates you dared. You can't mean to keep them ! Good God alive, man, they're all I've got in the world ! '

Torpenhow watched Dick's face and whistled.

Dick walked up and down, thinking. He saw the whole of his little stock-in-trade, the first weapon of his equipment, annexed at the outset of his campaign by an elderly gentleman whose name Dick had not caught aright, who said that he represented a syndicate, which was a thing for which Dick had not the least reverence. The injustice of the proceedings did not much move him. He had seen the strong hand prevail too often in other places to be squeamish over the moral aspects of right and wrong. But he ardently desired the blood of the gentleman in the frock-coat, and when he spoke again it was with a strained sweetness that Torpenhow knew well for the beginning of strife.

' Forgive me, sir, but you have no—no

younger man who can arrange this business
with me?'

'I speak for the syndicate. I see no reason for
a third party to——'

'You will in a minute. Be good enough to
give back my sketches.'

The man stared blankly at Dick, and then at
Torpenhow, who was leaning against the wall.
He was not used to ex-employees who ordered
him to be good enough to do things.

'Yes, it is rather a cold-blooded steal,' said
Torpenhow critically; 'but I'm afraid, I am very
much afraid, you've struck the wrong man. Be
careful, Dick. Remember, this isn't the Sudan.'

'Considering what services the syndicate have
done you in putting your name before the
world——'

This was not a fortunate remark; it reminded
Dick of certain vagrant years lived out in loneliness
and strife and unsatisfied desires. The memory
did not contrast well with the prosperous gentleman who proposed to enjoy the fruit of those
years.

'I don't know quite what to do with you,'
began Dick meditatively. 'Of course you're a
thief, and you ought to be half killed, but in
your case you'd probably die. I don't want you
dead on this floor, and, besides, it's unlucky just
as one's moving in. Don't hit, sir; you'll only
excite yourself.' He put one hand on the man's
forearm and ran the other down the plump body
beneath the coat. 'My goodness!' said he to
Torpenhow, 'and this grey beast dares to be a

thief! I have seen an Esneh camel-driver have the black hide taken off his body in strips for stealing half a pound of wet dates, and *he* was as tough as whipcord. This thing's soft all over—like a woman.'

There are few things more poignantly humiliating than being handled by a man who does not intend to strike. The head of the syndicate began to breathe heavily. Dick walked round him, pawing him, as a cat paws a soft hearthrug. Then he traced with his forefinger the leaden pouches underneath the eyes, and shook his head. ' You were going to steal my things,—mine, mine, mine!—you, who don't know when you may die. Write a note to your office,—you say you're the head of it,—and order them to give Torpenhow my sketches,—every one of them. Wait a minute : your hand's shaking. Now! ' He thrust a pocket-book before him. The note was written. Torpenhow took it and departed without a word, while Dick walked round and round the spellbound captive, giving him such advice as he conceived best for the welfare of his soul. When Torpenhow returned with a gigantic portfolio, he heard Dick say, almost soothingly, ' Now, I hope this will be a lesson to you ; and if you worry me when I have settled down to work with any nonsense about actions for assault, believe me, I'll catch you and manhandle you, and you'll die. You haven't very long to live, anyhow. Go! *Imshi, Vootsak!*—Get out ! ' The man departed, staggering and dazed. Dick drew a long breath : ' Phew ! what a lawless lot these people are ! The first thing a poor orphan meets is gang robbery—organised burglary! Think of the hideous blackness of that man's mind! Are my sketches all right, Torp?'

'Yes; one hundred and forty-seven of them. Well, I *must* say, Dick, you've begun well.'

'He was interfering with me. It only meant a few pounds to him, but it was everything to me. I don't think he'll bring an action. I gave him some medical advice gratis about the state of his body. It was cheap at the little flurry it cost him. Now let's look at my things.'

Two minutes later Dick had thrown himself down on the floor and was deep in the portfolio, chuckling lovingly as he turned the drawings over and thought of the price at which they had been bought.

The afternoon was well advanced when Torpenhow came to the door and saw Dick dancing a wild saraband under the skylight.

'I builded better than I knew, Torp,' he said, without stopping the dance. 'They're good! They're damned good! They'll go like smoke! I shall have an exhibition of them on my own brazen hook. And that man would have cheated me out of it! Do you know that I'm sorry now that I didn't actually hit him?'

'Go out,' said Torpenhow,—'go out and pray to be delivered from the sin of arrogance, which you never will be. Bring your things up from whatever place you're staying in, and we'll try to make this barn a little more shipshape.'

'And then—oh, then,' said Dick, still capering, 'we'll spoil the Egyptians!'

CHAPTER IV

The wolf-cub at even lay hid in the corn,
  When the smoke of the cooking hung grey :
He knew where the doe made a couch for her fawn,
  And he looked to his strength for his prey.
  But the moon swept the smoke-wreaths away ;
And he turned from his meal in the villager's close,
And he bayed to the moon as she rose.

In Seeonee.

'WELL, and how does success taste?' said Torpenhow, some three months later, He had just returned to the chambers after a holiday in the country.

'Good,' said Dick, as he sat licking his lips before the easel in the studio. 'I want more,—heaps more. The lean years have passed, and I approve of these fat ones.'

'Be careful, old man. That way lies bad work.'

Torpenhow was sprawling in a long chair with a small fox-terrier asleep on his chest, while Dick was preparing a canvas. A dais, a background, and a lay-figure were the only fixed objects in the place. They rose from a wreck of oddments that began with felt-covered water-bottles, belts, and regimental badges, and ended with a small

45

bale of second-hand uniforms and a stand of
mixed arms. The mark of muddy feet on the
dais showed that a military model had just
gone away. The watery autumn sunlight was
failing, and shadows sat in the corners of the
studio.

'Yes,' said Dick deliberately, 'I like the
power; I like the fun; I like the fuss; and
above all I like the money. I almost like the
people who make the fuss and pay the money.
Almost. But they're a queer gang,—an amazingly
queer gang!'

'They have been good enough to you, at any
rate. That tin-pot exhibition of your sketches
must have paid. Did you see that the papers
called it the "Wild Work Show"?'

'Never mind. I sold every shred of canvas
I wanted to; and, on my word, I believe it was
because they believed I was a self-taught flag-
stone artist. I should have got better prices if
I had worked my things on wool or scratched
them on camel-bone instead of using mere black
and white and colour. But they are a queer gang,
these people. Limited isn't the word to describe
'em. I met a fellow the other day who told me
that it was impossible that shadows on white
sand should be blue,—ultramarine,—as they are.
I found out, later, that that man had been as far
as Brighton beach; but he knew all about Art,
confound him. He gave me a lecture on it, and
recommended me to go to school to learn technique. I wonder what old Kami would have said
to that.'

'When were you under Kami, man of extraordinary beginnings ? '

'I studied with him for two years in Paris. He taught by personal magnetism. All he ever said was, " *Continuez, mes enfants,*" and you had to make the best you could of that. He had a divine touch, and he knew something about colour. Kami used to dream colour. I swear he could never have seen the genuine article ; but he evolved it, and it was good.'

'Recollect some of those views in the Sudan ? ' said Torpenhow, with a provoking drawl.

Dick squirmed in his place. 'Don't! It makes me want to get out there again. What colour that was! Opal and umber and amber and claret and brick-red and sulphur—cockatoo-crest sulphur—against brown, with a nigger-black rock sticking up in the middle of it all, and a decorative frieze of camels festooning in front of a pure pale turquoise sky.' He began to walk up and down. 'And yet, you know, if you try to give these people the thing as God gave it keyed down to their comprehension and according to the powers He has given you——'

'Modest man ! Go on.'

'Half-a-dozen epicene young pagans who haven't even been to Algiers will tell you, first, that your notion is borrowed, and, secondly, that it isn't Art.'

'This comes of my leaving Town for a month. Dickie, you've been promenading among the toy-shops and hearing people talk.'

'I couldn't help it,' said Dick penitently.

' You weren't here, and it was lonely these long evenings. A man can't work for ever.'

' A man might have gone to a pub, and got decently drunk.'

' I wish I had ; but I foregathered with some men of sorts. They said they were artists, and I knew some of them could draw,—but they wouldn't draw. They gave me tea,—tea at five in the afternoon !—and talked about Art and the state of their souls. As if their souls mattered ! I've heard more about Art and seen less of her in the last six months than in the whole of my life. Do you remember Cassavetti, who worked for some continental syndicate, out with the desert column ? He was a regular Christmas-tree of contraptions when he took the field in full fig, with his water-bottle, lanyard, revolver, writing-case, housewife, gig-lamps, and the Lord knows what all. He used to fiddle about with 'em and show us how they worked ; but he never seemed to do much except fudge his reports from the Nilghai. See ? '

' Dear old Nilghai ! He's in Town, fatter than ever. He ought to be up here this evening. I see the comparison perfectly. You should have kept clear of all that man-millinery. Serves you right, and I hope it will unsettle your mind.'

' It won't. It has taught me what Art—holy sacred Art—means.'

' You've learnt something while I've been away. What is Art ? '

' Give 'em what they know, and when you've done it once do it again.' Dick dragged forward

a canvas laid face to the wall. ' Here's a sample
of real Art. It's going to be a facsimile reproduction for a weekly. I called it " His Last Shot."
It's worked up from the little water-colour I
made outside El Maghrib. Well, I lured my
model, a beautiful rifleman, up here with drink;
I drored him, and I redrored him, and I tre-
drored him, and I made him a flushed, dishe-
velled, bedevilled scallawag, with his helmet at
the back of his head, and the living fear of death
in his eye, and the blood oozing out of a cut over
his ankle-bone. He wasn't pretty, but he was
all soldier and very much man.'

' Once more, modest child ! '

Dick laughed. ' Well, it's only to you I'm
talking. I did him just as well as I knew how,
making allowance for the slickness of oils. Then
the art-manager of that abandoned paper said that
his subscribers wouldn't like it. It was brutal
and coarse and violent,—man being naturally
gentle when he's fighting for his life. They
wanted something more restful, with a little more
colour. I could have said a good deal, but you
might as well talk to a sheep as an art-manager.
I took my " Last Shot " back. Behold the result !
I put him into a lovely red coat without a speck
on it. That is Art. I polished his boots,—
observe the high light on the toe. That is Art.
I cleaned his rifle,—rifles are always clean on
service,—because that is Art. I pipeclayed his
helmet,—pipeclay is always used on active service, and is indispensable to Art. I shaved his
chin, I washed his hands, and gave him an air

of fatted peace. Result, military tailor's pattern-plate. Price, thank Heaven, twice as much as for the first sketch, which was moderately decent.'

'And do you suppose you're going to give that thing out as your work?'

'Why not? I did it. Alone I did it, in the interests of sacred, home-bred Art and *Dickenson's Weekly.*'

Torpenhow smoked in silence for a while. Then came the verdict, delivered from rolling clouds: 'If you were only a mass of blathering vanity, Dick, I wouldn't mind,—I'd let you go to the deuce on your own mahl-stick; but when I consider what you are to me, and when I find that to vanity you add the twopenny-halfpenny pique of a twelve-year-old girl, then I bestir myself in your behalf. Thus!'

The canvas ripped as Torpenhow's booted foot shot through it, and the terrier jumped down, thinking rats were about.

'If you have any bad language to use, use it. You have not. I continue. You are an idiot, because no man born of woman is strong enough to take liberties with his public, even though they be—which they ain't—all you say they are.'

'But they don't know any better. What can you expect from creatures born and bred in this light?' Dick pointed to the yellow fog. 'If they want furniture-polish, let them have furniture-polish, so long as they pay for it. They are only men and women. You talk as though they were gods.'

'That sounds very fine, but it has nothing to

do with the case. They are the people you have
to work for, whether you like it or not. They
are your masters. Don't be deceived, Dickie, you
aren't strong enough to trifle with them,—or
with yourself, which is more important. Moreover,—Come back, Binkie: that red daub isn't
going anywhere,—unless you take precious good
care you will fall under the damnation of the
cheque-book, and that's worse than death. You
will get drunk—you're half drunk already—on
easily-acquired money. For that money and your
own infernal vanity you are willing to deliberately
turn out bad work. You'll do quite enough bad
work without knowing it. And, Dickie, as I love
you and as I know you love me, I am not going to
let you cut off your nose to spite your face for all
the gold in England. That's settled. Now swear.'

'Don't know,' said Dick. ' I've been trying
to make myself angry, but I can't; you're so
abominably reasonable. There will be a row on
Dickenson's Weekly, I fancy.'

'Why the Dickenson do you want to work
on a weekly paper? It's slow bleeding of power.'

' It brings in the very desirable dollars,' said
Dick, his hands in his pockets.

Torpenhow watched him with large contempt.
' Why, I thought it was a man ! ' said he. ' It's
a child.'

' No, it isn't,' said Dick, wheeling quickly.
' You've no notion what the certainty of cash
means to a man who has always wanted it badly.
Nothing will pay me for some of my life's joys.
On that Chinese pig-boat, for instance, when we

ate bread and jam for every meal, because Ho-
Wang wouldn't allow us anything better, and it
all tasted of pig,—Chinee pig. I've worked for
this, I've sweated and I've starved for this, line
on line and month after month. And now I've
got it I am going to make the most of it while it
lasts. Let them pay—they've no knowledge.'

'What does Your Majesty please to want?
You can't smoke more than you do ; you won't
drink ; you're a gross feeder ; and you dress in the
dark, by the look of you. You wouldn't keep a
horse the other day when I suggested, because, you
said, it might fall lame, and whenever you cross
the street you take a hansom. Even you are not
foolish enough to suppose that theatres and all the
live things you can buy thereabouts mean Life.
What earthly need have you for money ? '

' It's there, bless its golden heart,' said Dick.
' It's there all the time. Providence has sent me
nuts while I have teeth to crack 'em with. I
haven't yet found the nut I wish to crack, but I'm
keeping my teeth filed. Perhaps some day you and
I will go for a walk round the wide earth.'

' With no work to do, nobody to worry us,
and nobody to compete with? You would be
unfit to speak to in a week. Besides, I shouldn't
go. I don't care to profit by the price of a man's
soul,—for that's what it would mean. Dick, it's
no use arguing. You're a fool.'

' Don't see it. When I was on that Chinese
pig-boat our captain got enormous credit for
saving about twenty-five thousand very seasick
little pigs, when our old tramp of a steamer fell

foul of a timber-junk.   Now, taking those pigs as a parallel——'

'Oh, confound your parallels!   Whenever I try to improve your soul you always drag in some irrelevant anecdote from your very shady past. Pigs aren't the British public; credit on the high seas isn't credit here; and self-respect is self-respect all the world over.   Go out for a walk and try to catch some self-respect.   And, I say, if the Nilghai comes up this evening can I show him your diggings?'

'Surely.   You'll be asking whether you must knock at my door next.'   And Dick departed, to take counsel with himself in the rapidly-gathering London fog.

Half an hour after he had left, the Nilghai laboured up the staircase.   He was the chiefest, as he was the hugest, of the war-correspondents, and his experiences dated from the birth of the needle-gun.   Saving only his ally, Keneu the Great War Eagle, there was no man mightier in the craft than he, and he always opened his conversation with the news that there would be trouble in the Balkans in the spring.   Torpenhow laughed as he entered.

'Never mind the trouble in the Balkans. Those little states are always screeching.   You've heard about Dick's luck?'

'Yes; he has been called up to notoriety, hasn't he?   I hope you keep him properly humble. He wants suppressing from time to time.'

'He does.   He's beginning to take liberties with what he thinks is his reputation.'

'Already! By Jove, he has cheek! I don't
know about his reputation, but he'll come a
cropper if he tries that sort of thing.'

'So I told him. I don't think he believes it.'

'They never do when they first start off.
What's that wreck on the ground there?'

'Specimen of his latest impertinence.' Torpenhow thrust the torn edges of the canvas
together and showed the well-groomed picture to
the Nilghai, who looked at it for a moment and
whistled.

'It's a chromo,' said he,—'a chromo-litholeo-
margarine fake! What possessed him to do it?
And yet how thoroughly he has caught the note
that catches a public who think with their boots
and read with their elbows! The cold-blooded
insolence of the work almost saves it; but he
mustn't go on with this. Hasn't he been praised
and cockered up too much? You know these
people here have no sense of proportion. They'll
call him a second Detaille and a third-hand
Meissonier while his fashion lasts. It's windy
diet for a colt.'

'I don't think it affects Dick much. You
might as well call a young wolf a lion and expect
him to take the compliment in exchange for a
shin-bone. Dick's soul is in the bank. He's
working for cash.'

'Now he has thrown up war work, I suppose he
doesn't see that the obligations of the service are
just the same, only the proprietors are changed.'

'How should he know? He thinks he is his
own master.'

' Does he ? I could undeceive him for his good if there's any virtue in print. He wants the whip-lash.'

' Lay it on with science, then. I'd flay him myself, but I like him too much.'

' I've no scruples. He had the audacity to try to cut me out with a woman at Cairo once. I forgot that, but I remember now.'

' Did he cut you out ? '

' You'll see when I have dealt with him. But, after all, what's the good ? Leave him alone and he'll come home, if he has any stuff in him, dragging or wagging his tail behind him. There's more in a week of life than in a lively weekly. None the less I'll slate him. I'll slate him ponderously in the *Cataclysm*.'

' Good luck to you ; but I fancy nothing short of a crowbar would make Dick wince. His soul seems to have been fired before we came across him. He's intensely suspicious and utterly lawless.'

' Matter of temper,' said the Nilghai. ' It's the same with horses. Some you wallop and they work, some you wallop and they jib, and some you wallop and they go out for a walk with their hands in their pockets.'

' That's exactly what Dick has done,' said Torpenhow. ' Wait till he comes back. In the meantime you can begin your slating here. I'll show you some of his last and worst work in his studio.'

Dick had instinctively sought running water for a comfort to his mood of mind. He was leaning over the Embankment wall, watching the rush of the Thames through the arches of Westminster Bridge. He began by thinking of Torpenhow's advice, but, as of custom, lost himself in the study of the faces flocking past. Some had death written on their features, and Dick marvelled that they could laugh. Others, clumsy and coarse-built for the most part, were alight with love; others were merely drawn and lined with work; but there was something, Dick knew, to be made out of them all. The poor at least should suffer that he might learn, and the rich should pay for the output of his learning. Thus his credit in the world and his cash balance at the bank would be increased. So much the better for him. He had suffered. Now he would take toll of the ills of others.

The fog was driven apart for a moment, and the sun shone, a blood-red wafer, on the water. Dick watched the spot till he heard the voice of the tide between the piers die down like the wash of the sea at low tide. A girl hard pressed by her lover shouted shamelessly, ' Ah, get away, you beast! ' and a shift of the same wind that had opened the fog drove across Dick's face the black smoke of a river-steamer at her berth below the wall. He was blinded for the moment, then spun round and found himself face to face with—Maisie.

There was no mistaking. The years had turned the child to a woman, but they had not altered the dark-grey eyes, the thin scarlet lips, or the firmly-modelled mouth and chin; and, that all should be as it was of old, she wore a closely-fitting grey dress.

Since the human soul is finite and not in the least under its own command, Dick, advancing, said, ' Hullo ! ' after the manner of schoolboys, and Maisie answered, ' Oh, Dick, is that you ? ' Then, against his will, and before the brain, newly released from considerations of the cash balance, had time to dictate to the nerves, every pulse of Dick's body throbbed furiously and his palate dried in his mouth. The fog shut down again, and Maisie's face was pearl-white through it. No word was spoken, but Dick fell into step at her side, and the two paced the Embankment together, keeping the step as perfectly as in their afternoon excursions to the mud-flats. Then Dick, a little hoarsely :

' What has happened to Amomma ? '

' He died, Dick. Not cartridges. Over-eating. He was always greedy. Isn't it funny ? '

' Yes. No. Do you mean Amomma ? '

' Ye—es. No. This. Where have you come from ? '

' Over there.' He pointed eastward through the fog. ' And you ? '

' Oh, I'm in the North,—the black North, across all the Park. I am very busy.'

' What do you do ? '

' I paint a great deal. That's all I have to do.'

' Why, what's happened ? You had three hundred a year.'

' I have that still. I'm painting ; that's all.'

' Are you alone, then ? '

'There's a girl living with me. Don't walk so fast, Dick. You're out of step.'

'Then you noticed it too?'

'Of course I did. You're always out of step.'

'So I am. I'm sorry. You went on with the painting?'

'Of course. I said I should. I was at the Slade, then at Merton's in St. John's Wood, the big studio, then I pepper-potted,—I mean I went to the National,—and now I'm working under Kami.'

'But Kami is in Paris surely?'

'No; he has his teaching-studio at Vitry-sur-Marne. I work with him in the summer, and I live in London in the winter. I'm a householder.'

'Do you sell much?'

'Now and again, but not often. There is my 'bus, I must take it or lose half an hour. Good-bye, Dick.'

'Good-bye, Maisie. Won't you tell me where you live? I must see you again; and perhaps I could help you. I—I paint a little myself.'

'I may be in the Park to-morrow if there is no working light. I walk from the Marble Arch down and back again; that is my little excursion. But of course I shall see you again.' She stepped into the omnibus and was swallowed up by the fog.

'Well,—I—am—damned!' exclaimed Dick, and returned to the chambers.

Torpenhow and Nilghai found him sitting on the steps to the studio door, repeating the phrase with an awful gravity.

'You'll be more damned when I've done with you,' said the Nilghai, upheaving his bulk from behind Torpenhow's shoulder and waving a sheaf of half-dry manuscript. 'Dick, it is of common report that you are suffering from swelled head.'

'Hullo, Nilghai. Back again? How are the Balkans and all the little Balkans? One side of your face is out of drawing, as usual.'

'Never mind that. I am commissioned to smite you in print. Torpenhow refuses from false delicacy. I've been overhauling the pot-boilers in your studio. They are simply disgraceful.'

'Oho! that's it, is it? If you think you can slate me, you're wrong. You can only describe, and you need as much room to turn in, on paper, as a cargo-boat. But continue, and be swift. I'm going to bed.'

'H'm! h'm! h'm! The first part only deals with your pictures. Here's the peroration : " For work done without conviction, for power wasted on trivialities, for labour expended with levity for the deliberate purpose of winning the easy applause of a fashion-driven public———" '

'That's " His Last Shot," second edition. Go on.'

'——" public, there remains but one end,— the oblivion that is preceded by toleration and cenotaphed with contempt. From that fate Mr. Heldar has yet to prove himself out of danger." '

'*Wow — wow — wow — wow — wow !* ' said Dick profanely. 'It's a clumsy ending and vile journalese, but it's quite true. And yet,'—he

sprang to his feet and snatched at the manuscript,—' you scarred, deboshed, battered old
gladiator! You're sent out when a war begins,
to minister to the blind, brutal, British public's
bestial thirst for blood. They have no arenas
now, but they must have special correspondents.
You're a fat gladiator who comes up through a
trap-door and talks of what he's seen. You stand
on precisely the same level as an energetic bishop,
an affable actress, a devastating cyclone, or—my
own sweet self. And you presume to lecture me
about my work! Nilghai, if it were worth while
I'd caricature you in four papers!'

The Nilghai winced. He had not thought of
this.

' As it is, I shall take this stuff and tear it
small—so!' The manuscript fluttered in slips
down the dark well of the staircase. ' Go home,
Nilghai,' said Dick. ' Go home to your lonely
little bed, and leave me in peace. I am about to
turn in till to-morrow.'

' Why, it isn't seven yet!' said Torpenhow,
with amazement.

' It shall be two in the morning, if I choose,'
said Dick, backing to the studio door. ' I go to
grapple with a serious crisis, and I shan't want
any dinner.'

The door shut and was locked.

' What can you do with a man like that?'
said the Nilghai.

' Leave him alone. He's as mad as a hatter.'

At eleven there was kicking on the studio door.
' Is the Nilghai with you still?' said a voice from

within. ' Then tell him he might have condensed the whole of his lumbering nonsense into an epigram: " Only the free are bond, and only the bond are free." Tell him he's an idiot, Torp, and tell him I'm another.'

' All right. Come out and have supper. You're smoking on an empty stomach.'

There was no answer.

CHAPTER V

'I have a thousand men,' said he,
  'To wait upon my will,
And towers nine upon the Tyne,
  And three upon the Till.'

'And what care I for your men,' said she,
  'Or towers from Tyne to Till,
Sith you must go with me,' she said,
  'To wait upon my will?'
                    Sir Hoggie and the Fairies.

NEXT morning Torpenhow found Dick sunk in
deepest repose of tobacco.

'Well, madman, how d'you feel?'

'I don't know. I'm trying to find out.'

'You had much better do some work.'

'Maybe; but I'm in no hurry. I've made a
discovery, Torp. There's too much Ego in my
Cosmos.'

'Not really! Is this revelation due to my
lectures, or the Nilghai's?'

'It came to me suddenly, all on my own
account. Much too much Ego; and now I'm
going to work.'

He turned over a few half-finished sketches,
drummed on a new canvas, cleaned three brushes,

set Binkie to bite the toes of the lay-figure, rattled through his collection of arms and accoutrements, and then went out abruptly, declaring that he had done enough for the day.

'This is positively indecent,' said Torpenhow, 'and the first time that Dick has ever broken up a light morning. Perhaps he has found out that he has a soul, or an artistic temperament, or something equally valuable. That comes of leaving him alone for a month. Perhaps he has been going out of evenings. I must look to this.' He rang for the bald-headed old housekeeper, whom nothing could astonish or annoy.

'Beeton, did Mr. Heldar dine out at all while I was out of town?'

'Never laid 'is dress-clothes out once, sir, all the time. Mostly 'e dined in; but 'e brought some most remarkable fancy young gentlemen up 'ere after theatres once or twice. Remarkable fancy they was. You gentlemen on the top floor does very much as you likes, but it do seem to me, sir, droppin' a walkin'-stick down five flights o' stairs an' then goin' down four abreast to pick it up again at half-past two in the mornin' singin', "Bring back the whisky, Willie darlin',"—not once or twice, but scores o' times,—ain't charity to the other tenants. What I say is, "Do as you would be done by." That's my motto.'

'Of course! of course! I'm afraid the top floor isn't the quietest in the house.'

'I make no complaints, sir. I have spoke to Mr. Heldar friendly, an' he laughed, an' did me a picture of the missis that is as good as a coloured print. It 'asn't the 'igh shine of a photograph, but what I say is, " Never look a gift-horse in the mouth." Mr. Heldar's dress-clothes 'aven't been on him for weeks.'

' Then it's all right,' said Torpenhow to himself. ' Orgies are healthy, and Dick has a head of his own, but when it comes to women making eyes I'm not so certain.—Binkie, never you be a man, little dorglums. They're contrary brutes, and they do things without any reason.'

Dick had turned northward across the Park, but he was walking in the spirit on the mud-flats with Maisie. He laughed aloud as he remembered the day when he had decked Amomma's horns with the ham-frills, and Maisie, white with rage, had cuffed him. How long those four years seemed in review, and how closely Maisie was connected with every hour of them! Storm across the sea, and Maisie in a grey dress on the beach, sweeping her drenched hair out of her eyes and laughing at the homeward race of the fishing-smacks; hot sunshine on the mud-flats, and Maisie sniffing scornfully, with her chin in the air; Maisie flying before the wind that threshed the foreshore and drove the sand like small shot about her ears; Maisie, very composed and independent, telling lies to Mrs. Jennett while Dick supported her with coarser perjuries; Maisie picking her way delicately from stone to stone, a pistol in her hand and her teeth firm-set; and Maisie in a grey dress sitting on the grass between the mouth of a cannon and a nodding yellow sea-poppy. The pictures passed

before him one by one, and the last stayed the
longest. Dick was perfectly happy with a quiet
peace that was as new to his mind as it was
foreign to his experience. It never occurred to
him that there might be other calls upon his
time than loafing across the Park in the fore-
noon.

'There's a good working light now,' he said,
watching his shadow placidly. 'Some poor devil
ought to be grateful for this. And there's
Maisie!'

She was walking towards him from the Marble
Arch, and he saw that no mannerism of her gait
had been changed. It was good to find her still
Maisie, and, so to speak, his next-door neighbour.
No greeting passed between them, because there
had been none in the old days.

'What are you doing out of your studio at
this hour?' said Dick, as one who was entitled
to ask.

'Idling. Just idling. I got angry with a
chin and scraped it out. Then I left it in a little
heap of paint-chips and came away.'

'I know what palette-knifing means. What
was the piccy?'

'A fancy head that wouldn't come right,—
horrid thing!'

'I don't like working over scraped paint when
I'm doing flesh. The grain comes up woolly as
the paint dries.'

'Not if you scrape properly.' Maisie waved
her hand to illustrate her methods. There was a
dab of paint on the white cuff. Dick laughed.

' You're as untidy as ever.'

' That comes well from you. Look at your own cuff ! '

' By Jove, yes ! It's worse than yours. I don't think we've much altered in anything. Let's see, though.' He looked at Maisie critically. The pale blue haze of an autumn day crept between the tree-trunks of the Park and made a background for the grey dress, the black velvet toque above the black hair, and the resolute profile.

' No, there's nothing changed. How good it is ! D'you remember when I fastened your hair into the snap of a hand-bag ? '

Maisie nodded, with a twinkle in her eyes, and turned her full face to Dick.

' Wait a minute,' said he. ' That mouth is down at the corners a little. Who's been worrying you, Maisie ? '

' No one but myself. I never seem to get on with my work, and yet I try hard enough, and Kami says——'

' " *Continuez, mesdemoiselles. Continuez toujours, mes enfants.*" Kami *is* depressing. I beg your pardon.'

' Yes, that's what he says. He told me last summer that I was doing better and he'd let me exhibit this year.'

' Not in this place, surely ? '

' Of course not. The Salon.'

' You fly high.'

' I've been beating my wings long enough. Where do you exhibit, Dick ? '

' I don't exhibit. I sell.'

' What is your line, then ? '

' Haven't you heard? ' Dick's eyes opened. Was this thing possible? He cast about for some means of conviction. They were not far from the Marble Arch. ' Come up Oxford Street a little and I'll show you.'

A small knot of people stood round a print-shop that Dick knew well. ' Some reproduction of my work inside,' he said, with suppressed triumph. Never before had success tasted so sweet upon the tongue. ' You see the sort of things I paint. D'you like it? '

Maisie looked at the wild whirling rush of a field-battery going into action under fire. Two artillerymen stood behind her in the crowd.

' They've chucked the off lead-'orse,' said one to the other. ' 'E's tore up awful, but they're makin' good time with the others. That lead-driver drives better nor you, Tom. See 'ow cunnin' 'e's nursin' 'is 'orse.'

' Number Three'll be off the limber, next jolt,' was the answer.

' No, 'e won't. See 'ow 'is foot's braced against the iron? ' E's all right.'

Dick watched Maisie's face and swelled with ioy—fine, rank, vulgar triumph. She was more interested in the little crowd than in the picture. That was something that she could understand.

' And I wanted it so ! Oh, I did want it so ! ' she said at last, under her breath.

' Me,—all me ! ' said Dick placidly. ' Look at their faces. It hits 'em. They don't know what makes their eyes and mouths open; but I know. And I know my work's right.'

' Yes. I see. Oh, what a thing to have come to one ! '

' Come to one, indeed ! I had to go out and look for it. What do you think ? '

' I call it success. Tell me how you got it.'

They returned to the Park, and Dick delivered himself of the saga of his own doings, with all the arrogance of a young man speaking to a woman. From the beginning he told the tale, the I—I—I's flashing through the records as telegraph-poles fly past the traveller. Maisie listened and nodded her head. The histories of strife and privation did not move her a hair's-breadth. At the end of each canto he would conclude, ' And *that* gave me some notion of handling colour,' or light, or whatever it might be that he had set out to pursue and understand. He led her breathless across half the world, speaking as he had never spoken in his life before. And in the flood-tide of his exaltation there came upon him a great desire to pick up this maiden who nodded her head and said, ' I understand. Go on,'—to pick her up and to carry her away with him, because she was Maisie, and because she understood, and because she was his right, and a woman to be desired above all women.

Then he checked himself abruptly. ' And so I took all I wanted,' he said, ' and I had to fight for it. Now you tell.'

Maisie's tale was almost as grey as her dress. It covered years of patient toil backed by savage pride that would not be broken though dealers laughed, and fogs delayed work, and Kami was unkind and even sarcastic, and girls in other studios were painfully polite. It had a few bright spots, in pictures accepted at provincial exhibitions, but it wound up with the oft‑repeated wail, ' And so you see, Dick, I had no success, though I worked so hard.'

Then pity filled Dick. Even thus had Maisie spoken when she could not hit the breakwater, half an hour before she had kissed him. And that had happened yesterday.

' Never mind,' he said. ' I'll tell you something if you'll believe it.' The words were shaping themselves of their own accord. ' The whole thing, lock, stock, and barrel, isn't worth one big yellow sea-poppy below Fort Keeling.'

Maisie flushed a little. ' It's all very well for you to talk, but you've had the success and I haven't.'

' Let me talk, then. I know you'll understand. Maisie, dear, it sounds a bit absurd, but those ten years never existed, and I've come back again. It really is just the same. Can't you see? You're alone now and I'm alone. What's the use of worrying? Come to me instead, darling ! '

Maisie poked the gravel with her parasol. They were sitting on a bench. ' I understand,' she said slowly. ' But I've got my work to do, and I must do it.'

' Do it with me, then, dear. I won't interrupt.'

' No, I couldn't. It's my work,—mine,— mine,—mine ! I've been alone all my life in myself, and I'm not going to belong to anybody except myself. I remember things as well as you do, but that doesn't count. We were babies then, and we didn't know what was before us. Dick, don't be selfish. I think I see my way to a little success next year. Don't take it away from me.'

' I beg your pardon, darling. It's my fault for speaking stupidly. I can't expect you to throw up all your life just because I'm back. I'll go to my own place and wait a little.'

' But, Dick, I don't want you to—go—out of —my life, now you've just come back.'

' I'm at your orders; forgive me.' Dick devoured the troubled little face with his eyes. There was triumph in them, because he could not conceive that Maisie should refuse sooner or later to love him, since he loved her.

' It's wrong of me,' said Maisie, more slowly than before; ' it's wrong and selfish. But, oh, I've been so lonely! No, you misunderstand. Now I've seen you again,—it's absurd, but I want to keep you in my life.'

' Naturally. We belong.'

' We don't; but you always understood me, and there is so much in my work that you could help me in. You know things and the ways of doing things. You must.'

' I do, I fancy, or else I don't know myself. Then I suppose you won't care to lose sight of me altogether, and you want me to help you in your work?'

' Yes; but remember, Dick, nothing will ever

come of it. That's why I feel so selfish. Let
things stay as they are. I *do* want your help.'

'You shall have it. But let's consider. I
must see your piccys first, and overhaul your
sketches, and find out about your tendencies.
You should see what the papers say about *my*
tendencies! Then I'll give you good advice, and
you shall paint according. Isn't that it, Maisie?'

Again there was unholy triumph in Dick's eye.

'It's too good of you,—much too good.
Because you are consoling yourself with what
will never happen, and I know that, and yet I
wish to keep you. Don't blame me later, please.'

'I'm going into the matter with my eyes open.
Moreover, the Queen can do no wrong. It isn't
your selfishness that impresses me. It's your
audacity in proposing to make use of *me*.'

'Pooh! You're only Dick,—and a print-
shop.'

'Very good: that's all I am. But, Maisie,
you believe, don't you, that I love you? I don't
want you to have any false notions about brothers
and sisters.'

Maisie looked up for a moment and dropped
her eyes.

'It's absurd, but—I believe. I wish I could
send you away before you get angry with me.
But—but the girl that lives with me is red-
haired, and an impressionist, and all our notions
clash.'

'So do ours, I think. Never mind. Three
months from to-day we shall be laughing at this
together.'

Maisie shook her head mournfully. ' I knew you wouldn't understand, and it will only hurt you more when you find out. Look at my face, Dick, and tell me what you see.'

They stood up and faced each other for a moment. The fog was gathering, and it stifled the roar of the traffic of London beyond the railings. Dick brought all his painfully-acquired knowledge of faces to bear on the eyes, mouth, and chin underneath the black velvet toque.

' It's the same Maisie, and it's the same me,' he said. ' We've both nice little wills of our own, and one or other of us has to be broken. Now about the future. I must come and see your pictures some day,—I suppose when the red-haired girl is on the premises.'

' Sundays are my best times. You must come on Sundays. There are such heaps of things I want to talk about and ask your advice about. Now I must get back to work.'

' Try to find out before next Sunday what I am,' said Dick. ' Don't take my word for anything I've told you. Good-bye, darling, and bless you.'

Maisie stole away like a little grey mouse. Dick watched her till she was out of sight, but he did not hear her say to herself, very soberly, ' I'm a wretch,—a horrid, selfish wretch. But it's Dick, and Dick will understand.'

No one has yet explained what actually happens when an irresistible force meets the immovable post, though many have thought deeply, even as Dick thought. He tried to assure himself that Maisie would be led in a few weeks by his mere presence and discourse to a better way of thinking.   Then he remembered much too distinctly her face and all that was written on it.

'If I know anything of heads,' he said, 'there's everything in that face but love. I shall have to put that in myself; and that chin and mouth won't be got for nothing. But she's right. She knows what she wants, and she's going to get it. What insolence! Me! Of all the people in the wide world, to use me! But then she's Maisie. There's no getting over that fact; and it's good to see her again. This business must have been simmering at the back of my head for years. . . . She'll use me as I used Binat at Port Said. She's quite right. It will hurt a little. I shall have to see her every Sunday,—like a young man courting a housemaid. She's sure to come round; and yet—that mouth isn't a yielding one. I shall be wanting to kiss her all the time, and I shall have to look at her pictures,—I don't even know what sort of work she does yet,—and I shall have to talk about Art,—Woman's Art! Therefore, particularly and perpetually, damn all varieties of Art. It did me a good turn once, and now it's in my way. I'll go home and do some Art.'

Half-way to the studio Dick was smitten with a terrible thought. The figure of a solitary woman in the fog suggested it.

'She's all alone in London, with a red-haired impressionist girl, who probably has the digestion of an ostrich. Most red-haired people have. Maisie's a bilious little body. They'll eat like lone women,—meals at all hours, and tea with all meals. I remember how the students in Paris used to pig along. She may fall ill at any minute, and I shan't be able to help. Whew! this is ten times worse than owning a wife.'

Torpenhow came into the studio at dusk, and looked at Dick with his eyes full of the austere love that springs up between men who have tugged at the same oar together and are yoked by custom and use and the intimacies of toil. This is a good love, and, since it allows, and even encourages strife, recrimination, and the most brutal sincerity, does not die, but increases, and is proof against any absence and evil conduct.

Dick was silent after he handed Torpenhow the filled pipe of council. He thought of Maisie and her possible needs. It was a new thing to think of anybody but Torpenhow, who could think for himself. Here at least was an outlet for that cash balance. He could adorn Maisie barbarically with jewelry,—a thick gold necklace round that little neck, bracelets upon the rounded arms, and rings of price upon her hands,—the cool, temperate, ringless hands that he had taken between his own. It was an absurd thought, for Maisie would not even allow him to put one ring on one finger, and she would laugh at golden trappings. It would be better to sit with her quietly in the dusk, his arm round her neck and her face on his shoulder, as befitted husband and wife. Torpenhow's boots creaked that night, and his strong voice jarred. Dick's brows contracted and he murmured an evil word because he had taken all his success as a right and part payment for past discomfort, and now he was checked in his stride by a woman who admitted all the success and did not instantly care for him.

' I say, old man,' said Torpenhow, who had made one or two vain attempts at conversation, ' I haven't put your back up by anything I've said lately, have I ? '

' You ! No. How could you ? '

' Liver out of order ? '

' The truly healthy man doesn't know he has a liver. I'm only a bit worried about things in general. I suppose it's my soul.'

' The truly healthy man doesn't know he has a soul. What business have you with luxuries of that kind ? '

' It came of itself. Who's the man that says that we're all islands shouting lies to each other across seas of misunderstanding ? '

' He's right, whoever he is,—except about the misunderstanding. I don't think we could misunderstand each other.'

The blue smoke curled back from the ceiling in clouds. Then Torpenhow, insinuatingly :—

' Dick, is it a woman ? '

' Be hanged if it's anything remotely resembling a woman ; and if you begin to talk like that, I'll hire a red-brick studio with white paint trimmings, and begonias and petunias and blue Hungarians to play among three-and-sixpenny pot-palms, and I'll mount all my piccys in aniline-dye plush plasters, and I'll invite every woman who yelps and maunders and moans over what her

guide-books tell her is Art, and you shall receive
'em, Torp,—in a snuff-brown velvet coat with
yellow trousers and an orange tie. You'll like
that.'

' Too thin, Dick. A better man than you
denied with cursing and swearing on a memor-
able occasion. You've overdone it, just as he did.
It's no business of mine, of course, but it's com-
forting to think that somewhere under the stars
there's saving up for you a tremendous thrashing.
Whether it'll come from Heaven or Earth I don't
know, but it's bound to come and break you up
a little. You want hammering.'

Dick shivered. ' All right,' said he. ' When
this island is disintegrated it will call for you.'

' I shall come round the corner and help to
disintegrate it some more. We're talking nonsense. Come along to a theatre.'

CHAPTER VI

' And you may lead a thousand men,
  Nor ever draw the rein,
But ere ye lead the Faery Queen
  'Twill burst your heart in twain.'

He has slipped his foot from the stirrup-bar,
  The bridle from his hand,
And he is bound by hand and foot
  To the Queen o' Faery-land.
                              Sir Hoggie and the Fairies.

SOME weeks later, on a very foggy Sunday, Dick
was returning across the Park to his studio.
' This,' he said, ' is evidently the thrashing that
Torp meant. It hurts more than I expected;
but the Queen can do no wrong; and she certainly has some notion of drawing.'

He had just finished a Sunday visit to Maisie,
—always under the green eyes of the red-haired
impressionist girl, whom he learned to hate at
sight,—and was tingling with a keen sense of
shame. Sunday after Sunday, putting on his
best clothes, he had walked over to the untidy
house north of the Park, first to see Maisie's
pictures, and then to criticise and advise upon
them as he realised that they were productions on

which advice would not be wasted. Sunday after Sunday, and his love grew with each visit, he had been compelled to cram his heart back from between his lips when it prompted him to kiss Maisie several times and very much indeed. Sunday after Sunday, the head above the heart had warned him that Maisie was not yet attainable, and that it would be better to talk as connectedly as possible upon the mysteries of the craft that was all in all to her. Therefore it was his fate to endure weekly torture in the studio built out over the clammy back garden of a frail, stuffy little villa where nothing was ever in its right place and nobody ever called,—to endure and to watch Maisie moving to and fro with the teacups. He abhorred tea, but, since it gave him a little longer time in her presence, he drank it devoutly, and the red-haired girl sat in an untidy heap and eyed him without speaking. She was always watching him. Once, and only once, when she had left the studio Maisie showed him an album that held a few poor cuttings from provincial papers,—the briefest of hurried notes on some of her pictures sent to outlying exhibitions. Dick stooped and kissed the paint-smudged thumb on the open page. ' Oh, my love, my love,' he muttered, ' do you value these things ? Chuck 'em into the waste-paper basket ! '

' Not till I get something better,' said Maisie, shutting the book.

Then Dick, moved by no respect for his public and a very deep regard for the maiden, did deliberately propose, in order to secure more of

these coveted cuttings, that he should paint a
picture which Maisie should sign.

' That's childish,' said Maisie, ' and I didn't
think it of you. It must be my work. Mine,—
mine,—mine ! '

' Go and design decorative medallions for rich
brewers' houses. You are thoroughly good at
that.' Dick was sick and savage.

' Better things than medallions, Dick,' was the
answer, in tones that recalled a grey-eyed atom's
fearless speech to Mrs. Jennett. Dick would
have abased himself utterly, but that the other
girl trailed in.

Next Sunday he laid at Maisie's feet small
gifts of pencils that could almost draw of themselves and colours in whose permanence he believed, and he was ostentatiously attentive to the
work in hand. It demanded, among other things,
an exposition of the faith that was in him. Torpenhow's hair would have stood on end had he
heard the fluency with which Dick preached his
own gospel of Art.

A month before, Dick would have been
equally astonished ; but it was Maisie's will and
pleasure, and he dragged his words together to
make plain to her comprehension all that had
been hidden to himself of the whys and where-
fores of work. There is not the least difficulty
in doing a thing if you only know how to do it ;
the trouble is to explain your method.

' I could put this right if I had a brush in my
hand,' said Dick despairingly, over the modelling
of a chin that Maisie complained would not ' look

flesh,'—it was the same chin that she had scraped
out with the palette-knife,—' but I find it almost
impossible to teach you. There's a queer grim
Dutch touch about your painting that I like ; but
I've a notion that you're weak in drawing. You
foreshorten as though you never used the model,
and you've caught Kami's pasty way of dealing
with flesh in shadow. Then, again, though you
don't know it yourself, you shirk hard work.
Suppose you spend some of your time on line
alone. Line doesn't allow of shirking. Oils do,
and three square inches of flashy, tricky stuff in
the corner of a pic sometimes carry a bad thing
off,—as I know. That's immoral. Do line-work
for a little while, and then I can tell more about
your powers, as old Kami used to say.'

Maisie protested. She did not care for the
pure line.

' I know,' said Dick. ' You want to do your
fancy heads with a bunch of flowers at the base
of the neck to hide bad modelling.' The red-
haired girl laughed a little. ' You want to do
landscapes with cattle knee-deep in grass to hide
bad drawing. You want to do a great deal more
than you can do. You *have* sense of colour, but
you want form. Colour's a gift,—put it aside and
think no more about it,—but form you can be
drilled into. Now, all your fancy heads—and
some of them are very good—will keep you
exactly where you are. With line you must go
forward or backward, and it will show up all your
weaknesses.'

' But other people——' began Maisie.

' You mustn't mind what other people do. If their souls were your soul it would be different. You stand and fall by your own work, remember, and it's waste of time to think of any one else in this battle.'

Dick paused, and the longing that had been so resolutely put away came back into his eyes. He looked at Maisie, and the look asked as plainly as words, Was it not time to leave all this barren wilderness of canvas and counsel and join hands with Life and Love?

Maisie assented to the new programme of schooling so adorably that Dick could hardly restrain himself from picking her up then and there and carrying her off to the nearest registrar's office. It was the implicit obedience to the spoken word and the blank indifference to the unspoken desire that baffled and buffeted his soul. He held authority in that house,—authority limited, indeed, to one-half of one afternoon in seven, but very real while it lasted. Maisie had learned to appeal to him on many subjects, from the proper packing of pictures to the condition of a smoky chimney. The red-haired girl never consulted him about anything. On the other hand, she accepted his appearances without pro-test, and watched him always. He discovered that the meals of the establishment were irregular and fragmentary. They depended chiefly on tea, pickles, and biscuit, as he had suspected from the beginning. The girls were supposed to market week and week about, but they lived, with the help of a charwoman, as casually as the young ravens. Maisie spent most of her income on models, and the other girl revelled in apparatus as refined as her work was rough. Armed with knowledge dear-bought from the Docks, Dick warned Maisie that the end of semi-starvation meant the crippling of power to work, which was considerably worse than death. Maisie took the warning, and gave more thought to what she ate and drank. When his trouble returned upon him, as it generally did in the long winter twilights, the remembrance of that little act of domestic authority and his coercion with a hearth-brush of the smoky drawing-room chimney stung Dick like a whip-lash.

He conceived that this memory would be the extreme of his sufferings, till, one Sunday, the red-haired girl announced that she would make a study of Dick's head, and that he would be good enough to sit still, and—quite as an afterthought —look at Maisie. He sat, because he could not well refuse, and for the space of half an hour he reflected on all the people in the past whom he had laid open for the purposes of his own craft. He remembered Binat most distinctly,—that Binat who had once been an artist and talked about degradation.

It was the merest monochrome roughing in of a head, but it presented the dumb waiting, the longing, and, above all, the hopeless enslavement of the man, in a spirit of bitter mockery.

' I'll buy it,' said Dick promptly, ' at your own price.'

' My price is too high, but I daresay you'll be

as grateful if——' The wet sketch fluttered from the girl's hand and fell into the ashes of the studio stove. When she picked it up it was hopelessly smudged.

'Oh, it's all spoiled!' said Maisie. 'And I never saw it. Was it like?'

'Thank you,' said Dick under his breath to the red-haired girl, and he removed himself swiftly.

'How that man hates me!' said the girl. 'And how he loves you, Maisie!'

'What nonsense! I know Dick's very fond of me, but he has his work to do, and I have mine.'

'Yes, he is fond of you, and I think he knows there is something in impressionism, after all. Maisie, can't you *see*?'

'See? See what?'

'Nothing; only I know that if I could get any man to look at me as that man looks at you, I'd—I don't know what I'd do. But he hates me. Oh, how he hates me!'

She was not altogether correct. Dick's hatred was tempered with gratitude for a few moments, and then he forgot the girl entirely. Only the sense of shame remained, and he was nursing it across the Park in the fog. 'There'll be an explosion one of these days,' he said wrathfully. 'But it isn't Maisie's fault; she's right, quite right, as far as she knows, and I can't blame her. This business has been going on for three months nearly. Three months!—and it cost me ten years' knocking about to get at the notion, the merest raw notion, of my work. That's true;

but then I didn't have pins, drawing-pins and palette-knives, stuck into me every Sunday. Oh, my little darling, if ever I break you, somebody will have a very bad time of it. No, she won't. I'd be as big a fool about her as I am now. I'll poison that red-haired girl on my wedding-day, —she's unwholesome,—and now I'll pass on these present bad times to Torp.'

Torpenhow had been moved to lecture Dick more than once lately on the sin of levity, and Dick had listened and replied not a word. In the weeks between the first few Sundays of his discipline he had flung himself savagely into his work, resolved that Maisie should at least know the full stretch of his powers. Then he had taught Maisie that she must not pay the least attention to any work outside her own, and Maisie had obeyed him all too well. She took his counsels, but was not interested in his pictures.

'Your things smell of tobacco and blood,' she said once. 'Can't you do anything except soldiers?'

'I could do a head of you that would startle you,' thought Dick,—this was before the red-haired girl had brought him under the guillotine, —but he only said, 'I am very sorry,' and harrowed Torpenhow's soul that evening with blasphemies against Art. Later, insensibly and to a large extent against his own will, he ceased to interest himself in his own work. For Maisie's sake, and to soothe the self-respect that it seemed to him he lost each Sunday, he would not consciously turn out bad stuff, but, since Maisie did

not care even for his best, it were better not to
do anything at all save wait and mark time
between Sunday and Sunday. Torpenhow was
disgusted as the weeks went by fruitless, and then
attacked him one Sunday evening when Dick felt
utterly exhausted after three hours' biting self-
restraint in Maisie's presence. There was Language, and Torpenhow withdrew to consult the
Nilghai, who had come in to talk continental
politics.

'Bone-idle, is he? Careless, and touched in
the temper?' said the Nilghai. 'It isn't worth
worrying over. Dick is probably playing the fool
with a woman.'

'Isn't that bad enough?'

'No. She may throw him out of gear and
knock his work to pieces for a while. She may
turn up here some day and make a scene on the
staircase. One never knows. But until Dick
speaks of his own accord you had better not
touch him. He is no easy-tempered man to
handle.'

'No; I wish he were. He is such an aggressive, cocksure, you-be-damned fellow.'

'He'll get that knocked out of him in time.
He must learn that he can't storm up and down
the world with a box of moist tubes and a slick
brush. You're fond of him?'

'I'd take any punishment that's in store for
him if I could; but the worst of it is, no man can
save his brother.'

'No, and the worser of it is, there is no dis-
charge in this war. Dick must learn his lesson

like the rest of us. Talking of war, there'll be trouble in the Balkans in the spring.'

' That trouble is long coming. I wonder if we could drag Dick out there when it comes off? '

Dick entered the room soon afterwards, and the question was put to him. ' Not good enough,' he said shortly. ' I'm too comfy where I am.'

' Surely you aren't taking all the stuff in the papers seriously? ' said the Nilghai. ' Your vogue will be ended in less than six months,— the public will know your touch and go on to something new,—and where will you be then? '

' Here, in England.'

' When you might be doing decent work among us out there? Nonsense ! I shall go, the Keneu will be there, Torp will be there, Cassavetti will be there, and the whole lot of us will be there, and we shall have as much as ever we can do, with unlimited fighting and the chance for you of seeing things that would make the reputation of three Verestchagins.'

' Um ! ' said Dick, pulling at his pipe.

' You prefer to stay here and imagine that all the world is gaping at your pictures? Just think how full an average man's life is of his own pursuits and pleasures. When twenty thousand of him find time to look up between mouthfuls and grunt something about something they aren't the least interested in, the net result is called fame, reputation, or notoriety, according to the taste and fancy of the speller, me lord.'

' I know that as well as you do. Give me credit for a little gumption.'

' Be hanged if I do ! '

' *Be* hanged, then ; you probably will be,— for a spy, by excited Turks. Heigh-ho ! I'm weary, dead weary, and virtue has gone out of me.' Dick dropped into a chair, and was fast asleep in a minute.

' That's a bad sign,' said the Nilghai, in an undertone.

Torpenhow picked the pipe from the waistcoat where it was beginning to burn, and put a pillow behind the head. ' We can't help ; we can't help,' he said. ' It's a good ugly sort of old coconut, and I'm fond of it. There's the scar of the wipe he got when he was cut over in the square.'

' Shouldn't wonder if that has made him a trifle mad.'

' *I* should. He's a most businesslike madman.'

Then Dick began to snore furiously.

' Oh, here, no affection can stand this sort of thing. Wake up, Dick, and go and sleep somewhere else, if you intend to make a noise about it.'

' When a cat has been out on the tiles all night,' said the Nilghai in his beard, ' I notice that she usually sleeps all day. This is natural history.'

Dick staggered away rubbing his eyes and yawning. In the night-watches he was overtaken with an idea, so simple and so luminous that he wondered he had never conceived it before. It was full of craft. He would seek Maisie on a week-day,—would suggest an excursion, and would take her by train to Fort Keeling, over the very ground that they two had trodden together ten years ago.

' As a general rule,' he explained to his chin-lathered reflection in the morning, ' it isn't safe to cross an old trail twice. Things remind one of things, and a cold wind gets up, and you feel sad. But this is an exception to every rule that ever was. I'll go to Maisie at once.'

Fortunately, the red-haired girl was out shopping when he arrived, and Maisie in a paint-spattered blouse was warring with her canvas. She was not pleased to see him ; for week-day visits were a stretch of the bond ; and it needed all his courage to explain his errand.

' I know you've been working too hard,' he concluded, with an air of authority. ' If you do that you'll break down. You had much better come.'

' Where ? ' said Maisie wearily. She had been standing before her easel too long, and was very tired.

' Anywhere you please. We'll take a train to-morrow and see where it stops. We'll have lunch somewhere, and I'll bring you back in the evening.'

' If there's a good working light to-morrow I lose a day.' Maisie balanced the heavy white chestnut palette irresolutely.

Dick held back an oath that was hurrying to his lips. He had not yet learned patience with the maiden to whom her work was all in all.

' You'll lose ever so many more, dear, if you use every hour of working light. Overwork's only murderous idleness. Don't be unreasonable. I'll call for you to-morrow after breakfast early.'

' But surely you are going to ask——'

' No, I am not. I want you and nobody else.
Besides, she hates me as much as I hate her. She
won't care to come. To-morrow, then ; and pray
that we get sunshine.'

Dick went away delighted, and by consequence
did no work whatever. He strangled a wild
desire to order a special train, but bought a
great grey kangaroo cloak lined with glossy black
marten, and then retired into himself to consider
things.

' I'm going out for the day to-morrow with
Dick,' said Maisie to the red-haired girl when the
latter returned, tired, from marketing in the
Edgware Road.

' He deserves it. I shall have the studio floor
thoroughly scrubbed while you're away. It's
very dirty.'

Maisie had enjoyed no sort of holiday for
months, and looked forward to the little excitement, but not without misgivings.

' There's nobody nicer than Dick when he
talks sensibly,' she thought, ' but I'm sure he'll
be silly and worry me, and I'm sure I can't tell
him anything he'd like to hear. If he'd only be
sensible I should like him so much better.'

Dick's eyes were full of joy when he made
his appearance next morning and saw Maisie,
grey-ulstered and black-velvet-hatted, standing in
the hall-way. Palaces of marble, and not sordid
imitations of grained wood, were surely the fittest
background for such a divinity. The red-haired
girl drew her into the studio for a moment and
kissed her hurriedly. Maisie's eyebrows climbed

to the top of her forehead. She was altogether
unused to these demonstrations. ' Mind my hat,'
she said, hurrying away, and ran down the steps
to Dick waiting by the hansom.

' Are you quite warm enough? Are you sure
you wouldn't like some more breakfast? Put
this cloak over your knees.'

' I'm quite comfy, thanks. Where are we
going, Dick? Oh, do stop singing like that.
People will think we're mad.'

' Let 'em think,—if the exertion doesn't kill
them. They don't know who we are, and I'm
sure I don't care who they are. My faith, Maisie,
you're looking lovely ! '

Maisie stared directly in front of her and did
not reply. The wind of a keen, clear winter
morning had put colour into her cheeks. Overhead, the creamy-yellow smoke-clouds were thin-
ning away one by one against a pale-blue sky,
and the improvident sparrows broke off from
water-spout committees and cab-rank cabals to
clamour of the coming of spring.

' It will be perfect weather in the country,'
said Dick.

' But where are we going? '

' Wait and see.'

They stopped at Victoria, and Dick sought
tickets. For less than half the fraction of an
instant it occurred to Maisie, comfortably settled
by the waiting-room fire, that it was much more
pleasant to send a man to the booking-office than
to elbow one's own way through the crowd. Dick
put her into a Pullman,—solely on account of the

warmth there; and she regarded the extravagance with grave scandalised eyes as the train moved out into the country.

'I wish I knew where we are going,' she repeated for the twentieth time. The name of a well-remembered station flashed by, towards the end of the run, and Maisie was enlightened.

'Oh, Dick, you villain!'

'Well, I thought you might like to see the place again. You haven't been here since old times, have you?'

'No. I never cared to see Mrs. Jennett again; and she was all that was ever there.'

'Not quite. Look out a minute. There's the windmill above the potato-fields; they haven't built villas there yet. D'you remember when I shut you up in it?'

'Yes. How she beat you for it! *I* never told it was you.'

'She guessed. I jammed a stick under the door and told you that I was burying Amomma alive in the potatoes, and you believed me. You had a trusting nature in those days.'

They laughed and leaned to look out, identifying ancient landmarks with many reminiscences. Dick fixed his weather eye on the curve of Maisie's cheek, very near his own, and watched the blood rise under the clear skin. He congratulated himself upon his cunning, and looked that the evening would bring him a great reward.

When the train stopped they went out to look at an old town with new eyes. First, but from a distance, they regarded the house of Mrs. Jennett.

'Suppose she should come out now, what would you do?' said Dick, with mock terror.

'I should make a face.'

'Show, then,' said Dick, dropping into the speech of childhood.

Maisie made that face in the direction of the mean little villa, and Dick laughed aloud.

'"This is disgraceful,"' said Maisie, mimicking Mrs. Jennett's tone. '"Maisie, you run in at once, and learn the collect, gospel, and epistle for the next three Sundays. After all I've taught you, too, and three helps every Sunday at dinner! Dick's always leading you into mischief. If you aren't a gentleman, Dick, you might at least——"'

The sentence ended abruptly. Maisie remembered when it had last been used.

'"Try to behave like one,"' said Dick promptly. 'Quite right. Now we'll get some lunch and go on to Fort Keeling,—unless you'd rather drive there?'

'We must walk, out of respect to the place. How little changed it all is!'

They turned in the direction of the sea through unaltered streets, and the influence of old things lay upon them. Presently they passed a confectioner's shop much considered in the days when their joint pocket-money amounted to a shilling a week.

'Dick, have you any pennies?' said Maisie, half to herself.

'Only three; and if you think you're going to have two of 'em to buy peppermints with, you're wrong. She says peppermints aren't ladylike.'

Again they laughed, and again the colour came into Maisie's cheeks as the blood boiled through Dick's heart. After a large lunch they went down to the beach and to Fort Keeling across the waste, wind-bitten land that no builder had thought it worth his while to defile. The winter breeze came in from the sea and sang about their ears.

'Maisie,' said Dick, 'your nose is getting a crude Prussian blue at the tip. I'll race you as far as you please for as much as you please.'

She looked round cautiously, and with a laugh set off, swiftly as the ulster allowed, till she was out of breath.

'We used to run miles,' she panted. 'It's absurd that we can't run now.'

'Old age, dear. This it is to get fat and sleek in Town. When I wished to pull your hair you generally ran for three miles, shrieking at the top of your voice. I ought to know, because those shrieks were meant to call up Mrs. Jennett with a cane and——'

'Dick, I never got you a beating on purpose in my life.'

'No, of course you never did. Good heavens, look at the sea.'

'Why, it's the same as ever!' said Maisie.

Torpenhow had gathered from Mr. Beeton that Dick, properly dressed and shaved, had left the house at half-past eight in the morning with a travelling-rug over his arm. The Nilghai rolled in at mid-day for chess and polite conversation.

'It's worse than anything I imagined,' said Torpenhow.

'Oh, the everlasting Dick, I suppose! You fuss over him like a hen with one chick. Let him run riot if he thinks it'll amuse him. You can whip a young pup off feather, but you can't whip a young man.'

'It isn't a woman. It's one woman; and it's a girl.'

'Where's your proof?'

'He got up and went out at eight this morning, —got up in the middle of the night, by Jove! a thing he never does except when he's on service. Even then, remember, we had to kick him out of his blankets before the fight at El-Maghrib. It's disgusting.'

'It looks odd; but maybe he's decided to buy a horse at last. He might get up for that, mightn't he?'

'Buy a blazing wheelbarrow! He'd have told us if there was a horse in the wind. It's a girl.'

'Don't be certain. Perhaps it's only a married woman.'

'Dick has some sense of humour, if you haven't. Who gets up in the grey dawn to call on another man's wife? It's a girl.'

'Let it be a girl, then. She may teach him that there's somebody else in the world besides himself.'

'She'll spoil his hand. She'll waste his time, and she'll marry him, and ruin his work for ever.

He'll be a respectable married man before we can
stop him, and—he'll never go on the long trail
again.'

'All quite possible, but the earth won't spin
the other way when it happens. . . . Ho! ho!
I'd give something to see Dick " go wooing with
the boys." Don't worry about it. These things
be with Allah, and we can only look on. Get the
chessmen.'

The red-haired girl was lying down in her own
room, staring at the ceiling. The footsteps of
people on the pavement sounded, as they grew
indistinct in the distance, like a many-times-
repeated kiss that was all one long kiss. Her
hands were by her side, and they opened and
shut savagely from time to time.

The charwoman in charge of the scrubbing
of the studio knocked at her door: 'Beg y'
pardon, miss, but in cleanin' of a floor there's
two, not to say three, kind of soap, which is yaller,
an' mottled, an' disinfectink. Now, jist before I
took my pail into the passage I thought it would
be pre'aps jest as well if I was to come up 'ere
an' ask you what sort of soap you was wishful
that I should use on them boards. The yaller
soap, miss——'

There was nothing in the speech to have
caused the paroxysm of fury that drove the red-
haired girl into the middle of the room, almost
shouting :—

'Do you suppose *I* care what you use? Any
kind will do!—*any* kind!'

The woman fled, and the red-haired girl looked at her own reflection in the glass for an instant and covered her face with her hands. It was as though she had shouted some shameful secret aloud.

CHAPTER VII

Roses red and roses white
Plucked I for my love's delight.
She would none of all my posies,—
Bade me gather her blue roses.

Half the world I wandered through,
Seeking where such flowers grew;
Half the world unto my quest
Answered but with laugh and jest.

It may be beyond the grave
She shall find what she would have.
Mine was but an idle quest,—
Roses white and red are best!

Blue Roses.

INDEED the sea had not changed. Its waters
were low on the mud-banks, and the Marazion
bell-buoy clanked and swung in the tideway.
On the white beach-sand dried stumps of sea-
poppy shivered and chattered together.

'I don't see the old breakwater,' said Maisie
under her breath.

'Let's be thankful that we have as much as
we have. I don't believe they've mounted a
single new gun on the fort since we were here.
Come and look.'

They came to the glacis of Fort Keeling, and
sat down in a nook sheltered from the wind
under the tarred throat of a forty-pounder cannon.

'Now, if Amomma were only here!' said
Maisie.

For a long time both were silent. Then Dick
took Maisie's hand and called her by her name.

She shook her head and looked out to sea.

'Maisie, darling, doesn't it make any difference?'

'No!' between clenched teeth. 'I'd—I'd
tell you if it did; but it doesn't. Oh, Dick,
please be sensible.'

'Don't you think that it ever will?'

'No, I'm sure it won't.'

'Why?'

Maisie rested her chin on her hand, and, still
regarding the sea, spoke hurriedly:

'I know what you want perfectly well, but I
can't give it you, Dick. It isn't my fault; indeed
it isn't. If I felt that I could care for any one——
But I don't feel that I care. I simply don't
understand what the feeling means.'

'Is that true, dear?'

'You've been very good to me, Dickie; and
the only way I can pay you back is by speaking
the truth. I daren't tell a fib. I despise myself
quite enough as it is.'

'What in the world for?'

'Because—because I take everything that you
give me and I give you nothing in return. It's
mean and selfish of me, and whenever I think
of it, it worries me.'

'Understand once for all, then, that I can manage my own affairs, and if I choose to do anything you aren't to blame. You haven't a single thing to reproach yourself with, darling.'

'Yes, I have, and talking only makes it worse.'

'Then don't talk about it.'

'How can I help myself? If you find me alone for a minute you are always talking about it; and when you aren't you look it. You don't know how I despise myself sometimes.'

'Great goodness!' said Dick, nearly jumping to his feet. 'Speak the truth now, Maisie, if you never speak it again! Do I—does this worrying bore you?'

'No. It does not.'

'You'd tell me if it did?'

'I should let you know, I think.'

'Thank you. The other thing is fatal. But you must learn to forgive a man when he's in love. He's always a nuisance. You must have known that?'

Maisie did not consider the last question worth answering, and Dick was forced to repeat it.

'There were other men, of course. They always worried just when I was in the middle of my work, and wanted me to listen to them.'

'Did you listen?'

'At first; they couldn't understand why I didn't care. And they used to praise my pictures; and I thought they meant it. I used to be proud of the praise, and tell Kami, and—I shall never forget—once Kami laughed at me.'

'You don't like being laughed at, Maisie, do you?'

'I hate it. I never laugh at other people unless—unless they do bad work. Dick, tell me honestly what you think of my pictures generally, —of everything of mine that you've seen.'

'"Honest, honest, and honest over!"' quoted Dick from a catchword of long ago. 'Tell me what Kami always says.'

Maisie hesitated. 'He—he says that there is feeling in them.'

'How dare you tell me a fib like that? Remember, I was under Kami for two years. I know exactly what he says.'

'It isn't a fib.'

'It's worse; it's a half-truth. Kami says, when he puts his head on one side,—so,—"*Il y a du sentiment, mais il n'y a pas de parti pris.*"' He rolled the *r* threateningly, as Kami used to do.

'Yes, that is what he says; and I'm beginning to think that he is right.'

'Certainly he is.' Dick admitted that two people in the world could do and say no wrong. Kami was the man.

'And now you say the same thing. It's so disheartening.'

'I'm sorry, but you asked me to speak the truth. Besides, I love you too much to pretend about your work. It's strong, it's patient sometimes,—not always,—and sometimes there's power in it, but there's no special reason why it should be done at all. At least, that's how it strikes me.'

' There's no special reason why anything in
the world should ever be done. You know that
as well as I do. I only want success.'

' You're going the wrong way to get it, then.
Hasn't Kami ever told you so?'

' Don't quote Kami to me. I want to know
what you think. My work's bad, to begin with.'

' I didn't say that, and I don't think it.'

' It's amateurish, then.'

' That it most certainly is not. You're a work-
woman, darling, to your boot-heels, and I respect
you for that.'

' You don't laugh at me behind my back?'

' No, dear. You see, you are more to me than
any one else. Put this cloak thing round you, or
you'll get chilled.'

Maisie wrapped herself in the soft marten
skins, turning the grey kangaroo fur to the
outside.

' This is delicious,' she said, rubbing her chin
thoughtfully along the fur. ' Well? Why am I
wrong in trying to get a little success?'

' Just because you try. Don't you understand,
darling? Good work has nothing to do with—
doesn't belong to—the person who does it. It's
put into him or her from outside.'

' But how does that affect——'

' Wait a minute. All we can do is to learn
how to do our work, to be masters of our materials
instead of servants, and never to be afraid of
anything.'

' I understand that.'

' Everything else comes from outside ourselves.

Very good. If we sit down quietly to work out
notions that are sent to us, we may or we may not
do something that isn't bad. A great deal depends on being master of the bricks and mortar
of the trade. But the instant we begin to think
about success and the effect of our work—to
play with one eye on the gallery—we lose power
and touch and everything else. At least that's
how I have found it. Instead of being quiet and
giving every power you possess to your work,
you're fretting over something which you can
neither help nor hinder by a minute. See?'

'It's so easy for you to talk in that way.
People like what you do. Don't you ever think
about the gallery?'

'Much too often; but I'm always punished
for it by loss of power. It's as simple as the
Rule of Three. If we make light of our work
by using it for our own ends, our work will make
light of us, and, as we're the weaker, we shall
suffer.'

'*I* don't treat my work lightly. You know
that it's everything to me.'

'Of course; but, whether you realise it or
not, you give two strokes for yourself to one for
your work. It isn't your fault, darling. I do
exactly the same thing, and know that I'm doing
it. Most of the French schools, and all the schools
here, drive the students to work for their own
credit, and for the sake of their pride. I was
told that all the world was interested in my work,
and everybody at Kami's talked turpentine, and
I honestly believed that the world needed elevat-

ing and influencing, and all manner of imperti-
nences, by my brushes. By Jove, I actually
believed that! When my little head was bursting
with a notion that I couldn't handle because I
hadn't sufficient knowledge of my craft, I used to
run about wondering at my own magnificence and
getting ready to astonish the world.'

' But surely one can do that sometimes?'

' Very seldom with malice aforethought, darling. And when it's done it's such a tiny thing,
and the world's so big, and all but a millionth
part of it doesn't care. Maisie, come with me
and I'll show you something of the size of the
world. One can no more avoid working than
eating,—that goes on by itself,—but try to see
what you are working for. I know such little
heavens that I could take you to,—islands tucked
away under the Line. You sight them after
weeks of crashing through water as black as black
marble because it's so deep, and you sit in the
fore-chains day after day and see the sun rise
almost afraid because the sea's so lonely.'

' Who is afraid?—you, or the sun?'

' The sun, of course. And there are noises
under the sea, and sounds overhead in a clear sky.
Then you find your island alive with hot moist
orchids that make mouths at you, and can do
everything except talk. There's a waterfall in it
three hundred feet high, just like a sliver of green
jade laced with silver; and millions of wild bees
live up in the rocks; and you can hear the fat
coconuts falling from the palms; and you order
an ivory-white servant to sling you a long yellow

hammock with tassels on it like ripe maize, and you put up your feet and hear the bees hum and the water fall till you go to sleep.'

' Can one work there? '

' Certainly. One must do something always. You hang your canvas up in a palm-tree and let the parrots criticise. When they scuffle you heave a ripe custard-apple at them, and it bursts in a lather of cream. There are hundreds of places. Come and see them.'

' I don't quite like that place. It sounds lazy. Tell me another.'

' What do you think of a big, red, dead city built of red sandstone, with raw green aloes growing between the stones, lying out neglected on honey-coloured sands? There are forty dead kings there, Maisie, each in a gorgeous tomb finer than all the others. You look at the palaces and streets and shops and tanks, and think that men must live there, till you find a wee grey squirrel rubbing its nose all alone in the market-place, and a jewelled peacock struts out of a carved doorway and spreads its tail against a marble screen as fine-pierced as point-lace. Then a monkey—a little black monkey—walks through the main square to get a drink from a tank forty feet deep. He slides down the creepers to the water's edge, and a friend holds him by the tail in case he should fall in.'

' Is all that true? '

' I have been there and seen. Then evening comes, and the lights change till it's just as though you stood in the heart of a king-opal. A little before sundown, as punctually as clockwork, a big bristly wild boar, with all his family following, trots through the city gate, churning the foam on his tusks. You climb on the shoulder of a blind black stone god and watch that pig choose himself a palace for the night and stump in wagging his tail. Then the night-wind gets up, and the sands move, and you hear the desert outside the city singing, " Now I lay me down to sleep," and everything is dark till the moon rises. Maisie, darling, come with me and see what the world is really like. It's very lovely, and it's very horrible, —but I won't let you see anything horrid,—and it doesn't care your life or mine for pictures or anything else except doing its own work and making love. Come, and I'll show you how to brew sangaree, and sling a hammock, and—oh, thousands of things, and you'll see for yourself what colour means, and we'll find out together what love means, and then, maybe, we shall be allowed to do some good work. Come away ! '

' Why ? ' said Maisie.

' How can you do anything until you have seen everything, or as much as you can? And besides, darling, I love you. Come along with me. You have no business here. You don't belong to this place ; you're half a gipsy,—your face tells that ; and I—even the smell of open water makes me restless. Come across the sea and be happy ! '

He had risen to his feet, and stood in the shadow of the gun, looking down at the girl. The very short winter afternoon had worn away, and, before they knew, the winter moon was

walking the untroubled sea. Long ruled lines of
silver showed where a ripple of the rising tide
was turning over the mud-banks. The wind had
dropped, and in the intense stillness they could
hear a donkey cropping the frosty grass many
yards away. A faint beating like that of a muffled
drum came out of the moon-haze.

'What's that?' said Maisie quickly. 'It
sounds like a heart beating. Where is it?'

Dick was so angry at this sudden wrench to his
pleadings that he could not trust himself to speak,
and in this silence caught the sound. Maisie
from her seat under the gun watched him with a
certain amount of fear. She wished so much
that he would be sensible and cease to worry her
with over-sea emotion that she both could and
could not understand. She was not prepared,
however, for the change in his face as he listened.

'It's a steamer,' he said,—'a twin-screw
steamer, by the beat. I can't make her out, but
she must be standing very close in-shore. Ah!'
as the red of a rocket streaked the haze, 'she's
standing in to signal before she clears the Channel.'

'Is it a wreck?' said Maisie, to whom these
words were as Greek.

Dick's eyes were turned to the sea. 'Wreck!
What nonsense! She's only reporting herself.
Red rocket forward—there's a green light aft
now, and two red rockets from the bridge.'

'What does that mean?'

'It's the signal of the Cross Keys Line running
to Australia. I wonder which boat it is.' The
note of his voice had changed. He seemed

to be talking to himself, and Maisie did not approve of it. The moonlight broke the haze for a moment, touching the black sides of a long steamer working down Channel. 'Four masts and three funnels—she's in deep draught, too. That must be the *Barralong*, or the *Bhutia*. No, the *Bhutia* has a clipper bow. It's the *Barralong*, to Australia. She'll lift the Southern Cross in a week,—lucky old tub!—oh, lucky old tub!'

He stared intently, and moved up the slope of the fort to get a better view, but the mist on the sea thickened again, and the beating of the screws grew fainter. Maisie called to him a little angrily, and he returned, still keeping his eyes to seaward. 'Have you ever seen the Southern Cross blazing right over your head?' he asked. 'It's superb!'

'No,' she said shortly, 'and I don't want to. If you think it's so lovely why don't you go and see it yourself?'

She raised her face from the soft blackness of the marten skins about her throat, and her eyes shone like diamonds. The moonlight on the grey kangaroo fur turned it to frosted silver of the coldest.

'By Jove, Maisie, you look like a little heathen idol tucked up there.' The eyes showed that they did not appreciate the compliment. 'I'm sorry,' he continued. 'The Southern Cross isn't worth looking at unless some one helps you to see. That steamer's out of hearing.'

'Dick,' she said quietly, 'suppose I were to come to you now,—be quiet a minute,—just as

I am, and caring for you just as much as I do.'

' Not as a brother, though? You said you didn't—in the Park.'

' I never had a brother. Suppose I said, " Take me to those places, and in time, perhaps, I might really care for you," what would you do? '

' Send you straight back to where you came from, in a cab. No, I wouldn't; I'd let you walk. But you couldn't do it, dear. And I wouldn't run the risk. You're worth waiting for till you can come without reservation.'

' Do you honestly believe that? '

' I have a hazy sort of idea that I do. Has it never struck you in that light ? '

' Ye—es. I feel so wicked about it.'

' Wickeder than usual? '

' You don't know all I think. It's almost too awful to tell.'

' Never mind. You promised to tell me the truth—at least.'

' It's so ungrateful of me, but—but, though I know you care for me, and I like to have you with me, I'd—I'd even sacrifice you, if that would bring me what I want.'

' My poor little darling! I know that state of mind. It doesn't lead to good work.'

' You aren't angry? Remember, I do despise myself.'

' I'm not exactly flattered,—I had guessed as much before,—but I'm not angry. I'm sorry for you. Surely you ought to have left a littleness like that behind you, years ago.'

' You've no right to patronise me! I only

want what I have worked for so long.   It came
to *you* without any trouble, and—and I don't
think it's fair.'

'What can I do?   I'd give ten years of my
life to get you what you want.   But I can't help
you; even I can't help.'

A murmur of dissent from Maisie.   He went
on:—

' And I know by what you have just said that
you're on the wrong road to success.   It isn't got
at by sacrificing other people,—I've had that much
knocked into me;   you must sacrifice yourself,
and live under orders, and never think for yourself, and never have real satisfaction in your work
except just at the beginning, when you're reaching
out after a notion.'

' How can you believe all that? '

' There's no question of belief or disbelief.
That's the law, and you take it or refuse it as
you please.   I try to obey, but I can't, and then
my work turns bad on my hands.   Under any
circumstances, remember, four-fifths of everybody's work must be bad.   But the remnant is
worth the trouble for its own sake.'

' Isn't it nice to get credit even for bad work? '

' It's much too nice.   But—— May I tell you
something?   It isn't a pretty tale, but you're so
like a man that I forget when I'm talking to you.'

' Tell me.'

' Once when I was out in the Sudan I went
over some ground that we had been fighting on
for three days.   There were twelve hundred dead;
and we hadn't had time to bury them.'

' How ghastly ! '

' I had been at work on a big double-sheet sketch, and I was wondering what people would think of it at home. The sight of that field taught me a good deal. It looked just like a bed of horrible toadstools in all colours, and—I'd never seen men in bulk go back to their beginnings before. So I began to understand that men and women were only material to work with, and that what they said or did was of no consequence. See? Strictly speaking, you might just as well put your ear down to the palette to catch what your colours are saying.'

' Dick, that's disgraceful ! '

' Wait a minute. I said, strictly speaking. Unfortunately, everybody must be either a man or a woman.'

' I'm glad you allow that much.'

' In your case I don't. You aren't a woman. But ordinary people, Maisie, must behave and work as such. That's what makes me so savage.' He hurled a pebble towards the sea as he spoke. ' I know that it is outside my business to care what people say; I can see that it spoils my output if I listen to 'em; and yet, confound it all,—another pebble flew seaward,—' I can't help purring when I'm rubbed the right way. Even when I can see on a man's forehead that he is lying his way through a clump of pretty speeches, those lies make me happy and play the mischief with my hand.'

' And when he doesn't say pretty things ? '

' Then, belovedest,'—Dick grinned,—' I forget that I am the steward of these gifts, and I want to make that man love and appreciate my work with a thick stick. It's too humiliating altogether; but I suppose even if one were an angel and painted humans altogether from outside, one would lose in touch what one gained in grip.'

Maisie laughed at the idea of Dick as an angel.

'But you seem to think,' she said, 'that everything nice spoils your hand.'

'I don't think. It's the law,—just the same as it was at Mrs. Jennett's. Everything that is nice *does* spoil your hand. I'm glad you see so clearly.'

'I don't like the view.'

'Nor I. But—have got orders. What can do? Are you strong enough to face it alone?'

'I suppose I must.'

'Let me help, darling. We can hold each other very tight and try to walk straight. We shall blunder horribly, but it will be better than stumbling apart. Maisie, can't you see reason?'

'I don't think we should get on together. We should be two of a trade, so we should never agree.'

'How I should like to meet the man who made that proverb! He lived in a cave and ate raw bear, I fancy. I'd make him chew his own arrow-heads. Well?'

'I should be only half married to you. I should worry and fuss about my work, as I do now. Four days out of the seven I'm not fit to speak to.'

' You talk as if no one else in the world had ever used a brush. D'you suppose that I don't know the feeling of worry and bother and can't-get-at-ness? You're lucky if you only have it four days out of the seven. What difference would that make?'

' A great deal—if you had it too.'

' Yes, but I could respect it. Another man might not. He might laugh at you. But there's no use talking about it. If you can think in that way you can't care for me—yet.'

The tide had nearly covered the mud-banks, and twenty little ripples broke on the beach before Maisie chose to speak.

' Dick,' she said slowly, ' I believe very much that you are better than I am.'

' This doesn't seem to bear on the argument—but in what way?'

' I don't quite know, but in what you said about work and things; and then you're so patient. Yes, you're better than I am.'

Dick considered rapidly the murkiness of an average man's life. There was nothing in the review to fill him with a sense of virtue. He lifted the hem of the cloak to his lips.

' Why,' said Maisie, making as though she had not noticed, ' can you see things that I can't? I don't believe what you believe; but you're right, I believe.'

' If I've seen anything, God knows I couldn't have seen it but for you, and I know that I couldn't have said it except to you. You seemed to make everything clear for a minute; but I

don't practise what I preach. You would help
me. . . . There are only us two in the world for
all purposes, and—and you like to have me with
you?'

'Of course I do. I wonder if you can realise
how utterly lonely I am!'

'Darling, I think I can.'

'Two years ago, when I first took the little
house, I used to walk up and down the back-
garden trying to cry. I never can cry. Can you?'

'It's some time since I tried. What was the
trouble? Overwork?'

'I don't know; but I used to dream that I
had broken down, and had no money, and was
starving in London. I thought about it all day,
and it frightened me—oh, how it frightened me!'

'I know that fear. It's the most terrible of
all. It wakes me up in the night sometimes.
You oughtn't to know anything about it.'

'How do *you* know?'

'Never mind. Is your three hundred a year
safe?'

'It's in Consols.'

'Very well. If any one comes to you and
recommends a better investment,—even if I
should come to you,—don't you listen. Never
shift the money for a minute, and never lend a
penny of it,—even to the red-haired girl.'

'Don't scold me so! I'm not likely to be
foolish.'

'The earth is full of men who'd sell their
souls for three hundred a year; and women
come and talk, and borrow a five-pound note

here and a ten-pound note there; and a woman
has no conscience in a money debt. Stick to
your money, Maisie. There's nothing more
ghastly in the world than poverty in London.
It's scared me. By Jove, it put the fear into *me*!
And one oughtn't to be afraid of anything.'

To each man is appointed his particular dread,
—the terror that, if he does not fight against it,
must cow him even to the loss of his manhood.
Dick's experience of the sordid misery of want
had entered into the deeps of him, and, lest he
might find virtue too easy, that memory stood
behind him, tempting to shame, when dealers
came to buy his wares. As the Nilghai quaked
against his will at the still green water of a lake
or a mill-dam, as Torpenhow flinched before any
white arm that could cut or stab and loathed
himself for flinching, Dick feared the poverty he
had once tasted half in jest. His burden was
heavier than the burdens of his companions.

Maisie watched the face working in the moonlight.

'You've plenty of pennies now,' she said
soothingly.

'I shall never get enough,' he began, with
vicious emphasis. Then, laughing, 'I shall
always be threepence short in my accounts.'

'Why threepence?'

'I carried a man's bag once from Liverpool
Street Station to Blackfriars Bridge. It was a
sixpenny job,—you needn't laugh; indeed it was,
—and I wanted the money desperately. He only
gave me threepence; and he hadn't even the

decency to pay in silver. Whatever money I make I shall never get that odd threepence out of the world.'

This was not language befitting the man who had preached of the sanctity of work. It jarred on Maisie, who preferred her payment in applause, which, since all men desire it, must be of the right. She hunted for her little purse and gravely took out a threepenny bit.

'There it is,' she said. 'I'll pay you, Dickie; and don't worry any more; it isn't worth while. Are you paid?'

'I am,' said the very human apostle of fair craft, taking the coin. 'I'm paid a thousand times, and we'll close that account. It shall live on my watch-chain; and you're an angel, Maisie.'

'I'm very cramped, and I'm feeling a little cold. Good gracious! the cloak is all white, and so is your moustache! I never knew it was so chilly.'

A light frost lay white on the shoulder of Dick's ulster. He, too, had forgotten the state of the weather. They laughed together, and with that laugh ended all serious discourse.

They ran inland across the waste to warm themselves, then turned to look at the glory of the full tide under the moonlight and the intense black shadows of the furze-bushes. It was an additional joy to Dick that Maisie could see colour even as he saw it,—could see the blue in the white of the mist, the violet that is in grey palings, and all things else as they are,—not of one hue, but a thousand. And the moonlight came into Maisie's soul, so that she, usually reserved, chattered of herself and of the things she took interest in,—of Kami, wisest of teachers, and of the girls in the studio,—of the Poles, who will kill themselves with overwork if they are not checked; of the French, who talk at great length of much more than they will ever accomplish; of the slovenly English, who toil hopelessly and cannot understand that inclination does not imply power; of the Americans, whose rasping voices in the hush of a hot afternoon strain tense-drawn nerves to breaking-point, and whose suppers lead to indigestion; of tempestuous Russians, neither to hold nor to bind, who tell the girls ghost-stories till the girls shriek; of stolid Germans, who come to learn one thing, and, having mastered that much, stolidly go away and copy pictures for evermore. Dick listened enraptured because it was Maisie who spoke. He knew the old life.

'It hasn't changed much,' he said. 'Do they still steal colours at lunch-time?'

'Not steal. "Attract" is the word. Of course they do. I'm good—I only attract ultramarine; but there are students who'd attract flake-white.'

'I've done it myself. You can't help it when the palettes are hung up. Every colour is common property once it runs down,—even though you start it with a drop of oil. It teaches people not to waste their tubes.'

'I should like to "attract" some of your colours, Dick. Perhaps I might catch your success with them.'

' I mustn't say a bad word, but I should like to. What in the world, which you've just missed a lovely chance of seeing, does success or want of success, or a three-storeyed success, matter compared with—— No, I won't open that question again. It's time to go back to Town.'

' I'm sorry, Dick, but——'

' You're much more interested in that than you are in me.'

' I don't know. I don't think I am.'

' What will you give me if I tell you a sure short-cut to everything you want,—the trouble and the fuss and the tangle and all the rest? Will you promise to obey me?'

' Of course.'

' In the first place, you must never forget a meal because you happen to be at work. You forgot your lunch twice last week,' said Dick, at a venture, for he knew with whom he was dealing.

' No, no,—only once, really.'

' That's bad enough. And you mustn't take a cup of tea and a biscuit in place of a regular dinner, because dinner happens to be a trouble.'

' You're making fun of me!'

' I never was more in earnest in my life. Oh, my love, my love, hasn't it dawned on you yet what you are to me? Here's the whole earth in a conspiracy to give you a chill, or run over you, or drench you to the skin, or cheat you out of your money, or let you die of overwork and under-feeding, and I haven't the mere right to look after you. Why, I don't even know if you have sense

enough to put on warm things when the weather's
cold.'

'Dick, you're the most awful boy to talk to—
really! How do you suppose I managed when
you were away?'

'I wasn't here, and I didn't know. But now
I'm back I'd give everything I have for the right
of telling you to come in out of the rain.'

'Your success too?'

This time it cost Dick a severe struggle to
refrain from bad words.

'As Mrs. Jennett used to say, you're a trial,
Maisie! You've been cooped up in the schools
too long, and you think every one is looking at
you. There aren't twelve hundred people in the
world who understand pictures. The others pretend and don't care. Remember, I've seen
twelve hundred men dead in toadstool-beds. It's
only the voice of the tiniest little fraction of
people that makes success. The real world
doesn't care a tinker's—doesn't care a bit. For
aught you or I know, every man in the world
may be arguing with a Maisie of his own.'

'Poor Maisie!'

'Poor Dick, I think. Do you believe while
he's fighting for what's dearer than his life he
wants to look at a picture? And even if he did,
and if all the world did, and a thousand million
people rose up and shouted hymns to my honour
and glory, would that make up to me for the
knowledge that you were out shopping in the
Edgware Road on a rainy day without an umbrella? Now we'll go to the station.'

'But you said on the beach——' persisted Maisie with a certain fear.

Dick groaned aloud: 'Yes, I know what I said. My work is everything I have, or am, or hope to be, to me, and I believe I've learnt the law that governs it; but I've some lingering sense of fun left,—though you've nearly knocked it out of me. I can just see that it isn't everything to all the world. "Do what I say, and not what I do."'

Maisie was careful not to reopen debatable matters, and they returned to London joyously. The terminus stopped Dick in the midst of an eloquent harangue on the beauties of exercise. He would buy Maisie a horse, — such a horse as never yet bowed head to bit,—would stable it, with a companion, some twenty miles from London, and Maisie, solely for her health's sake, should ride with him twice or thrice a week.

'That's absurd,' said she. 'It wouldn't be proper.'

'Now who in all London to-night would have sufficient interest or audacity to call us two to account for anything we chose to do?'

Maisie looked at the lamps, the fog, and the hideous turmoil. Dick was right; but horse-flesh did not make for Art as she understood it.

'You're very nice sometimes, but you're very foolish more times. I'm not going to let you give me horses, or take you out of your way to-night. I'll go home by myself. Only I want you to promise me something. You won't think any more about that extra threepence, will you?

Remember, you've been paid; and I won't allow
you to be spiteful and do bad work for a little
thing like that. You can be so big that you
mustn't be tiny.'

This was turning the tables with a vengeance.
There remained only to put Maisie into her
hansom.

'Good-bye,' she said simply. 'You'll come
on Sunday. It has been a beautiful day, Dick.
Why can't it be like this always?'

'Because love's like line-work: you must go
forward or backward; you can't stand still. By
the way, go on with your line-work. Good-night,
and, for my—for any sake, take care of yourself.'

He turned to walk home, meditating. The
day had brought him nothing that he hoped for,
but—surely this was worth many days—it had
brought him nearer to Maisie. The end was only
a question of time now, and the prize well worth
the waiting. By instinct, once more, he turned
to the river.

'And she understood at once,' he said, looking
at the water. 'She found out my pet besetting
sin on the spot, and paid it off. My God, how
she understood! And she said I was better than
she was! Better than she was!' He laughed at
the absurdity of the notion. 'I wonder if girls
guess at one-half a man's life. They can't, or—
they wouldn't marry us.' He took her gift out
of his pocket, and considered it in the light of a
miracle and a pledge of the comprehension that,
one day, would lead to perfect happiness. Meantime Maisie was alone in London, with none to

save her from danger. And the packed wilderness was very full of danger.

Dick made his prayer to Fate disjointedly after the manner of the heathen as he threw the piece of silver into the river. If any evil were to befall, let him bear the burden and let Maisie go unscathed, since the threepenny piece was dearest to him of all his possessions. It was a small coin in itself, but Maisie had given it, and the Thames held it, and surely the Fates would be bribed for this once.

The drowning of the coin seemed to cut him free from thought of Maisie for the moment. He took himself off the bridge and went whistling to his chambers with a strong yearning for some man-talk and tobacco after his first experience of an entire day spent in the society of a woman. There was a stronger desire at his heart when there rose before him an unsolicited vision of the *Barralong* dipping deep and sailing free for the Southern Cross.

CHAPTER VIII

And these two, as I have told you,
Were the friends of Hiawatha,
Chibiabos, the musician,
And the very strong man, Kwasind.
Hiawatha.

TORPENHOW was paging the last sheets of some manuscript, while the Nilghai, who had come for chess and remained to talk tactics, was reading through the first part, commenting scornfully the while.

' It's picturesque enough and it's sketchy,' said he ; ' but as a serious consideration of affairs in Eastern Europe, it's not worth much.'

' It's off my hands at any rate. . . . Thirty-seven, thirty-eight, thirty-nine slips altogether, aren't there ? That should make between eleven and twelve pages of valuable misinformation. Heigho ! ' Torpenhow shuffled the writing together and hummed :—

' Young lambs to sell, young lambs to sell,
If I'd as much money as I could tell,
I never would cry, Young lambs to sell ! '

Dick entered, self-conscious and a little defiant, but in the best of tempers with all the world.

'Back at last?' said Torpenhow.

'More or less. What have you been doing?'

'Work. Dickie, you behave as though the Bank of England were behind you. Here's Sunday, Monday, and Tuesday gone and you haven't done a line. It's scandalous.'

'The notions come and go, my children—they come and go like our 'baccy,' he answered, filling his pipe. 'Moreover,'—he stooped to thrust a spill into the grate—'Apollo does not always stretch his—— Oh, confound your clumsy jests, Nilghai!'

'This is not the place to preach the theory of direct inspiration,' said the Nilghai, returning Torpenhow's large and workmanlike bellows to their nail on the wall. 'We believe in cobblers' wax. *Là!*—where you sit down.'

'If you weren't so big and fat,' said Dick, looking round for a weapon, 'I'd——'

'No skylarking in my rooms. You two smashed half my furniture last time you threw the cushions about. You might have the decency to say How d'you do? to Binkie. Look at him.'

Binkie had jumped down from the sofa and was fawning round Dick's knee, and scratching at his boots.

'Dear man!' said Dickie, snatching him up, and kissing him on the black patch above his right eye. 'Did ums was, Binks? Did that ugly Nilghai turn you off the sofa? Bite him, Mr. Binkle.' He pitched him on the Nilghai's stomach, as the big man lay at ease, and Binkie pretended to destroy the Nilghai inch by inch, till a sofa-cushion extinguished him, and panting he stuck out his tongue at the company.

' The Binkie-boy went for a walk this morning before you were up, Torp. I saw him making love to the butcher at the corner when the shutters were being taken down—just as if he hadn't enough to eat in his own proper house,' said Dick.

' Binks, is that a true bill? ' said Torpenhow severely. The little dog retreated under the sofa-cushion, and showed by the fat white back of him that he really had no further interest in the discussion.

' Strikes me that another disreputable dog went for a walk, too,' said the Nilghai. ' What made you get up so early? Torp said you might be buying a horse? '

' He knows it would need three of us for a serious business like that. No, I felt lonesome and unhappy, so I went out to look at the sea, and watch the pretty ships go by.'

' Where did you go? '

' Somewhere on the Channel. Progly or Snigly, or some one-horse watering-place was its name; I've forgotten; but it was only two hours' run from London and the ships went by.'

' Did you see anything you knew? '

' Only the *Barralong* outwards to Australia, and an Odessa grain-boat loaded down by the head. It was a thick day, but the sea smelt good.'

' Wherefore put on one's best trousers to see the *Barralong*? ' said Torpenhow, pointing.

' Because I've nothing except these things and

my painting duds.   Besides, I wanted to do honour
to the sea.'

'Did she make you feel restless?' asked the
Nilghai keenly.

'Crazy. Don't speak of it. I'm sorry I went.'

Torpenhow and the Nilghai exchanged a look
as Dick, stooping, busied himself among the
former's boots and trees.

'These will do,' he said at last; 'I can't say I
think much of your taste in slippers, but the fit's
the thing.' He slipped his feet into a pair of
socklike sambhur-skin foot-coverings, found a
long chair, and lay at length.

'They're my own pet pair,' Torpenhow said.
'I was just going to put them on myself.'

'All your reprehensible selfishness. Just because you see me happy for a minute, you want
to worry me and stir me up. Find another pair.'

'Good for you that Dick can't wear your
clothes, Torp. You two live communistically,'
said the Nilghai.

'Dick never has anything that I can wear.
He's only useful to sponge upon.'

'Confound you, have you been rummaging
round among my caches, then?' said Dick. 'I
put a sovereign in the tobacco-jar yesterday.
How do you expect a man to keep his accounts
properly if you——'

Here the Nilghai began to laugh, and Torpenhow joined him.

'Hid a sovereign yesterday! You're no sort
of a financier. You lent me a fiver about a month
back. Do you remember?' Torpenhow said.

'Yes, of course.'

'Do you remember that I paid it you ten days later, and you put it at the bottom of the tobacco?'

'By Jove, did I? I thought it was in one of my colour-boxes.'

'You thought! About a week ago I went into your studio to get some 'baccy and found it.'

'What did you do with it?'

'Took the Nilghai to a theatre and fed him.'

'You couldn't feed the Nilghai under twice the money—not though you gave him Army beef. Well, I suppose I should have found it out sooner or later. What is there to laugh at?'

'You're a most amazing cuckoo in many directions,' said the Nilghai, still chuckling over the thought of the dinner. 'Never mind. We had both been working very hard, and it was your unearned increment we spent, and as you're only a loafer it didn't matter.'

'That's pleasant—from the man who is bursting with my meat, too. I'll get that dinner back one of these days. Suppose we go to a theatre now.'

'Put our boots on,—and dress,—and wash?' The Nilghai spoke very lazily.

'I withdraw the motion.'

'Suppose, just for a change—as a startling variety, you know—we, that is to say we, get our charcoal and our canvas and go on with our work.' Torpenhow spoke pointedly, but Dick only wriggled his toes inside the soft leather moccasins.

'What a one-idea'd clucker it is! If I had any unfinished figures on hand, I haven't any model;

if I had my model, I haven't any spray, and I never leave charcoal unfixed overnight; and if I had my spray and twenty photographs of backgrounds, I couldn't do anything to-night. I don't feel that way.'

' Binkie-dog, he's a lazy hog, isn't he? ' said the Nilghai.

' Very good, I *will* do some work,' said Dick, rising swiftly. ' I'll fetch the Nungapunga Book, and we'll add another picture to the Nilghai Saga.'

' Aren't you worrying him a little too much? ' asked the Nilghai, when Dick had left the room.

' Perhaps, but I know what he can turn out if he likes. It makes me savage to hear him praised for past work when I know what he ought to do. You and I are arranged for—'

' By Kismet and our own powers, more's the pity. I have dreamed of a good deal.'

' So have I, but we know our limitations now. I'm dashed if I know what Dick's may be when he gives himself to his work. That's what makes me so keen about him.'

' And when all's said and done, you will be put aside—quite rightly—for a female girl.'

' I wonder . . . . Where do you think he has been to-day? '

' To the sea. Didn't you see the look in his eyes when he talked about her? He's as restless as a swallow in autumn.'

' Yes ; but did he go alone? '

' I don't know, and I don't care, but he has the beginnings of the go-fever upon him. He wants to up-stakes and move out. There's no mistaking the signs. Whatever he may have said before, he has the call upon him now.'

' It might be his salvation,' Torpenhow said.

' Perhaps—if you care to take the responsibility of being a saviour : I'm averse to tampering with souls myself.'

Dick returned with a great clasped sketch-book that the Nilghai knew well and did not love too much. In it Dick had drawn in his playtime all manner of moving incidents, experienced by himself or related to him by the others, of all the four corners of the earth. But the wider range of the Nilghai's body and life attracted him most. When truth failed here he fell back on fiction of the wildest, and represented incidents in the Nilghai's career that were unseemly,—his marriages with many African princesses, his shameless betrayal, for Arab wives, of army corps to the Mahdi, his tattooment by skilled operators in Burma, his interview (and his fears) with the yellow headsman in the blood-stained execution-ground of Canton, and finally, the passings of his spirit into the bodies of whales, elephants, and toucans. Torpenhow from time to time had added rhymed descriptions, and the whole was a curious piece of art, because Dick decided, having regard to the name of the book, which being interpreted means ' naked,' that it would be wrong to draw the Nilghai with any clothes on, under any circumstances. Consequently the last sketch, representing that much-enduring man calling on the War Office to press his claims to the Egyptian medal, was hardly delicate. He settled himself comfortably at Torpenhow's table and turned over the pages.

'What a fortune you would have been to Blake, Nilghai!' he said. 'There's a succulent pinkness about some of these sketches that's more than life-like. "The Nilghai surrounded while bathing by the Mahdieh"—that was founded on fact, eh?'

'It was very nearly my last bath, you irreverent dauber. Has Binkie come into the Saga yet?'

'No; the Binkie-boy hasn't done anything except eat and kill cats. Let's see. Here you are as a stained-glass saint in a church. Deuced decorative lines about your anatomy; you ought to be grateful for being handed down to posterity in this way. Fifty years hence you'll exist in rare and curious fascimiles at ten guineas each. What shall I try this time? The domestic life of the Nilghai?'

'Hasn't got any.'

'The undomestic life of the Nilghai, then. Of course. Mass-meeting of his wives in Trafalgar Square. That's it. They came from the ends of the earth to attend the Nilghai's wedding to an English bride. This shall be in sepia. It's a sweet material to work with.'

'It's a scandalous waste of time,' said Torpenhow.

'Don't worry; it keeps one's hand in—specially when you begin without the pencil.' He set to work rapidly. 'That's Nelson's Column. Presently the Nilghai will appear shinning up it.'

' Give him some clothes this time.'

' Certainly—a veil and an orange-wreath, because he's been married.'

' Gad, that's clever enough ! ' said Torpenhow
over his shoulder, as Dick brought out of the
paper with three twirls of the brush a very fat
back and labouring shoulder pressed against the
stone.

' Just imagine,' Dick continued, ' if we could
publish a few of these dear little things every
time the Nilghai subsidises a man who can write,
to give the public an honest opinion of my
pictures.'

' Well, you'll admit I always tell you when I
have done anything of that kind. I know I can't
hammer you as you ought to be hammered, so I
give the job to another. Young Maclagan, for
instance——'

' No-o—one half-minute, old man ; stick your
hand out against the dark of the wall-paper—
you only burble and call me names. That left
shoulder's out of drawing. I must literally throw
a veil over that. Where's my penknife? Well,
what about Maclagan?'

' I only gave him his riding-orders to—to
lambaste you on general principles for not pro-
ducing work that will last.'

' Whereupon that young fool,'—Dick threw
back his head and shut one eye as he shifted the
page under his hand,—' being left alone with an
ink-pot and what he conceived were his own
notions, went and spilt them both over me in the
papers. You might have engaged a grown man

for the business, Nilghai. How do you think the bridal veil looks now, Torp?'

'How the deuce do three dabs and two scratches make the stuff stand away from the body as it does?' said Torpenhow, to whom Dick's methods were always new.

'It just depends on where you put 'em. If Maclagan had known that much about his business he might have done better.'

'Why don't you put the damned dabs into something that will stay, then?' insisted the Nilghai, who had really taken considerable trouble in hiring for Dick's benefit the pen of a young gentleman who devoted most of his waking hours to an anxious consideration of the aims and ends of Art, which, he wrote, was one and indivisible.

'Wait a minute till I see how I am going to manage my procession of wives. You seem to have married extensively, and I must rough 'em in with the pencil—Medes, Parthians, Edomites. . . . Now, setting aside the weakness and the wickedness and—and the fat-headedness of deliberately trying to do work that will live, as they call it, I'm content with the knowledge that I've done my best up to date, and I shan't do anything like it again for some hours at least—probably years. Most probably never.'

'What! any stuff you have in stock your best work?' said Torpenhow.

'Anything you've sold?' said the Nilghai.

'Oh no. It isn't here and it isn't sold. Better than that, it can't be sold, and I don't think any one knows where it is. I'm sure I don't. . . .

And yet more and more wives, on the north side of the Square. Observe the virtuous horror of the lions ! '

' You may as well explain,' said Torpenhow, and Dick lifted his head from the paper.

' The sea reminded me of it,' he said slowly. ' I wish it hadn't. It weighs some few thousand tons—unless you cut it out with a cold chisel.'

' Don't be an idiot. You can't pose with us here,' said the Nilghai.

' There's no pose in the matter at all. It's a fact. I was loafing from Lima to Auckland in a big, old, condemned passenger-ship turned into a cargo-boat and owned by a second-hand Italian firm. She was a crazy basket. We were cut down to fifteen ton of coal a day, and we thought ourselves lucky when we kicked seven knots out of her. Then we used to stop and let the bearings cool down, and wonder whether the crack in the shaft was spreading.'

' Were you a steward or a stoker in those days ? '

' I was flush for the time being, so I was a passenger, or else I should have been a steward, I think,' said Dick with perfect gravity, returning to the procession of angry wives. ' I was the only other passenger from Lima, and the ship was half empty, and full of rats and cockroaches and scorpions.'

' But what has this to do with the picture ? '

' Wait a minute. She had been in the China passenger trade and her lower deck had bunks for two thousand pigtails. Those were all taken down and she was empty up to her nose, and the lights came through the port-holes—most annoying lights to work in till you got used to them. I hadn't anything to do for weeks. The ship's charts were in pieces and our skipper daren't run south for fear of catching a storm. So he did his best to knock all the Society Islands out of the water one by one, and I went into the lower deck, and did my picture on the port side as far forward in her as I could go. There was some brown paint and some green paint that they used for the boats, and some black paint for ironwork, and that was all I had.'

'The passengers must have thought you mad.'

'There was only one, and it was a woman; but it gave me the notion of my picture.'

'What was she like?' said Torpenhow.

'She was a sort of Negroid-Jewess-Cuban; with morals to match. She couldn't read or write, and she didn't want to, but she used to come down and watch me paint, and the skipper didn't like it, because he was paying her passage and had to be on the bridge occasionally.'

'I see. That must have been cheerful.'

'It was the best time I ever had. To begin with, we didn't know whether we should go up or go down any minute when there was a sea on; and when it was calm it was Paradise; and the woman used to mix the paints and talk broken English, and the skipper used to steal down every few minutes to the lower deck, because he said he was afraid of fire. So, you see, we could never tell when we might be caught, and I had a splendid notion to work out in only three keys of colour.'

'What was the notion?'

'Two lines in Poe—

'Neither the angels in Heaven above nor the demons down
    under the sea,
Can ever dissever my soul from the soul of the beautiful
    Annabel Lee.

It came out of the sea—all by itself. I drew that fight, fought out in green water over the naked, choking soul, and the woman served as the model for the devils and the angels both—sea-devils and sea-angels, and the soul half drowned between them. It doesn't sound much, but when there was a good light on the lower deck it looked very fine and creepy. It was seven by fourteen feet, all done in shifting light for shifting light.'

'Did the woman inspire you much?' said Torpenhow.

'She and the sea between them—immensely. There was a heap of bad drawing in that picture. I remember I went out of my way to foreshorten for sheer delight of doing it, and I foreshortened damnably, but for all that it's the best thing I've ever done; and now I suppose the ship's broken up or gone down. Whew! What a time that was!'

'What happened after all?'

'It all ended. They were loading her with wool when I left the ship, but even the stevedores kept the picture clear to the last. The eyes of the demons scared them, I honestly believe.'

'And the woman?'

'She was scared too when it was finished. She used to cross herself before she went down to look at it. Just three colours and no chance of getting any more, and the sea outside and unlimited love-making inside, and the fear of death atop of everything else, O Lord!' He had ceased to look at the sketch, but was staring straight in front of him across the room.

'Why don't you try something of the same kind now?' said the Nilghai.

'Because those things come not by fasting and prayer. When I find a cargo-boat and a Jewess-Cuban and another notion and the same old life, I may.'

'You won't find them here,' said the Nilghai.

'No, I shall not.' Dick shut the sketch-book with a bang. 'This room's as hot as an oven. Open the window, some one.'

He leaned into the darkness, watching the greater darkness of London below him. The chambers stood much higher than the other houses, commanding a hundred chimneys — crooked cowls that looked like sitting cats as they swung round, and other uncouth brick and zinc mysteries supported by iron stanchions and clamped by S-pieces. Northward the lights of Piccadilly Circus and Leicester Square threw a copper-coloured glare above the black roofs, and southward lay all the orderly lights of the Thames. A train rolled out across one of the railway bridges, and its thunder drowned for a minute the dull roar of the streets. The Nilghai looked at his watch and said shortly, 'That's the Paris night-mail. You can book from here to St. Petersburg if you choose.'

Dick crammed head and shoulders out of the window and looked across the river. Torpenhow came to his side, while the Nilghai passed over quietly to the piano and opened it. Binkie, making himself as large as possible, spread out upon the sofa with the air of one who is not to be lightly disturbed.

'Well,' said the Nilghai to the two pairs of shoulders, 'have you never seen this place before?'

A steam-tug on the river hooted as she towed her barges to wharf. Then the boom of the traffic came into the room. Torpenhow nudged Dick. 'Good place to bank in—bad place to bunk in, Dickie, isn't it?'

Dick's chin was in his hand as he answered, in the words of a general not without fame, still looking out on the darkness: ' " My God, what a city to loot ! " '

Binkie found the night air tickling his whiskers and sneezed plaintively.

'We shall give the Binkie-dog a cold,' said Torpenhow. ' Come in,' and they withdrew their heads. ' You'll be buried in Kensal Green, Dick, one of these days, if it isn't closed by the time you want to go there—buried within two feet of some one else, his wife and his family.'

'Allah forbid ! I shall get away before that time comes. Give a man room to stretch his legs, Mr. Binkle.' Dick flung himself down on the sofa and tweaked Binkie's velvet ears, yawning heavily the while.

' You'll find that wardrobe-case very much out of tune,' Torpenhow said to the Nilghai. ' It's never touched except by you.'

' A piece of gross extravagance,' Dick grunted. ' The Nilghai only comes when I'm out.'

' That's because you're always out. Howl, Nilghai, and let him hear.'

> ' The life of the Nilghai is fraud and slaughter,
> His writings are watered Dickens and water;
> But the voice of the Nilghai raised on high
> Makes even the Mahdieh glad to die ! '

Dick quoted from Torpenhow's letterpress in the Nungapunga Book. ' How do they call moose in Canada, Nilghai ? '

The man laughed. Singing was his one polite accomplishment, as many Press-tents in far-off lands had known.

' What shall I sing ? ' said he, turning in the chair.

' " Moll Roe in the Morning," ' said Torpenhow at a venture.

' No,' said Dick sharply, and the Nilghai opened his eyes. The old chanty whereof he, among a very few, possessed all the words was not a pretty one, but Dick had heard it many times before without wincing. Without prelude he launched into that stately tune that calls together and troubles the hearts of the gipsies of the sea :—

> ' Farewell and adieu to you, fair Spanish ladies,
> Farewell and adieu to you, ladies of Spain.'

Dick turned uneasily on the sofa, for he could hear the bows of the *Barralong* crashing into the green seas on her way to the Southern Cross. Then came the chorus :—

> ' We'll rant and we'll roar like true British sailors,
> We'll rant and we'll roar across the salt seas,
> Until we take soundings in the Channel of Old England,
> From Ushant to Scilly 'tis forty-five leagues.'

' Thirty-five—thirty-five,' said Dick petulantly. ' Don't tamper with Holy Writ.   Go on, Nilghai.'

> ' The first land we made it was called the Deadman,'

and they sang to the end very vigorously.

' That would be a better song if her head were turned the other way—to the Ushant light, for instance,' said the Nilghai.

' Flinging its arms about like a mad windmill,' said Torpenhow.   ' Give us something else, Nilghai.   You're in fine fog-horn form to-night.'

' Give us " The Ganges Pilot " : you sang that in the square the night before El-Maghrib.   By the way, I wonder how many of the chorus are alive to-night,' said Dick.

Torpenhow considered for a minute.   ' By Jove ! I believe only you and I.   Raynor, Vickery, and Deenes—all dead ; Vincent caught smallpox in Cairo, carried it here and died of it.   Yes, only you and I and the Nilghai.'

' Umph ! And yet the men here who've done their work in a well-warmed studio all their lives, with a policeman at each corner, say that I charge too much for my pictures.'

' They are buying your work, not your insurance policies, dear child,' said the Nilghai.

' I gambled with one to get at the other.

Don't preach. Go on with the " Pilot." Where in the world did you get that song?'

'On a tombstone,' said the Nilghai. 'On a tombstone in a distant land. I made it an accompaniment with heaps of bass chords.'

'Oh, Vanity! Begin.' And the Nilghai began :—

'I have slipped my cable, messmates, I'm drifting down with the tide,
I have my sailing orders, while ye at anchor ride.
And never on fair June morning have I put out to sea
With clearer conscience or better hope, or a heart more light and free.

'Shoulder to shoulder, Joe, my boy, into the crowd like a wedge.
Strike with the hangers, messmates, but do not cut with the edge.
Cries Charnock, " Scatter the faggots, double that Brahmin in two.
The tall pale widow for me, Joe, the little brown girl for you ! "

'Young Joe (you're nearing sixty), why is your hide so dark?
Katie has soft fair blue eyes, who blackened yours?—Why, hark ! '

They were all singing now, Dick with the roar of the wind of the open sea about his ears as the deep bass voice let itself go.

'The morning gun—Ho, steady !—the arquebuses to me !
I ha' sounded the Dutch High Admiral's heart as my lead doth sound the sea.

'Sounding, sounding the Ganges, floating down with the tide,
Moor me close to Charnock, next to my nut-brown bride.
My blessing to Kate at Fairlight—Holwell, my thanks to you ;
Steady ! We steer for Heaven, through sand-drifts cold and blue.'

'Now what is there in that nonsense to make a man restless?' said Dick, hauling Binkie from his feet to his chest.

'It depends on the man,' said Torpenhow.

'The man who has been down to look at the sea,' said the Nilghai.

'I didn't know she was going to upset me in this fashion.'

'That's what men say when they go to say good-bye to a woman. It's more easy, though, to get rid of three women than a piece of one's life and surroundings.'

'But a woman can be——' began Dick unguardedly.

'A piece of one's life,' continued Torpenhow. 'No, she can't.' His face darkened for a moment. 'She says she wants to sympathise with you and help you in your work, and everything else that clearly a man must do for himself. Then she sends round five notes a day to ask why the dickens you haven't been wasting your time with her.'

'Don't generalise,' said the Nilghai. 'By the time you arrive at five notes a day you must have gone through a good deal and behaved accordingly. Shouldn't begin these things, my son.'

'I shouldn't have gone down to the sea,' said Dick, just a little anxious to change the conversation. 'And you shouldn't have sung.'

'The sea isn't sending you five notes a day,' said the Nilghai.

'No, but I'm fatally compromised. She's an enduring old hag, and I'm sorry I ever met her.

Why wasn't I born and bred and dead in a three-pair back?'

'Hear him blaspheming his first love! Why in the world shouldn't you listen to her?' said Torpenhow.

Before Dick could reply the Nilghai lifted up his voice with a shout that shook the windows, in ' The Men of the Sea,' that begins, as all know, ' The sea is a wicked old woman,' and after racing through eight lines whose imagery is truthful, ends in a refrain, slow as the clacking of a capstan when the boat comes unwillingly up to the bars where the men sweat and tramp in the shingle.

> ' " Ye that bore us, oh, restore us!
>   She is kinder than ye;
>   For the call is on our heart-strings! "
>   Said The Men of the Sea.'

The Nilghai sang that verse twice, with simple craft, intending that Dick should hear. But Dick was waiting for the farewell of the men to their wives.

> ' " Ye that love us, can ye move us?
>   She is dearer than ye;
>   And your sleep will be the sweeter,"
>   Said The Men of the Sea.'

The rough words beat like the blows of the waves on the bows of the rickety boat from Lima in the days when Dick was mixing paints, making love, drawing devils and angels in the half-dark, and wondering whether the next minute would place the Italian captain's knife between his shoulder - blades. And the go - fever, which is more real than many doctor's diseases, waked and raged, urging him who loved Maisie beyond anything in the world to go away and taste the old hot, unregenerate life again,—to scuffle, swear, gamble, and love light loves with his fellows; to take ship and know the sea once more, and by her beget pictures; to talk to Binat among the sands of Port Said while Yellow 'Tina mixed the drinks; to hear the crackle of musketry, and see the smoke roll outward, thin and thicken again till the shining black faces came through, and in that hell every man was strictly responsible for his own head, and his own alone, and struck with an unfettered arm. It was impossible, utterly impossible, but—

> ' " Oh, our fathers, in the churchyard,
> She is older than ye,
> And our graves will be the greener,"
> Said The Men of the Sea.'

' What *is* there to hinder?' said Torpenhow, in the long hush that followed the song.

' You said a little time since that you wouldn't come for a walk round the world, Torp.'

' That was months ago, and I only objected to your making money for travelling expenses. You've shot your bolt here and it has gone home. Go away and do some work, and see some things.'

' Get some of the fat off you; you're disgracefully out of condition,' said the Nilghai, making a plunge from the chair and grasping a handful of Dick generally over the right ribs. ' Soft as putty—pure tallow born of over-feeding. Train it off, Dickie.'

'We're all equally gross, Nilghai. Next time you have to take the field you'll sit down, wink your eyes, gasp, and die in a fit.'

'Never mind. You go away on a ship. Go to Lima again, or to Brazil. There's always trouble in South America.'

'Do you suppose I want to be told where to go? Great Heavens, the only difficulty is to know where I'm to stop. But I shall stay here, as I told you before.'

'Then you'll be buried in Kensal Green and turn into adipocere with the others,' said Torpenhow. Are you thinking of commissions in hand? Pay forfeit and go. You've money enough to travel as a king if you please.'

'You've the grisliest notions of amusement, Torp. I think I see myself shipping first class on a six-thousand-ton hotel, and asking the third engineer what makes the engines go round, and whether it isn't very warm in the stokehold. Ho! ho! I should ship as a loafer if ever I shipped at all, which I'm not going to do. I shall compromise, and go for a small trip to begin with.'

'That's something at any rate. Where will you go?' said Torpenhow. 'It would do you all the good in the world, old man.'

The Nilghai saw the twinkle in Dick's eye and refrained from speech.

'I shall go in the first place to Rathray's stable, where I shall hire one horse, and take him very carefully as far as Richmond Hill. Then I shall walk him back again, in case he should accidentally burst into a lather and make Rathray angry. I shall do that to-morrow for the sake of air and exercise.'

'Bah!' Dick had barely time to throw up his arm and ward off the cushion that the disgusted Torpenhow heaved at his head.

'Air and exercise indeed,' said the Nilghai, sitting down heavily on Dick. 'Let's give him a little of both. Get the bellows, Torp.'

At this point the conference broke up in disorder, because Dick would not open his mouth till the Nilghai held his nose fast, and there was some trouble in forcing the nozzle of the bellows between his teeth; and even when it was there he weakly tried to puff against the force of the blast, and his cheeks blew up with a great explosion; and the enemy becoming helpless with laughter he so beat them over the head with a soft sofa-cushion that that became unsewn and distributed its feathers, and Binkie, interfering in Torpenhow's interests, was bundled into the half-empty bag and advised to scratch his way out, which he did after a while, travelling rapidly up and down the floor in the shape of an agitated green haggis, and when he came out looking for satisfaction, the three pillars of his world were picking feathers out of their hair.

'A prophet has no honour in his own country,' said Dick ruefully, dusting his knees. 'This filthy stuff will never brush off my bags.'

'It was all for your good,' said the Nilghai. 'Nothing like air and exercise.'

'All for your good,' said Torpenhow, not in the least with reference to past clowning. 'It would let you focus things at their proper worth and prevent your becoming slack in this hothouse of a town. Indeed it would, old man. I shouldn't have spoken if I hadn't thought so. Only, you make a joke of everything.'

'Before God, I do no such thing,' said Dick quickly and earnestly. 'You don't know me if you think that.'

'*I* don't think it,' said the Nilghai.

'How can fellows like ourselves, who know what life and death really mean, dare to make a joke of anything? I know we pretend it, to save ourselves from breaking down or going to the other extreme. Can't I see, old man, how you're always anxious about me, and try to advise me to make my work better? Do you suppose I don't think about that myself? But you can't help me—you can't help me—not even you. I must play my own hand alone in my own way.'

'Hear, hear,' from the Nilghai.

'What's the one thing in the Nilghai Saga that I've never drawn in the Nungapunga Book?' Dick continued to Torpenhow, who was a little astonished at the outburst.

Now there was one blank page in the book given over to the sketch that Dick had not drawn of the crowning exploit in the Nilghai's life; when that man, being young and forgetting that his body and bones belonged to the paper that employed him, had ridden over sunburned slippery grass in the rear of Bredow's brigade on the day that the troopers flung themselves at

Canrobert's artillery, and for aught they knew twenty battalions in front, to save the battered 24th German Infantry, to give time to decide the fate of Vionville, and to learn ere their remnant came back to Flavigny that cavalry can attack and crumple and break unshaken infantry. Whenever he was inclined to think over a life that might have been better, an income that might have been larger, and a soul that might have been considerably cleaner, the Nilghai would comfort himself with the thought, ' I rode with Bredow's brigade at Vionville,' and take heart for any lesser battle the next day might bring.

' I know,' he said very gravely. ' I was always glad that you left it out.'

' I left it out because Nilghai taught me what the German Army learned then, and what Schmidt taught their cavalry. I don't know German. What is it? " Take care of the time and the dressing will take care of itself." I must ride my own line to my own beat, old man.'

' *Tempo ist Richtung*. You've learned your lesson well,' said the Nilghai. ' He must go alone. He speaks truth, Torp.'

' Maybe I'm as wrong as I can be—hideously wrong. I must find that out for myself, as I have to think things out for myself, but I daren't turn my head to dress by the next man. It hurts me a great deal more than you know not to be able to go, but I cannot, that's all. I must do my own work and live my own life in my own way, because I'm responsible for both. Only don't think I frivol about it, Torp. I have my own matches and sulphur, and I'll make my own Hell, thanks.'

There was an uncomfortable pause. Then Torpenhow said blandly, ' What did the Governor of North Carolina say to the Governor of South Carolina?'

' Excellent notion. It *is* a long time between drinks. There are the makings of a very fine prig in you, Dick,' said the Nilghai.

' I've liberated my mind, estimable Binkie, with the feathers in his mouth.' Dick picked up the still indignant one and shook him tenderly. ' You're tied up in a sack and made to run about blind, Binkie-wee, without any reason, and it has hurt your little feelings. Never mind. *Sic volo, sic jubeo, stet pro ratione voluntas*, and don't sneeze in my eye because I talk Latin. Good-night.'

He went out of the room.

' That's distinctly one for you,' said the Nilghai. ' I told you it was hopeless to meddle with him. He's not pleased.'

' He'd swear at me if he weren't. I can't make it out. He has the go-fever upon him and he won't go. I only hope that he mayn't have to go some day when he doesn't want to,' said Torpenhow.

.   .   .   .   .

In his own room Dick was settling a question with himself—and the question was whether all the world, and all that was therein, and a burning desire to exploit both, was worth one threepenny piece thrown into the Thames.

' It came of seeing the sea, and I'm a cur to think about it,' he decided. ' After all, the

honeymoon will be that tour—with reservations ;
only . . . only I didn't realise that the sea was so
strong.   I didn't feel it so much when I was with
Maisie.   Those damnable songs did it.   He's
beginning again.'

But it was only Herrick's Nightpiece to Julia
that the Nilghai sang, and before it was ended
Dick reappeared on the threshold, not altogether
clothed indeed, but in his right mind, thirsty and
at peace.

The mood had come and gone with the rising
and the falling of the tide by Fort Keeling.

CHAPTER IX

' If I have taken the common clay
    And wrought it cunningly
In the shape of a God that was digged a clod,
    The greater honour to me.'

' If thou hast taken the common clay,
    And thy hands be not free
From the taint of the soil, thou hast made thy spoil
    The greater shame to thee.'

The Two Potters.

HE did no work of any kind for the rest of the week. Then came another Sunday. He dreaded and longed for the day always, but since the red-haired girl had sketched him there was rather more dread than desire in his mind.

He found that Maisie had entirely neglected his suggestions about line-work. She had gone off at score filled with some absurd notion for a ' fancy head.' It cost Dick something to command his temper.

' What's the good of suggesting anything?' he said pointedly.

' Ah, but this will be a picture,—a real picture ; and I know that Kami will let me send it to the Salon. You don't mind, do you?'

' I suppose not.   But you won't have time for the Salon.'

Maisie hesitated a little.   She even felt uncomfortable.

' We're going over to France a month sooner because of it.   I shall get the idea sketched out here and work it up at Kami's.'

Dick's heart stood still, and he came very near to being disgusted with his Queen who could do no wrong.   ' Just when I thought I had made some headway, she goes off chasing butterflies. It's maddening ! '

There was no possibility of arguing, for the red-haired girl was in the studio.   Dick could only look unutterable reproach.

' I'm sorry,' he said, ' and I think you make a mistake.   But what's the idea of your new picture ? '

' I took it from a book.'

' That's bad, to begin with.   Books aren't the places for pictures.   And——'

' It's this,' said the red-haired girl behind him. ' I was reading it to Maisie the other day from *The City of Dreadful Night*.   D'you know the book ? '

' A little.   I'm sorry I spoke.   There are pictures in it.   What has taken her fancy ? '

' The description of the Melancolia :——

> ' Her folded wings as of a mighty eagle,
>   But all too impotent to lift the regal
>   Robustness of her earth-born strength and pride.

And here again.   (Maisie, get the tea, dear.)

> ' The forehead charged with baleful thoughts and dreams,
>   The household bunch of keys, the housewife's gown,
>   Voluminous indented, and yet rigid
>   As though a shell of burnished metal frigid,
>   Her feet thick-shod to tread all weakness down.'

There was no attempt to conceal the scorn of the lazy voice. Dick winced.

' But that has been done already by an obscure artist of the name of Dürer,' said he. ' How does the thing run?—

> ' Three centuries and threescore years ago,
>   With phantasies of his peculiar thought.

You might as well try to rewrite *Hamlet*. It will be waste of time.'

' No, it won't,' said Maisie, putting down the teacups with clatter to reassure herself. ' And I mean to do it. Can't you see what a beautiful thing it would make?'

' How in perdition can one do work when one hasn't had the proper training? Any fool can get a notion. It needs training to drive the thing through,—training and conviction; not rushing after the first fancy.' Dick spoke between his teeth.

' You don't understand,' said Maisie. ' I think I can do it.'

Again the voice of the girl behind him:—

> ' Baffled and beaten back, she works on still;
>   Weary and sick of soul, she works the more.
> Sustained by her indomitable will,
>   The hands shall fashion, and the brain shall pore,
>   And all her sorrow shall be turned to labour——

I fancy Maisie means to embody herself in the picture.'

'Sitting on a throne of rejected pictures? No, I shan't, dear. The notion in itself has fascinated me.—Of course you don't care for fancy heads, Dick. I don't think you could do them. You like blood and bones.'

'That's a direct challenge. If you can do a Melancolia that isn't merely a sorrowful female head, I can do a better one. And I will, too. What d'you know about Melancolias?' Dick firmly believed that he was even then tasting three-quarters of all the sorrow in the world.

'She was a woman,' said Maisie, 'and she suffered a great deal,—till she could suffer no more. Then she began to laugh at it all, and then I painted her and sent her to the Salon.'

The red-haired girl rose up and left the room, laughing.

Dick looked at Maisie humbly and hopelessly.

'Never mind about the picture,' he said. 'Are you really going back to Kami's a month before your time?'

'I must, if I want to get the picture done.'

'And that's all you want?'

'Of course. Don't be stupid, Dick.'

'You haven't the power. You have only the ideas—the ideas and the little cheap impulses. How you could have kept at your work for ten years steadily is a mystery to me. So you are really going,—a month before you need?'

'I must do my work.'

'Your work—bah! . . . No, I didn't mean that. It's all right, dear. Of course you must do your work, and—I think I'll say good-bye for this week.'

'Won't you even stay for tea?'

'No, thank you. Have I your leave to go, dear? There's nothing more you particularly want me to do, and the line-work doesn't matter.'

'I wish you could stay, and then we could talk over my picture. If only one single picture's a success it draws attention to all the others. I *know* some of my work is good, if only people could see. And you needn't have been so rude about it.'

'I'm sorry. We'll talk the Melancolia over some one of the other Sundays. There are four more—yes, one, two, three, four—before you go. Good-bye, Maisie.'

Maisie stood by the studio window, thinking, till the red-haired girl returned, a little white at the corners of her lips.

'Dick's gone off,' said Maisie. 'Just when I wanted to talk about the picture. Isn't it selfish of him?'

Her companion opened her lips as if to speak, shut them again, and went on reading *The City of Dreadful Night*.

Dick was in the Park, walking round and round a tree that he had chosen as his confidante for many Sundays past. He was swearing audibly, and when he found that the infirmities of the English tongue hemmed in his rage, he sought consolation in Arabic, which is expressly designed for the use of the afflicted. He was not pleased with the reward of his patient service; nor was he pleased with himself; and it was long before he arrived at the proposition that the Queen could do no wrong.

' It's a losing game,' he said. ' I'm worth nothing when a whim of hers is in question. But in a losing game at Port Said we used to double the stakes and go on. She do a Melancolia! She hasn't the power, or the insight, or the training. Only the desire. She's cursed with the curse of Reuben. She won't do line-work, because it means real work; and yet she's stronger than I am. I'll make her understand that I can beat her on her own Melancolia. Even then she wouldn't care. She says I can only do blood and bones. I don't believe she has blood in her veins. All the same I love her; and I must go on loving her; and if I can humble her vanity I will. I'll do a Melancolia that shall be something like a Melancolia,—" the Melancolia that transcends all wit." I'll do it at once, con—bless her.'

He discovered that the notion would not come to order, and that he could not free his mind for an hour from the thought of Maisie's departure. He took very small interest in her rough studies for the Melancolia when she showed them next week. The Sundays were racing past, and the time was at hand when all the church bells in London could not ring Maisie back to him. Once or twice he said something to Binkie about ' hermaphroditic futilities,' but the little dog received so many confidences both from Torpenhow and Dick that he did not trouble his tulip-ears to listen.

Dick was permitted to see the girls off. They were going by the Dover night-boat, and they hoped to return in August. It was then February, and Dick felt that he was being hardly used. Maisie was so busy stripping the small house across the Park, and packing her canvases, that she had no time for thought. Dick went down to Dover and wasted a day there fretting over a wonderful possibility. Would Maisie at the very last allow him one small kiss? He reflected that he might capture her by the strong arm, as he had seen women captured in the Southern Sudan, and lead her away; but Maisie would never be led. She would turn her grey eyes upon him and say, ' Dick, how selfish you are!' Then his courage would fail him. It would be better, after all, to beg for that kiss.

Maisie looked more than usually kissable as she stepped from the night-mail on to the windy pier, in a grey waterproof and a little grey cloth travelling-cap. The red-haired girl was not so lovely. Her green eyes were hollow and her lips were dry. Dick saw the trunks aboard, and went to Maisie's side in the darkness under the bridge. The mail-bags were thundering into the forehold, and the red-haired girl was watching them.

' You'll have a rough passage to-night,' said Dick. ' It's blowing outside. I suppose I may come over and see you if I'm good?'

' You mustn't. I shall be busy. At least, if I want you I'll send for you. But I shall write from Vitry-sur-Marne. I shall have heaps of things to consult you about. Oh, Dick, you have been so good to me!—So good to me!'

'Thank you for that, dear. It hasn't made any difference, has it?'

'I can't tell a fib. It hasn't—in that way. But don't think I'm not grateful.'

'Damn the gratitude!' said Dick huskily to the paddle-box.

'What's the use of worrying? You know I should ruin your life, and you'd ruin mine, as things are now. You remember what you said when you were so angry that day in the Park? One of us has to be broken. Can't you wait till that day comes?'

'No, love. I want you unbroke—all to myself.'

Maisie shook her head. 'My poor Dick, what can I say?'

'Don't say anything. Give me a kiss? Only one kiss, Maisie. I'll swear I won't take any more. You might as well, and then I can be sure you're grateful.'

Maisie put her cheek forward, and Dick took his reward in the darkness. It was only one kiss, but, since there was no time-limit specified, it was a long one. Maisie wrenched herself free angrily, and Dick stood abashed and tingling from head to heel.

'Good-bye, darling. I didn't mean to scare you. I'm sorry. Only—keep well and do good work,—specially the Melancolia. I'm going to do one, too. Remember me to Kami, and be careful what you drink. Country drinking-water is bad everywhere, but it's worst in France. Write to me if you want anything, and good-bye.

Say good-bye to the what-you-call-um girl, and—can't I have another kiss? No. You're quite right. Good-bye.'

A shout told him that it was not seemly to charge up the mail-bag incline. He reached the pier as the steamer began to move off, and he followed her with his heart.

'And there's nothing—nothing in the wide world—to keep us apart except her obstinacy. These Calais night-boats are much too small. I'll get Torp to write to the papers about it. She's beginning to pitch already.'

Maisie stood where Dick had left her till she heard a little gasping cough at her elbow. The red-haired girl's eyes were alight with cold flame.

'He kissed you!' she said. 'How could you let him, when he wasn't anything to you? How dared you take a kiss from him? Oh, Maisie, let's go to the ladies' cabin. I'm sick,—deadly sick.'

'We aren't into open water yet. Go down, dear, and I'll stay here. I don't like the smell of the engines. . . . Poor Dick! He deserved one,—only one. But I didn't think he'd frighten me so.'

Dick returned to Town next day just in time for lunch, for which he had telegraphed. To his disgust, there were only empty plates in the studio. He lifted up his voice like all the bears in the fairy-tale, and Torpenhow entered, looking very guilty.

'H'sh!' said he. 'Don't make such a noise. I took it. Come into my rooms, and I'll show you why.'

Dick paused amazed at the threshold, for on Torpenhow's sofa lay a girl asleep and breathing heavily. The little cheap sailor hat, the blue-and-white dress, fitter for June than for February, dabbled with mud at the skirts, the jacket trimmed with imitation astrakhan and ripped at the shoulder-seams, the one-and-elevenpenny umbrella, and, above all, the disgraceful condition of the kid-topped boots, declared all things.

'Oh, I say, old man, this is too bad! You mustn't bring this sort up here. They steal things from the rooms.'

'It looks bad, I admit, but I was coming in after lunch, and she staggered into the hall. I thought she was drunk at first, but it was collapse. I couldn't leave her as she was, so I brought her up here and gave her your lunch. She was fainting from want of food. She went fast asleep the minute she had finished.'

'I know something of that complaint. She's been living on sausages, I suppose. Torp, you should have handed her over to a policeman for presuming to faint in a respectable house. Poor little wretch! Look at that face! There isn't an ounce of immorality in it. Only folly,—slack, fatuous, feeble, futile folly. It's a typical head. D'you notice how the skull begins to show through the flesh-padding on the face and cheek-bone?'

'What a cold-blooded barbarian it is! Don't hit a woman when she's down. Can't we do anything? She was simply dropping with starvation. She almost fell into my arms, and when she got to the food she ate like a wild beast. It was horrible.'

' I can give her money, which she would probably spend in drinks. Is she going to sleep for ever?'

The girl opened her eyes and glared at the men between terror and effrontery.

' Feeling better?' said Torpenhow.

' Yes. Thank you. There aren't many gentlemen that are as kind as you are. Thank you.'

' When did you leave service?' said Dick, who had been watching the scarred and chapped hands.

' How did you know I was in service? I was. General servant. I didn't like it.'

' And how do you like being your own mistress?'

' Do I look as if I liked it?'

' I suppose not. One moment. Would you be good enough to turn your face to the window?'

The girl obeyed, and Dick watched her face keenly,—so keenly that she made as if to hide behind Torpenhow.

' The eyes have it,' said Dick, walking up and down. ' They are superb eyes for my business. And, after all, every head depends on the eyes. This has been sent from Heaven to make up for— what was taken away. Now the weekly strain's off my shoulders, I can get to work in earnest. Evidently sent from Heaven. Yes. Raise your chin a little, please.'

' Gently, old man, gently. You're scaring somebody out of her wits,' said Torpenhow, who could see the girl trembling.

'Don't let him hit me! Oh, please don't let him hit me! I've been hit cruel to-day because I spoke to a man. Don't let him look at me like that! He's reg'lar wicked, that one. Don't let him look at me like that, neither! Oh, I feel as if I hadn't nothing on when he looks at me like that!'

The overstrained nerves in the frail body gave way, and the girl wept like a little child and began to scream. Dick threw open the window, and Torpenhow flung the door back.

'There you are,' said Dick soothingly. 'My friend here can call for a policeman, and you can run through that door. Nobody is going to hurt you.'

The girl sobbed convulsively for a few minutes, and then tried to laugh.

'Nothing in the world to hurt you. Now listen to me for a minute. I'm what they call an artist by profession. You know what artists do?'

'They draw the things in red and black ink on the pop-shop labels.'

'I daresay. I haven't risen to pop-shop labels yet. Those are done by the Academicians. I want to draw your head.'

'What for?'

'Because it's pretty. That is why you will come to the room across the landing three times a week at eleven in the morning, and I'll give you three quid a week just for sitting still and being drawn. And there's a quid on account.'

'For nothing? Oh, my!' The girl turned the sovereign in her hand, and with more foolish tears : ' Ain't neither o' you two gentlemen afraid of my bilking you?'

' No. Only ugly girls do that. Try and remember this place. And, by the way, what's your name?'

' I'm Bessie,—Bessie—— It's no use giving the rest. Bessie Broke,—Stone-broke if you like. What's your names? But there,—no one ever gives the real ones.'

Dick consulted Torpenhow with his eyes.

' My name's Heldar, and my friend's called Torpenhow ; and you must be sure to come here. Where do you live?'

' South-the-water,—one room,—five and sixpence a week. Aren't you making fun of me about that three quid?'

' You'll see later on. And, Bessie, next time you come, remember, you needn't wear that paint. It's bad for the skin, and I have all the colours you'll be likely to need.'

Bessie withdrew, scrubbing her cheek with a ragged pocket - handkerchief. The two men looked at each other.

' You're a man,' said Torpenhow.

' I'm afraid I've been a fool. It isn't our business to run about the earth reforming Bessie Brokes. And a woman of any kind has no right on this landing.'

' Perhaps she won't come back.'

' She will if she thinks she can get food and warmth here. I know she will, worse luck. But remember, old man, she isn't a woman. She's my model; and be careful.'

'The idea! She's a dissolute little scarecrow, — gutter-snippet and nothing more.'

'So you think. Wait till she has been fed a little and freed from fear. That fair type recovers itself very quickly. You won't know her in a week or two, when that abject funk has died out of her eyes. She'll be too happy and smiling for my purposes.'

'But surely you're taking her out of charity? —to please me?'

'I am not in the habit of playing with hot coals to please anybody. She has been sent from Heaven, as I may have remarked before, to help me with my Melancolia.'

'Never heard a word about the lady before.'

'What's the use of having a friend if you must sling your notions at him in words? *You* ought to know what I'm thinking about. You've heard me grunt lately?'

'Even so; but grunts mean anything in your language, from bad 'baccy to wicked dealers. And I don't think I've been much in your confidence for some time.'

'It was a high and soulful grunt. You ought to have understood that it meant the Melancolia.' Dick walked Torpenhow up and down the room, keeping silence. Then he smote him in the ribs. '*Now* don't you see it? Bessie's abject futility, and the terror in her eyes, welded on to one or two details in the way of sorrow that have come under my experience lately. Likewise some orange and black,—two keys of each. But I can't explain on an empty stomach.'

'It sounds mad enough. You'd better stick to your soldiers, Dick, instead of maundering about heads and eyes and experiences.'

'Think so?' Dick began to dance on his heels, singing :—

'They're as proud as a turkey when they hold the ready cash,
　You ought to 'ear the way they laugh an' joke!
They are tricky an' they're funny when they've got the ready
　money,—
　Ow! but see 'em when they're all stone-broke!'

Then he sat down to pour out his heart to Maisie in a four-sheet letter of counsel and encouragement, and registered an oath that he would get to work with an undivided heart as soon as Bessie should reappear.

The girl kept her appointment unpainted and unadorned, afraid and overbold by turns. When she found that she was merely expected to sit still, she grew calmer, and criticised the appointments of the studio with freedom and some point. She liked the warmth and the comfort and the release from fear of physical pain. Dick made two or three studies of her head in monochrome, but the actual notion of the Melancolia would not arrive.

'What a mess you keep your things in!' said Bessie, some days later, when she felt herself thoroughly at home. 'I s'pose your clothes are just as bad. Gentlemen never think what buttons and tape are made for.'

'I buy things to wear, and wear 'em till they go to pieces. I don't know what Torpenhow does.'

Bessie made diligent inquiry in the latter's

room, and unearthed a bale of disreputable socks.
' Some of these I'll mend now,' she said, ' and
some I'll take home. D'you know, I sit all day
long at home doing nothing, just like a lady, and
no more noticing them other girls in the house
than if they was so many flies? I don't have any
unnecessary words, but I put 'em down quick, I
can tell you, when they talk to me. No; it's
quite nice these days. I lock my door, and they
can only call me names through the keyhole, and
I sit inside, just like a lady, mending socks. Mr.
Torpenhow wears his socks out both ends at
once.'

' Three quid a week from me, and the delights
of my society. No socks mended. Nothing from
Torp except a nod on the landing now and again,
and all his socks mended. Bessie is very much a
woman,' thought Dick; and he looked at her
between half-shut eyes. Food and rest had trans-
formed the girl, as Dick knew they would.

' What are you looking at me like that for?'
she said quickly. ' Don't. You look reg'lar bad
when you look that way. You don't think much
o' me, do you?'

' That depends on how you behave.'

Bessie behaved beautifully. Only it was difficult at the end of a sitting to bid her go out into
the grey streets. She very much preferred the
studio and a big chair by the stove, with some
socks in her lap as an excuse for delay. Then
Torpenhow would come in, and Bessie would be
moved to tell strange and wonderful stories of
her past, and still stranger ones of her present

improved circumstances. She would make them tea as though she had a right to make it; and once or twice on these occasions Dick caught Torpenhow's eyes fixed on the trim little figure, and because Bessie's flittings about the room made Dick ardently long for Maisie, he realised whither Torpenhow's thoughts were tending. And Bessie was exceedingly careful of the condition of Torpenhow's linen. She spoke very little to him, but sometimes they talked together on the landing.

'I was a great fool,' Dick said to himself. 'I know what red firelight looks like when a man's trampling through a strange town; and ours is a lonely, selfish sort of life at the best. I wonder Maisie doesn't feel that sometimes. But I can't order Bessie away. That's the worst of beginning things. One never knows where they'll stop.'

One evening after a sitting prolonged to the last limit of the light, Dick was roused from a nap by a broken voice in Torpenhow's room. He jumped to his feet. 'Now what ought I to do? It looks foolish to go in.—Oh, bless you, Binkie!' The little terrier thrust Torpenhow's door open with his nose and came out to take possession of Dick's chair. The door swung wide unheeded, and Dick across the landing could see Bessie in the half-light making her little supplication to Torpenhow. She was kneeling by his side, and her hands were clasped across his knees.

'I know,—I know,' she said thickly. ''Tisn't right o' me to do this, but I can't help it; and you were so kind,—so kind; and you never took any

notice o' me. And I've mended all your things
so carefully,—I did. Oh, please, 'tisn't as if I
was asking you to marry me. I wouldn't think
of it. But cou—couldn't you take and live with
me till Miss Right comes along? I'm only Miss
Wrong, I know, but I'd work my hands to the
bare bones for you. And I'm not ugly to look at.
Say you will?'

Dick hardly recognised Torpenhow's voice in
reply :—

'But look here. It's no use. I'm liable to
be ordered off anywhere at a minute's notice if a
war breaks out. At a minute's notice—dear.'

'What does that matter? Until you go, then.
Until you go. 'Tisn't much I'm asking, and—
you don't know how good I can cook.' She had
put an arm round his neck and was drawing his
head down.

'Until—I—go, then.'

'Torp,' said Dick across the landing. He
could hardly steady his voice. 'Come here a
minute, old man. I'm in trouble.—Heaven send
he'll listen to me!' There was something very
like an oath from Bessie's lips. She was afraid of
Dick, and disappeared down the staircase in
panic, but it seemed an age before Torpenhow
entered the studio. He went to the mantelpiece,
buried his head on his arms, and groaned like a
wounded bull.

'What the devil right have you to interfere?'
he said, at last.

'Who's interfering with which? Your own
sense told you long ago you couldn't be such a

fool. It was a tough rack, St. Anthony, but you're all right now.'

'I oughtn't to have seen her moving about these rooms as if they belonged to her. That's what upset me. It gives a lonely man a sort of hankering, doesn't it?' said Torpenhow piteously.

'Now you talk sense. It does. But, since you aren't in a condition to discuss the disadvantages of double housekeeping, do you know what you're going to do?'

'I don't. I wish I did.'

'You're going away for a season on a brilliant tour to regain tone. You're going to Brighton, or Scarborough, or Prawle Point, to see the ships go by. And you're going at once. Isn't it odd? I'll take care of Binkie, but out you go immediately. Never resist the Devil. He holds the bank. Fly from him. Pack your things and go.'

'I believe you're right. Where shall I go?'

'And you call yourself a special correspondent! Pack first and inquire afterwards.'

An hour later Torpenhow was despatched into the night in a hansom. 'You'll probably think of some place to go to while you're moving,' said Dick. 'Go to Euston, to begin with, and—oh yes—get drunk to-night.'

He returned to the studio, and lighted more candles, for he found the room very dark.

'Oh, you Jezebel! you futile little Jezebel! Won't you hate me to-morrow?—Binkie, come here.'

Binkie turned over on his back on the hearth-rug, and Dick stirred him with a meditative foot.

' I said she was not immoral. I was wrong. She said she could cook. That showed premeditated sin. Oh, Binkie, if you are a man you will go to perdition ; but if you are a woman, and say that you can cook, you will go to a much worse place.'

CHAPTER X

What's yon that follows at my side?—
    The foe that ye must fight, my lord.—
That hirples swift as I can ride?—
    The shadow of your might, my lord.
Then wheel my horse against the foe!—
    He's down and overpast, my lord.
Ye war against the sunset glow:
    The darkness gathers fast, my lord.
           The Fight of Heriot's Ford.

'This is a cheerful life,' said Dick, some days later. 'Torp's away; Bessie hates me; I can't get at the notion of the Melancolia; Maisie's letters are scrappy; and I believe I have indigestion. What gives a man pains across his head and spots before his eyes, Binkie? Shall us take some liver pills?'

Dick had just gone through a lively scene with Bessie. She had for the fiftieth time reproached him for sending Torpenhow away. She explained her enduring hatred for Dick, and made it clear to him that she only sat for the sake of his money. 'And Mr. Torpenhow's ten times a better man than you,' she concluded.

'He is. That's why he went away. *I* should have stayed and made love to you.'

The girl sat with her chin on her hand, scowling. ' To me! I'd like to catch you! If I wasn't afraid o' being hung I'd kill you. That's what I'd do. D'you believe me?'

Dick smiled wearily. It is not pleasant to live in the company of a notion that will not work out, a fox-terrier that cannot talk, and a woman who talks too much. He would have answered, but at that moment there unrolled itself from one corner of the studio a veil, as it were, of the filmiest gauze. He rubbed his eyes, but the grey haze would not go.

' This is disgraceful indigestion. Binkie, we will go to a medicine-man. We can't have our eyes interfered with, for by these we get our bread; also mutton-chop bones for little dogs.'

The doctor was an affable local practitioner with white hair, and he said nothing till Dick began to describe the grey film in the studio.

' We all want a little patching and repairing from time to time,' he chirped. ' Like a ship, my dear sir,—exactly like a ship. Sometimes the hull is out of order, and we consult the surgeon; sometimes the rigging, and then I advise; sometimes the engines, and we go to the brain-specialist; sometimes the look-out on the bridge is tired, and then we see an oculist. I should recommend you to see an oculist. A little patching and repairing from time to time is all we want. An oculist, by all means.'

Dick sought an oculist,—the best in London. He was certain that the local practitioner did not know anything about his trade, and more certain that Maisie would laugh at him if he were forced to wear spectacles.

' I've neglected the warnings of my lord the stomach too long. Hence these spots before the eyes, Binkie. I can see as well as I ever could.'

As he entered the dark hall that led to the consulting-room a man cannoned against him. Dick saw the face as it hurried out into the street.

' That's the writer-type. He has the same modelling of the forehead as Torp. He looks very sick. Probably heard something he didn't like.'

Even as he thought, a great fear came upon Dick, a fear that made him hold his breath as he walked into the oculist's waiting-room, with the heavy carved furniture, the dark-green paper, and the sober-hued prints on the wall. He recognised a reproduction of one of his own sketches.

Many people were waiting their turn before him. His eye was caught by a flaming red-and-gold Christmas-carol book. Little children came to that eye-doctor, and they needed large-type amusement.

' That's idolatrous bad Art,' he said, drawing the book towards himself. ' From the anatomy of the angels, it has been made in Germany.' He opened it mechanically, and there leaped to his eyes a verse printed in red ink :—

> The next good joy that Mary had,
> It was the joy of three,
> To see her good Son Jesus Christ
> Making the blind to see ;

Making the blind to see, good Lord,
    And happy may we be.
Praise Father, Son, and Holy Ghost
    To all eternity!

Dick read and re-read the verse till his turn came, and the doctor was bending above him seated in an arm-chair. The blaze of a gas-microscope in his eyes made him wince. The doctor's hand touched the scar of the sword-cut on Dick's head, and Dick explained briefly how he had come by it. When the flame was removed, Dick saw the doctor's face, and the fear came upon him again. The doctor wrapped himself in a mist of words. Dick caught allusions to ' scar,' ' frontal bone,' ' optic nerve,' ' extreme caution,' and the ' avoidance of mental anxiety.'

'Verdict?' he said faintly. 'My business is painting, and I daren't waste time. What do you make of it?'

Again the whirl of words, but this time they conveyed a meaning.

'Can you give me anything to drink?'

Many sentences were pronounced in that darkened room, and the prisoners often needed cheering. Dick found a glass of liqueur brandy in his hand.

'As far as I can gather,' he said, coughing above the spirit, 'you call it decay of the optic nerve, or something, and therefore hopeless. What is my time-limit, avoiding all strain and worry?'

'Perhaps one year.'

'My God! And if I don't take care of myself?'

' I really could not say. One cannot ascertain the exact amount of injury inflicted by the sword-cut. The scar is an old one, and—exposure to the strong light of the desert, did you say?—with excessive application to fine work? I really could not say.'

' I beg your pardon, but it has come without any warning. If you will let me, I'll sit here for a minute, and then I'll go. You have been very good in telling me the truth. . . . Without any warning . . . without any warning. Thanks.'

Dick went into the street, and was rapturously received by Binkie. ' We've got it very badly, little dog! Just as badly as we can get it. We'll go to the Park to think it out.'

They headed for a certain tree that Dick knew well, and they sat down to think, because his legs were trembling under him and there was cold fear at the pit of his stomach.

' How could it have come without any warning? It's as sudden as being shot. It's the living death, Binkie. We're to be shut up in the dark in one year if we're careful, and we shan't see anybody, and we shall never have anything we want, not though we live to be a hundred.' Binkie wagged his tail joyously. ' Binkie, we must think. Let's see how it feels to be blind.' Dick shut his eyes, and flaming commas and Catherine-wheels floated inside the lids. Yet when he looked across the Park the scope of his vision was not contracted. He could see perfectly, until a procession of slow-wheeling fireworks defiled across his eyeballs.

'Little dorglums, we aren't at all well. Let's go home. If only Torp were back, now!'

But Torpenhow was in the South of England, inspecting dockyards in the company of the Nilghai. His letters were brief and full of mystery.

Dick had never asked anybody to help him in his joys or his sorrows. He argued, in the loneliness of the studio, henceforward to be decorated with a film of grey gauze in one corner, that, if his fate were blindness, all the Torpenhows in the world could not save him. 'I can't call him off his trip to sit down and sympathise with me. I must pull through the business alone,' he said. He was lying on the sofa, eating his moustache and wondering what the darkness of the night would be like. Then came to his mind the memory of a quaint scene in the Sudan. A soldier had been nearly hacked in two by a broad-bladed Arab spear. For one instant the man felt no pain. Looking down, he saw that his life-blood was going from him. The stupid bewilderment on his face was so intensely comic that both Dick and Torpenhow, still panting and unstrung from a fight for life, had roared with laughter, in which the man seemed as if he would join, but, as his lips parted in a sheepish grin, the agony of death came upon him, and he pitched grunting at their feet. Dick laughed again, remembering the horror. It seemed so exactly like his own case. 'But I have a little more time allowed me,' he said. He paced up and down the room, quietly at first, but afterwards with the hurried feet of fear. It was as though a black shadow stood at his elbow and urged him to go forward; and there were only weaving circles and floating pin-dots before his eyes.

'We must be calm, Binkie. We must be calm.' He talked aloud for the sake of distraction. 'This isn't nice at all. What shall we do? We must do something. Our time is short. I shouldn't have believed that this morning; but now things are different. Binkie, where was Moses when the light went out?'

Binkie smiled from ear to ear, as a well-bred terrier should, but made no suggestion.

'"Were there but world enough and time, This coyness, Binkie, were no crime. . . . But at my back I always hear——"' He wiped his forehead, which was unpleasantly damp. 'What can I do? What can I do? I haven't any notions left, and I can't think connectedly, but I must do something, or I shall go off my head.'

The hurried walk recommenced, Dick stopping every now and again to drag forth long-neglected canvases and old notebooks; for he turned to his work by instinct, as a thing that could not fail. 'You won't do, and you won't do,' he said, at each inspection. 'No more soldiers. I couldn't paint 'em. Sudden death comes home too nearly, and this is battle and murder both for me.'

The day was failing, and Dick thought for a moment that the twilight of the blind had come upon him unawares. 'Allah Almighty!' he cried despairingly, 'help me through the time of waiting, and I won't whine when my punishment comes. What can I do now, before the light goes?'

There was no answer. Dick waited till he could regain some sort of control over himself. His hands were shaking, and he prided himself on their steadiness; he could feel that his lips were quivering, and the sweat was running down his face. He was lashed by fear, driven forward by the desire to get to work at once and accomplish something, and maddened by the refusal of his brain to do more than repeat the news that he was about to go blind. 'It's a humiliating exhibition,' he thought, 'and I'm glad Torp isn't here to see. The doctor said I was to avoid mental worry. Come here and let me pet you, Binkie.'

The little dog yelped because Dick nearly squeezed the bark out of him. Then he heard the man speaking in the twilight, and, doglike, understood that his trouble stood off from him :—

'Allah is good, Binkie. Not quite so gentle as we could wish, but we'll discuss that later. I think I see my way to it now. All those studies of Bessie's head were nonsense, and they nearly brought your master into a scrape. I have the notion now as clear as crystal,—" the Melancolia that transcends all wit." There shall be Maisie in that head, because I shall never get Maisie; and Bess, of course, because she knows all about Melancolia, though she doesn't know she knows; and there shall be some drawing in it, and it shall all end up with a laugh. That's for myself. Shall she giggle or grin? No, she shall laugh right out of the canvas, and every man and woman that ever had a sorrow of their own shall —what is it the poem says?——

' Understand the speech and feel a stir
Of fellowship in all disastrous fight.

" In all disastrous fight "? That's better than painting the thing merely to pique Maisie. I can do it now because I have it inside me. Binkie, I'm going to hold you up by your tail. You're an omen. Come here.'

Binkie swung head downward for a moment without speaking.

' 'Rather like holding a guinea-pig; but you're a brave little dog, and you don't yelp when you're hung up. It *is* an omen.'

Binkie went to his own chair, and as often as he looked saw Dick walking up and down, rubbing his hands and chuckling. That night Dick wrote a letter to Maisie full of the tenderest concern for her health, but saying very little about his own, and dreamed of the Melancolia to be born. Not till morning did he remember that something might happen to him in the future.

He fell to work, whistling softly, and was swallowed up in the clean, clear joy of creation, which does not come to man too often, lest he should consider himself the equal of his God, and so refuse to die at the appointed time. He forgot Maisie, Torpenhow, and Binkie at his feet, but remembered to stir Bessie, who needed very little stirring, into a tremendous rage, that he might

watch the smouldering lights in her eyes. He
threw himself without reservation into his work,
and did not think of the doom that was to over-
take him, for he was possessed with his notion,
and the things of this world had no power upon
him.

'You're pleased to-day?' said Bessie.

Dick waved his mahl-stick in mystic circles
and went to the sideboard for a drink. In the
evening, when the exaltation of the day had died
down, he went to the sideboard again, and after
some visits became convinced that the eye-doctor
was a liar, since he still could see everything very
clearly. He was of opinion that he would even
make a home for Maisie, and that whether she
liked it or not she should be his wife. The mood
passed next morning, but the sideboard and all
upon it remained for his comfort. Again he set
to work, and his eyes troubled him with spots and
dashes and blurs till he had taken counsel with
the sideboard, and the Melancolia both on the
canvas and in his own mind appeared lovelier
than ever. There was a delightful sense of
irresponsibility upon him, such as they feel who
walking among their fellow-men know that the
death-sentence of disease is upon them, and,
since fear is but waste of the little time left, are
riotously happy. The days passed without event.
Bessie arrived punctually always, and, though her
voice seemed to Dick to come from a distance,
her face was always very near, and the Melancolia
began to flame on the canvas, in the likeness of
a woman who had known all the sorrow in the

world and was laughing at it. It was true that the corners of the studio draped themselves in grey film and retired into the darkness, that the spots in his eyes and the pains across his head were very troublesome, and that Maisie's letters were hard to read and harder still to answer. He could not tell her of his trouble, and he could not laugh at her accounts of her own Melancolia which was always going to be finished. But the furious days of toil and the nights of wild dreams made amends for all, and the sideboard was his best friend on earth. Bessie was singularly dull. She used to shriek with rage when Dick stared at her between half-closed eyes. Now she sulked, or watched him with disgust, saying very little.

Torpenhow had been absent for six weeks. An incoherent note heralded his return. ' News ! great news ! ' he wrote. ' The Nilghai knows, and so does the Keneu. We're all back on Thursday. Get lunch and clean your accoutrements.'

Dick showed Bessie the letter, and she abused him for that he had ever sent Torpenhow away and ruined her life.

' Well,' said Dick brutally, ' you're better as you are, instead of making love to some drunken beast in the street.' He felt that he had rescued Torpenhow from great temptation.

' I don't know if that's any worse than sitting to a drunken beast in a studio. *You* haven't been sober for three weeks. You've been soaking the whole time ; and yet you pretend you're better than me ! '

' What do you mean ? ' said Dick.

' Mean! You'll see when Mr. Torpenhow comes back.'

It was not long to wait. Torpenhow met Bessie on the staircase without a sign of feeling. He had news that was more to him than many Bessies, and the Keneu and the Nilghai were trampling behind him, calling for Dick.

' Drinking like a fish,' Bessie whispered. ' He's been at it for nearly a month.' She followed the men stealthily to hear judgment done.

They came into the studio, rejoicing, to be welcomed over - effusively by a drawn, lined, shrunken, haggard wreck,—unshaven, blue-white about the nostrils, stooping in the shoulders, and peering under his eyebrows nervously.   The drink had been at work as steadily as Dick.

' Is this you?' said Torpenhow.

' All that's left of me.   Sit down.   Binkie's quite well, and I've been doing some good work.' He reeled where he stood.

' You've done some of the worst work you've ever done in your life.   Man alive, you're——'

Torpenhow turned to his companions appealingly, and they left the room to find lunch elsewhere.   Then he spoke ; but, since the reproof of a friend is much too sacred and intimate a thing to be printed, and since Torpenhow used figures and metaphors which were unseemly, and contempt untranslatable, it will never be known what was actually said to Dick, who blinked and winked and picked at his hands.   After a time the culprit began to feel the need of a little self-respect.   He was quite sure that he had not in any way departed from virtue, and there were reasons, too, of which Torpenhow knew nothing. He would explain.

He rose, tried to straighten his shoulders, and spoke to the face he could hardly see.

'You are right,' he said. 'But I am right, too. After you went away I had some trouble with my eyes. So I went to an oculist, and he turned a gasogene—I mean a gas-engine—into my eye. That was very long ago. He said, " Scar on the head,—sword-cut and optic nerve." Make a note of that. So I am going blind. I have some work to do before I go blind, and I suppose that I must do it. I cannot see much now, but I can see best when I am drunk. I did not know I was drunk till I was told, but I must go on with my work. If you want to see it, there it is.' He pointed to the all but finished Melancolia and looked for applause.

Torpenhow said nothing, and Dick began to whimper feebly, for joy at seeing Torpenhow again, for grief at misdeeds—if indeed they were misdeeds—that made Torpenhow remote and unsympathetic, and for childish vanity hurt, since Torpenhow had not given a word of praise to his wonderful picture.

Bessie looked through the keyhole after a long pause, and saw the two walking up and down as usual, Torpenhow's hand on Dick's shoulder. Hereat she said something so improper that it shocked even Binkie, who was dribbling patiently on the landing in the hope of seeing his master again.

CHAPTER XI

The lark will make her hymn to God,
  The partridge call her brood,
While I forget the heath I trod,
  The fields wherein I stood.
'Tis dule to know not night from morn,
  But deeper dule to know
I can but hear the hunter's horn
  That once I used to blow.

Ballad.

I T was the third day after Torpenhow's return,
and his heart was heavy.

' Do you mean to tell me that you can't see to
work without whisky? It's generally the other
way about.'

' Can a drunkard swear on his honour? ' said
Dick.

' Yes, if he has been as good a man as you.'

' Then I give you my word of honour,' said
Dick, speaking hurriedly through parched lips.
' Old man, I can hardly see your face now.
You've kept me sober for two days,—if I ever
was drunk,—and I've done no work. Don't keep
me back any more. I don't know when my eyes
may give out. The spots and dots and the pains
and things are crowding worse than ever. I swear

I can see all right when I'm—when I'm moderately screwed, as you say. Give me three more sittings from Bessie and all the—stuff I want, and the picture will be done. I can't kill myself in three days. It only means a touch of D.T. at the worst.'

' If I give you three days more will you promise me to stop work and—the other thing, whether the picture's finished or not? '

'I can't. You don't know what that picture means to me. But surely you could get the Nilghai to help you, and knock me down and tie me up. I shouldn't fight for the whisky, but I should for the work.'

' Go on, then. I give you three days; but you're breaking my heart.'

Dick returned to his work, toiling as one possessed; and the yellow devil of whisky stood by him and chased away the spots in his eyes. The Melancolia was nearly finished, and was all or nearly all that he had hoped she would be. Dick jested with Bessie, who reminded him that he was ' a drunken beast '; but the reproof did not move him.

' You can't understand, Bess. We are in sight of land now, and soon we shall lie back and think about what we've done. I'll give you three months' pay when the picture's finished, and next time I have any more work in hand—but that doesn't matter. Won't three months' pay make you hate me less? '

' No, it won't! I hate you, and I'll go on hating you. Mr. Torpenhow won't speak to me

any more. He's always looking at map-things
and red-backed books.'

Bessie did not say that she had again laid siege
to Torpenhow, or that he had at the end of her
passionate pleading picked her up, given her a
kiss, and put her outside the door with a recom-
mendation not to be a little fool. He spent most
of his time in the company of the Nilghai, and
their talk was of war in the near future, the hiring
of transports, and secret preparations among the
dockyards. He did not care to see Dick till the
picture was finished.

'He's doing first-class work,' he said to the
Nilghai, 'and it's quite out of his regular line.
But, for the matter of that, so's his infernal
soaking.'

'Never mind. Leave him alone. When he
has come to his senses again we'll carry him off
from this place and let him breathe clean air.
Poor Dick! I don't envy you, Torp, when his
eyes fail.'

'Yes, it will be a case of " God help the man
who's chained to our Davie." The worst is that
we don't know when it will happen ; and I believe
the uncertainty and the waiting have sent Dick
to the whisky more than anything else.'

'How the Arab who cut his head open would
grin if he knew ! '

'He's at perfect liberty to grin if he can.
He's dead. That's poor consolation now.'

In the afternoon of the third day Torpenhow
heard Dick calling for him. 'All finished ! ' he
shouted. 'I've done it ! Come in ! Isn't she a

beauty? Isn't she a darling? I've been down to Hell to get her; but isn't she worth it?'

Torpenhow looked at the head of a woman who laughed,—a full-lipped, hollow-eyed woman who laughed from out of the canvas as Dick had intended she should.

'Who taught you how to do it?' said Torpenhow. 'The touch and notion have nothing to do with your regular work. What a face it is! What eyes, and what insolence!' Unconsciously he threw back his head and laughed with her. 'She's seen the game played out,—I don't think she had a good time of it,—and now she doesn't care. Isn't that the idea?'

'Exactly.'

'Where did you get the mouth and chin from? They don't belong to Bess.'

'They're—some one else's. But isn't it good? Isn't it thundering good? Wasn't it worth the whisky? I did it. Alone I did it, and it's the best I can do.' He drew his breath sharply, and whispered, 'Just God! what could I not do ten years hence, if I can do this now!—By the way, what do you think of it, Bess?'

The girl was biting her lips. She loathed Torpenhow because he had taken no notice of her.

'I think it's just the horridest, beastliest thing I ever saw,' she answered, and turned away.

'More than you will be of that way of thinking, young woman.—Dick, there's a sort of murderous, viperine suggestion in the poise of the head that I don't understand,' said Torpenhow.

'That's trick-work,' said Dick, chuckling with delight of being completely understood. 'I couldn't resist one little bit of sheer swagger. It's a French trick, and you wouldn't understand; but it's got at by slewing round the head a trifle, and a tiny, tiny foreshortening of one side of the face from the angle of the chin to the top of the left ear. That, and deepening the shadow under the lobe of the ear. It was flagrant trick-work; but, having the notion fixed, I felt entitled to play with it.—Oh, you beauty!'

'Amen! She is a beauty. I can feel it.'

'So will every man who has any sorrow of his own,' said Dick, slapping his thigh. 'He shall see his trouble there, and, by the Lord Harry, just when he's feeling properly sorry for himself he shall throw back his head and laugh,—as she is laughing. I've put the life of my heart and the light of my eyes into her, and I don't care what comes. . . . I'm tired,—awfully tired. I think I'll get to sleep. Take away the whisky, it has served its turn, and give Bessie thirty-six quid, and three over for luck. Cover the picture.'

He dropped asleep in the long chair, his face white and haggard, almost before he had finished the sentence. Bessie tried to take Torpenhow's hand. 'Aren't you never going to speak to me no more?' she said; but Torpenhow was looking at Dick.

'What a stock of vanity the man has! I'll take him in hand to-morrow and make much of him. He deserves it.—Eh! what was that, Bess?'

'Nothing. I'll put things tidy here a little, and then I'll go. You couldn't give me that three months' pay now, could you? He said you were to.'

Torpenhow gave her a cheque and went to his own rooms. Bessie faithfully tidied up the studio, set the door ajar for flight, emptied half a bottle of turpentine on a duster, and began to scrub the face of the Melancolia viciously. The paint did not smudge quickly enough. She took a palette-knife and scraped, following each stroke with the wet duster. In five minutes the picture was a formless, scarred muddle of colours. She threw the paint-stained duster into the studio stove, stuck out her tongue at the sleeper, and whispered, 'Bilked!' as she turned to run down the staircase. She would never see Torpenhow any more, but she had at least done harm to the man who had come between her and her desire and who used to make fun of her. Cashing the cheque was the very cream of the jest to Bessie. Then the little privateer sailed across the Thames, to be swallowed up in the grey wilderness of South-the-water.

Dick slept till late into the evening, when Torpenhow dragged him off to bed. His eyes were as bright as his voice was hoarse. 'Let's have another look at the picture,' he said, insistently as a child.

'You—go—to—bed,' said Torpenhow. 'You aren't at all well, though you mayn't know it. You're as jumpy as a cat.'

'I reform to-morrow. Good-night.'

As he repassed through the studio, Torpenhow lifted the cloth above the picture, and almost betrayed himself by outcries: ' Wiped out!—scraped out and turped out! If Dick knows this to-night he'll go raving mad. He's on the verge of jumps as it is. That's Bess,—the little devil! Only a woman could have done that!—with the ink not dry on the cheque, too! Dick will be off his head to-morrow. It was all my fault for trying to help gutter-devils. Oh, my poor Dick, the Lord is hitting you very hard! '

Dick could not sleep that night, partly for pure joy, and partly because the well-known Catherine-wheels inside his eyes had given place to crackling volcanoes of many-coloured fire. ' Spout away,' he said aloud. ' I've done my work, and now you can do what you please.' He lay still, staring at the ceiling, the long-pent-up delirium of drink in his veins, his brain on fire with racing thoughts that would not stay to be considered, and his hands crisped and dry. He had just discovered that he was painting the face of the Melancolia on a revolving dome ribbed with millions of lights, and that all his wondrous thoughts stood embodied hundreds of feet below his tiny swinging plank, shouting together in his honour, when something cracked inside his temples like an overstrained bowstring, the glittering dome broke inward, and he was alone in the thick night.

' I'll go to sleep. The room's very dark. Let's light a lamp and see how the Melancolia looks. There ought to have been a moon.'

It was then that Torpenhow heard his name called by a voice he did not know,—in the rattling accents of deadly fear.

'He's looked at the picture,' was his first thought, as he hurried into the bedroom and found Dick sitting up and beating the air with his hands.

'Torp! Torp! Where are you? For pity's sake, come to me!'

'What's the matter?'

Dick clutched at his shoulder. 'Matter! I've been lying here for hours in the dark, and you never heard me. Torp, old man, don't go away. I'm all in the dark. In the dark, I tell you!'

Torpenhow held the candle within a foot of Dick's eyes, but there was no answer in those eyes. He lit the gas, and Dick heard the flame catch. The grip of his fingers on Torpenhow's shoulder made Torpenhow wince.

'Don't leave me. You wouldn't leave me alone now, would you? I can't see. D'you understand? It's black,—quite black,—and I feel as if I was falling through it all.'

'Steady does it.' Torpenhow put his arm round Dick and began to rock him gently to and fro.

'That's good. Now don't talk. If I keep very quiet for a while this darkness will lift. It seems just on the point of breaking. H'sh!' Dick knit his brows, and stared desperately in front of him. The night air was chilling Torpenhow's toes.

'Can you stay like that a minute?' he said. 'I'll get my dressing-gown and some slippers.'

Dick clutched the bed-head with both hands and waited for the darkness to clear away. 'What a time you've been!' he cried, when Torpenhow returned. 'It's as black as ever. What are you banging about in the doorway?'

'Long chair,—horse-blanket,—pillow. Going to sleep by you. Lie down now; you'll be better in the morning.'

'I shan't!' The voice rose to a wail. 'My God! I'm blind! I'm blind, and the darkness will never go away.' He made as if to leap from the bed, but Torpenhow's arms were round him, and Torpenhow's chin was on his shoulder, and his breath was squeezed out of him. He could only gasp, 'Blind!' and wriggle feebly.

'Steady, Dickie, steady!' said the deep voice in his ear, and the grip tightened. 'Bite on the bullet, old man, and don't let them think you're afraid.' The grip could draw no closer. Both men were breathing heavily. Dick threw his head from side to side and groaned.

'Let me go,' he panted. 'You're cracking my ribs. We—we mustn't let them think we're afraid, must we,—all the Powers of Darkness and that lot?'

'Lie down. It's all over now.'

'Yes,' said Dick obediently. 'But would you mind letting me hold your hand? I feel as if I wanted something to hold on to. One drops through the dark so.'

Torpenhow thrust out a large and hairy paw

from the long chair. Dick clutched it tightly, and in half an hour had fallen asleep. Torpenhow withdrew his hand, and, stooping over Dick, kissed him lightly on the forehead, as men do sometimes kiss a wounded comrade in the hour of death, to ease his departure.

In the grey dawn Torpenhow heard Dick talking to himself. He was adrift on the shoreless tides of delirium, speaking very quickly :—

'It's a pity,—a great pity; but it's helped, and it must be eaten, Master George. . . . Sufficient unto the day is the blindness thereof, and, further, putting aside all Melancolias and false humours, it is of obvious notoriety—such as mine was—that the Queen can do no wrong. Torp doesn't know that. I'll tell him when we're a little farther into the desert. What a bungle those boatmen are making of the steamer-ropes! They'll have that four-inch hawser chafed through in a minute. I told you so—there she goes! . . . White foam on green water, and the steamer slewing round. How good that looks! I'll sketch it. No, I can't. I'm afflicted with ophthalmia. That was one of the ten plagues of Egypt, and it extends up the Nile in the shape of cataract. Ha! that's a joke, Torp. Laugh, you graven image, and stand clear of the hawser. . . . It'll knock you into the water and make your dress all dirty, Maisie dear.'

'Oh!' said Torpenhow. 'This happened before. That night on the river.'

'She'll be sure to say it's my fault if you get muddy, and you're quite near enough to the

breakwater. . . . Maisie, that's not fair. Ah!
I knew you'd miss. Low and to the left, dear.
But you've no conviction. Everything in the
world except conviction. Don't be angry, darling.
I'd cut my hand off if it would give you anything
more than obstinacy. My right hand, if it would
serve.'

'Now we mustn't listen. Here's an island
shouting across seas of misunderstanding with a
vengeance. But it's shouting truth, I fancy,'
said Torpenhow.

The babble continued. It all bore upon
Maisie. Sometimes Dick lectured at length on
his craft, then he cursed himself for his folly in
being enslaved. He pleaded to Maisie for a kiss
—only one kiss—before she went away, and
called to her to come back from Vitry-sur-Marne,
if she would; but through all his ravings he bade
Heaven and Earth witness that the Queen could
do no wrong.

Torpenhow listened attentively, and learned
every detail of Dick's life that had been hidden
from him. For three days Dick raved through
his past, and then slept a natural sleep. 'What
a strain he has been running under, poor chap!'
said Torpenhow. 'Dick, of all men, handing
himself over like a dog! And I was lecturing
him on arrogance! I ought to have known that
it is no use to judge a man. But I did it. What
a demon that girl must be! Dick's given her
his life,—confound him!—and she's given him
one kiss apparently.'

'Torp,' said Dick from the bed, 'go out for

a walk. You've been here too long. I'll get up. Hi! This is annoying. I can't dress myself. Oh, it's too absurd!'

Torpenhow helped him into his clothes and led him to the big chair in the studio. He sat quietly waiting under strained nerves for the darkness to lift. It did not lift that day, nor the next. Dick adventured on a voyage round the walls. He hit his shins against the stove, and this suggested to him that it would be better to crawl on all-fours, one hand in front of him. Torpenhow found him on the floor.

'I'm trying to get the geography of my new possessions,' said he. 'D'you remember that nigger you gouged in the square? Pity you didn't keep the odd eye. It would have been useful. Any letters for me? Give me all the ones in fat grey envelopes with a sort of crown thing outside. They're of no importance.'

Torpenhow gave him a letter with a black M. on the envelope flap. Dick put it into his pocket. There was nothing in it that Torpenhow might not have read, but it belonged to himself and to Maisie, who would never belong to him.

'When she finds that I don't write she'll stop writing. It's better so. I couldn't be any use to her now,' Dick argued, and the tempter suggested that he should make known his condition. Every nerve in him revolted. 'I have fallen low enough already. I'm not going to beg for pity. Besides, it would be cruel to her.' He strove to put Maisie out of his thoughts; but the blind have many opportunities for thinking, and as the tides of his

strength came back to him in the long employless
days of dead darkness, Dick's soul was troubled
to the core. Another letter, and another, came
from Maisie. Then there was silence, and Dick
sat by the window, the pulse of summer in the
air, and pictured her being won by another man,
stronger than himself. His imagination, the
keener for the dark background it worked against,
spared him no single detail that might send him
raging up and down the studio, to stumble over
the stove that seemed to be in four places at once.
Worst of all, tobacco would not taste in the darkness. The arrogance of the man had disappeared,
and in its place were settled despair that Torpenhow knew, and blind passion that Dick confided
to his pillow at night. The intervals between the
paroxysms were filled with intolerable waiting
and the weight of intolerable darkness.

'Come out into the Park,' said Torpenhow.
'You haven't stirred out since the beginning of
things.'

'What's the use? There's no movement in
the dark ; and, besides,'—he paused irresolutely
at the head of the stairs,—'something will run
over me.'

'Not if I'm with you. Proceed gingerly.'

The roar of the streets filled Dick with nervous terror, and he clung to Torpenhow's arm.
'Fancy having to feel for a gutter with your
foot ! ' he said petulantly, as he turned into the
Park. 'Let's curse God and die.'

'Sentries are forbidden to pay unauthorised
compliments. By Jove, there are the Guards! '

Dick's figure straightened. 'Let's get near 'em. Let's go in and look. Let's get on the grass and run. I can smell the trees.'

'Mind the low railing. That's all right!' Torpenhow kicked out a tuft of grass with his heel. Smell that,' he said. 'Isn't it good?' Dick snuffed luxuriously. 'Now pick up your feet and run.' They approached as near to the regiment as was possible. The clank of bayonets being unfixed made Dick's nostrils quiver.

'Let's get nearer. They're in column, aren't they?'

'Yes. How did you know?'

'Felt it. Oh, my men!—my beautiful men!' He edged forward as though he could see. 'I could draw those chaps once. Who'll draw 'em now?'

'They'll move off in a minute. Don't jump when the band begins.'

'Huh! I'm not a new charger. It's the silences that hurt. Nearer, Torp!—nearer! Oh, my God, what wouldn't I give to see 'em for a minute!—one half-minute!'

He could hear the armed life almost within reach of him, could hear the slings tighten across the bandsman's chest as he heaved the big drum from the ground.

'Sticks crossed above his head,' whispered Torpenhow.

'I know. *I* know! Who should know if I don't? H'sh!'

The drumsticks fell with a boom, and the men swung forward to the crash of the band.

Dick felt the wind of the massed movement in his face, heard the maddening tramp of feet and the friction of the pouches on the belts. The big drum pounded out the tune. It was a music-hall refrain that made a perfect quickstep :—

> He must be a man of decent height,
>   He must be a man of weight,
> He must come home on a Saturday night
>   In a thoroughly sober state ;
> He must know how to love me,
>   And he must know how to kiss ;
> And if he's enough to keep us both
>   I can't refuse him bliss.

'What's the matter?' said Torpenhow, as he saw Dick's head fall when the last of the regiment had departed.

'Nothing. I feel a little bit out of the running, —that's all. Torp, take me back. Why did you bring me out?'

CHAPTER XII

There were three friends that buried the fourth,
   The mould in his mouth and the dust in his eyes;
And they went south, and east, and north,—
   The strong man fights, but the sick man dies.

There were three friends that spoke of the dead,—
   The strong man fights, but the sick man dies.—
' And would he were here with us now,' they said,
   ' The sun in our face and the wind in our eyes.'
                              Ballad.

THE Nilghai was angry with Torpenhow. Dick
had been sent to bed,—blind men are ever under
the orders of those who can see,—and since he
had returned from the Park had fluently sworn at
Torpenhow because he was alive, and all the world
because it was alive and could see, while he, Dick,
was dead in the death of the blind, who, at the
best, are only burdens upon their associates.
Torpenhow had said something about a Mrs.
Gummidge, and Dick had retired in a black fury
to handle and rehandle three unopened letters from
Maisie.

The Nilghai, fat, burly, and aggressive, was
in Torpenhow's rooms. Behind him sat the
Keneu, the Great War Eagle, and between them

lay a large map embellished with black- and white-headed pins.

'I was wrong about the Balkans,' said the Nilghai. 'But I'm not wrong about this business. The whole of our work in the Southern Sudan must be done over again. The public doesn't care, of course, but the Government does, and they are making their arrangements quietly. You know that as well as I do.'

'I remember how the people cursed us when our troops withdrew from Omdurman. It was bound to crop up sooner or later. But I can't go,' said Torpenhow. He pointed through the open door; it was a hot night. 'Can you blame me?'

The Keneu purred above his pipe like a large and very happy cat :—

'Don't blame you in the least. It's uncommonly good of you, and all the rest of it, but every man—even you, Torp—must consider his work. I know it sounds brutal, but Dick's out of the race,—down,—*gastado*, expended, finished, done for. He has a little money of his own. He won't starve, and you can't pull out of your stride for his sake. Think of your own reputation.'

'Dick's was five times bigger than mine and yours put together.'

'That was because he signed his name to everything he did. It's all ended now. You must hold yourself in readiness to move out. You can command your own prices, and you do better work than any three of us.'

'Don't tell me how tempting it is. I'll stay here to look after Dick for a while. He's as

cheerful as a bear with a sore head, but I think
he likes to have me near him.'

The Nilghai said something uncomplimentary
about soft-headed fools who throw away their
careers for other fools. Torpenhow flushed
angrily. The constant strain of attendance on
Dick had worn his nerves thin.

'There remains a third fate,' said the Keneu
thoughtfully. 'Consider this, and be not larger
fools than is necessary. Dick is—or rather was
—an able-bodied man of moderate attractions and
a certain amount of audacity.'

'Oho!' said the Nilghai, who remembered an
affair at Cairo. 'I begin to see.—Torp, I'm
sorry.'

Torpenhow nodded forgiveness : 'You were
more sorry when he cut you out, though.—Go
on, Keneu.'

'I've often thought, when I've seen men die
out in the desert, that if the news could be sent
through the world, and the means of transport
were quick enough, there would be one woman
at least at each man's bedside.'

'There would be some mighty quaint revela-
tions. Let us be grateful things are as they are,'
said the Nilghai.

'Let us rather reverently consider whether
Torp's three-cornered ministrations are exactly
what Dick needs just now.—What do you think
yourself, Torp?'

'I know they aren't. But what can I do?'

'Lay the matter before the Board. We are all
Dick's friends here. You've been most in his life.'

' But I picked it up when he was off his head.'

' The greater chance of its being true. I thought we should arrive. Who is she?'

Then Torpenhow told a tale in plain words, as a special correspondent who knows how to make a verbal *précis* should tell it. The men listened without interruption.

' Is it possible that a man can come back across the years to his calf-love?' said the Keneu. ' Is it possible?'

' I give the facts. He says nothing about it now, but he sits fumbling three letters from her when he thinks I'm not looking. What am I to do?'

' Speak to him,' said the Nilghai.

' Oh yes! Write to her,—I don't know her full name, remember,—and ask her to accept him out of pity. I believe you once told Dick you were sorry for him, Nilghai. You remember what happened, eh? Go into the bedroom and suggest full confession and an appeal to this Maisie girl, whoever she is. I honestly believe he'd try to kill you ; and the blindness has made him rather muscular.'

' Torpenhow's course is perfectly clear,' said the Keneu. ' He will go to Vitry-sur-Marne, which is on the Bézières-Landes Railway,—single track from Tourgas. The Prussians shelled it out in '70 because there was a poplar on the top of a hill eighteen hundred yards from the church spire. There's a squadron of cavalry quartered there,—or ought to be. Where this studio Torp spoke about may be I cannot tell. That is Torp's business. I have given him his route. He will dispassionately explain the situation to the girl, and she will come back to Dick,—the more especially because, to use Dick's words, " there is nothing but her damned obstinacy to keep them apart." '

' And they have four hundred and twenty pounds a year between 'em. Dick never lost his head for figures, even in his delirium. You haven't the shadow of an excuse for not going,' said the Nilghai.

Torpenhow looked very uncomfortable. ' But it's absurd and impossible. I can't drag her back by the hair.'

' Our business—the business for which we draw our money—is to do absurd and impossible things,—generally with no reason whatever except to amuse the public. Here we have a reason. The rest doesn't matter. I shall share these rooms with the Nilghai till Torpenhow returns. There will be a batch of unbridled " specials " coming to Town in a little while, and these will serve as their headquarters. Another reason for sending Torpenhow away. Thus Providence helps those who help others, and '—here the Keneu dropped his measured speech—' we can't have you tied by the leg to Dick when the trouble begins. It's your only chance of getting away ; and Dick will be grateful.'

' He will,—worse luck ! I can but go and try. I can't conceive a woman in her senses refusing Dick.'

' Talk that out with the girl. I have seen you

wheedle an angry Mahdieh woman into giving
you dates. This won't be a tithe as difficult.
You had better not be here to-morrow afternoon,
because the Nilghai and I will be in possession.
It is an order. Obey.'

'Dick,' said Torpenhow next morning, 'can
I do anything for you?'

'No! Leave me alone. How often must I
remind you that I'm blind?'

'Nothing I could go for to fetch for to carry
for to bring?'

'No. Take those infernal creaking boots of
yours away.'

'Poor chap!' said Torpenhow to himself. 'I
must have been sitting on his nerves lately. He
wants a lighter step.' Then, aloud, 'Very well.
Since you're so independent I'm going off for
four or five days. Say good-bye at least. The
housekeeper will look after you, and Keneu has
my rooms.'

Dick's face fell. 'You won't be longer than
a week at the outside? I know I'm touched in
the temper, but I can't get on without you.'

'Can't you? You'll have to do without me in
a little time, and you'll be glad I'm gone.'

Dick felt his way back to the big chair, and
wondered what these things might mean. He
did not wish to be tended by the housekeeper,
and yet Torpenhow's constant tenderness jarred
on him. He did not exactly know what he wanted.
The darkness would not lift, and Maisie's unopened letters felt worn and old from much
handling. He could never read them for himself

as long as life endured; but Maisie might have sent him some fresh ones to play with. The Nilghai entered with a gift,—a piece of red modelling-wax. He fancied that Dick might find interest in using his hands. Dick poked and patted the stuff for a few minutes, and, ' Is it like anything in the world?' he said drearily. ' Take it away. I may get the touch of the blind in fifty years. Do you know where Torpenhow has gone?'

The Nilghai knew nothing. ' We're staying in his rooms till he comes back. Can we do anything for you?'

' I'd like to be left alone, please. Don't think I'm ungrateful, but I'm best alone.'

The Nilghai chuckled, and Dick resumed his drowsy brooding and sullen rebellion against fate. He had long since ceased to think about the work he had done in the old days, and the desire to do more work had departed from him. He was exceedingly sorry for himself, and the completeness of his tender grief soothed him. But his soul and his body cried for Maisie,—Maisie who would understand. His mind pointed out that Maisie, having her own work to do, would not care. His experience had taught him that when money was exhausted women went away, and that when a man was knocked out of the race the others trampled on him. ' Then at the least,' said Dick in reply, ' she could use me as I used Binat,—for some sort of a study. I wouldn't ask more than to be near her again, even though I knew that another man was making love to her. Ugh! what a dog I am!'

A voice on the staircase began to sing joyfully :—

When we go—go—go away from here,
  Our creditors will weep and they will wail,
Our absence much regretting when they find that we've been
    getting
  Out of England by next Tuesday's Indian mail.

Following the trampling of feet, slamming of Torpenhow's door, and the sound of voices in strenuous debate, some one squeaked, ' And see, you good fellows, I have found a new water-bottle,—firs'-class patent—eh, how you say? Open himself inside out.'

Dick sprang to his feet. He knew the voice well. ' That's Cassavetti, back from the Continent. Now I know why Torp went away. There's a row somewhere, and—I'm out of it ! '

The Nilghai commanded silence in vain. ' That's for my sake,' Dick said bitterly. ' The birds are getting ready to fly, and they wouldn't tell me. I can hear Morten - Sutherland and Mackaye. Half the war-correspondents in London are there ;—and I'm out of it.'

He stumbled across the landing and plunged into Torpenhow's room. He could feel that it was full of men. ' Where's the trouble? ' said he. ' In the Balkans at last? Why didn't some one tell me? '

' We thought you wouldn't be interested,' said the Nilghai shamefacedly. ' It's the Sudan, as usual.'

' You lucky dogs ! Let me sit here while you talk. I shan't be a skeleton at the feast.—Cassa-

vetti, where are you?   Your English is as bad
as ever.'

Dick was led into a chair.   He heard the rustle
of the maps, and the talk swept forward, carrying
him with it.   Everybody spoke at once, discussing
Press censorships, railway-routes, transport, water-
supply, the capacities of generals,—these in language that would have horrified a trusting public,
—ranting, asserting, denouncing, and laughing
at the top of their voices.   There was the glorious
certainty of war in the Sudan at any moment.
The Nilghai said so, and it was well to be in
readiness.   The Keneu had telegraphed to Cairo
for horses ; Cassavetti had stolen a perfectly
inaccurate list of troops that would be ordered
forward, and was reading it out amid profane
interruptions, and the Keneu introduced to Dick
some man unknown who would be employed as
war artist by the Central Southern Syndicate.
' It's his first outing,' said the Keneu.   ' Give him
some tips—about riding camels.'

' Oh, those camels ! ' groaned Cassavetti.   ' I
shall learn to ride him again, and now I am so
much all soft !   Listen, you good fellows.   I know
your military arrangement very well.   There will
go the Royal Argalshire Sutherlanders.   So it was
read to me upon best authority.'

A roar of laughter interrupted him.

' Sit down,' said the Nilghai.   ' The lists
aren't even made out in the War Office.'

' Will there be any force at Suakin ? ' said a
voice.

Then the outcries redoubled, and grew mixed,

thus : ' How many Egyptian troops will they use ? ——God help the Fellaheen !——There's a railway in Plumstead marshes doing duty as a fivescourt.——We shall have the Suakin-Berber line built at last.——Canadian voyageurs are too careful. Give me a half-drunk Krooman in a whaleboat.——Who commands the Desert column? ——No, they never blew up the big rock at the Ghizeh bend. We shall have to be hauled up, as usual.——Somebody tell me if there's an Indian contingent, or I'll break everybody's head. ——Don't tear the map in two.—It's a war of occupation, I tell you, to connect with the African Companies in the South.——There's guineaworm in most of the wells on that route.' Then the Nilghai, despairing of peace, bellowed like a fog-horn and beat upon the table with both hands.

' But what becomes of Torp ? ' said Dick, in the silence that followed.

' Torp's in abeyance just now. He's off lovemaking somewhere, I suppose,' said the Nilghai.

' He said he was going to stay at home,' said the Keneu.

' Is he ? ' said Dick with an oath. ' He won't. I'm not much good now, but if you and the Nilghai hold him down I'll engage to trample on him till he sees reason. He stay behind, indeed ! He's the best of you all. There'll be some tough work by Omdurman. We shall come there to stay, this time. But I forgot. . . . I wish I were going with you.'

' So do we all, Dickie,' said the Keneu.

' And I most of all,' said the new artist of the

Central Southern Syndicate. 'Could you tell me——'

'I'll give you one piece of advice,' Dick answered, moving towards the door. 'If you happen to be cut over the head in a scrimmage, don't guard. Tell the man to go on cutting. You'll find it cheapest in the end. Thanks for letting me look in.'

'There's grit in Dick,' said the Nilghai, an hour later, when the room was emptied of all save the Keneu.

'It was the sacred call of the war-trumpet. Did you notice how he answered to it? Poor fellow! Let's look at him,' said the Keneu.

The excitement of the talk had died away. Dick was sitting by the studio table, with his head on his arms, when the men came in. He did not change his position.

'It hurts,' he moaned. 'God forgive me, but it hurts cruelly; and yet, y'know, the world has a knack of spinning round all by itself. Shall I see Torp before he goes?'

'Oh yes. You'll see him,' said the Nilghai.

CHAPTER XIII

The sun went down an hour ago,
  I wonder if I face towards home,
If I lost my way in the light of day
  How shall I find it now night is come?
                  Old Song.

'Maisie, come to bed.'

'It's so hot I can't sleep. Don't worry.'

Maisie put her elbows on the window-sill and looked at the moonlight on the straight, poplar-flanked road. Summer had come upon Vitry-sur-Marne and parched it to the bone. The grass was dry-burnt in the meadows, the clay by the bank of the river was caked to brick, the roadside flowers were long since dead, and the roses in the garden hung withered on their stalks. The heat in the little low bedroom under the eaves was almost intolerable. The very moonlight on the wall of Kami's studio across the road seemed to make the night hotter, and the shadow of the big bell-handle by the closed gate cast a bar of inky black that caught Maisie's eye and annoyed her.

'Horrid thing! It should be all white,' she murmured. 'And the gate isn't in the middle of the wall, either. I never noticed that before.'

Maisie was hard to please at that hour. First, the heat of the past few weeks had worn her down; secondly, her work, and particularly the study of a female head intended to represent the Melancolia and not finished in time for the Salon, was unsatisfactory; thirdly, Kami had said as much two days before; fourthly,—but so completely fourthly that it was hardly worth thinking about,—Dick, her property, had not written to her for more than six weeks. She was angry with the heat, with Kami, and with her work, but she was exceedingly angry with Dick.

She had written to him three times,—each time proposing a fresh treatment of her Melancolia. Dick had taken no notice of these communications. She had resolved to write no more. When she returned to England in the autumn— for her pride's sake she could not return earlier— she would speak to him. She missed the Sunday afternoon conferences more than she cared to admit. All that Kami said was, ' *Continuez, mademoiselle, continuez toujours,*' and he had been repeating his wearisome counsel through the hot summer, exactly like a cicala,—an old grey cicala in a black alpaca coat, white trousers, and a huge felt hat. But Dick had tramped masterfully up and down her little studio north of the cool green London park, and had said things ten times worse than *Continuez*, before he snatched the brush out of her hand and showed her where her error lay. His last letter, Maisie remembered, contained some trivial advice about not sketching in the sun or drinking water at wayside farmhouses ; and he had said that not once, but three times,—as if he did not know that Maisie could take care of herself.

But what was he doing, that he could not trouble to write? A murmur of voices in the road made her lean from the window. A cavalry-man of the little garrison in the town was talking to Kami's cook. The moonlight glittered on the scabbard of his sabre, which he was holding in his hand lest it should clank inopportunely. The cook's cap cast deep shadows on her face, which was close to the conscript's. He slid his arm round her waist, and there followed the sound of a kiss.

'Faugh!' said Maisie, stepping back.

'What's that?' said the red-haired girl, who was tossing uneasily outside her bed.

'Only a conscript kissing the cook,' said Maisie. 'They've gone away now.' She leaned out of the window again, and put a shawl over her nightgown to guard against chills. There was a very small night-breeze abroad, and a sun-baked rose below nodded its head as one who knew unutterable secrets. Was it possible that Dick should turn his thoughts from her work and his own and descend to the degradation of Suzanne and the conscript? He could not! The rose nodded its head and one leaf therewith. It looked like a naughty little devil scratching its ear. Dick could not, ' because,' thought Maisie, ' he is mine, —mine,—mine. He said he was. I'm sure I don't care what he does. It will only spoil his work if he does ; and it will spoil mine too.'

The rose continued to nod in the futile way peculiar to flowers. There was no earthly reason why Dick should not disport himself as he chose, except that he was called by Providence, which was Maisie, to assist Maisie in her work. And her work was the preparation of pictures that went sometimes to English provincial exhibitions, as the notices in the scrap-book proved, and that were invariably rejected by the Salon when Kami was plagued into allowing her to send them up. Her work in the future, it seemed, would be the preparation of pictures on exactly similar lines which would be rejected in exactly the same way——

(The red-haired girl threshed distressfully across the sheets. ' It's too hot to sleep,' she moaned ; and the interruption jarred.)

Exactly the same way. Then she would divide her years between the little studio in England and Kami's big studio at Vitry-sur-Marne. No, she would go to another master, who would force her into the success that was her right, if patient toil and desperate endeavour gave one a right to anything. Dick had told her that he had worked ten years to understand his craft. She had worked ten years, and ten years were nothing. Dick had said that ten years were nothing,—but that was in regard to herself only. He had said—this very man who could not find time to write—that he would wait ten years for her, and that she was bound to come back to him sooner or later. He had said this in the absurd letter about sunstroke and diphtheria ; and then he had stopped writing. He was wandering up

and down moonlit streets, kissing cooks. She
would like to lecture him now,—not in her nightgown, of course, but properly dressed, severely
and from a height. Yet if he was kissing other
girls he certainly would not care whether she
lectured him or not. He would laugh at her.
Very good. She would go back to her studio and
prepare pictures that went, etc. etc. The mill-
wheel of thought swung round slowly, that no
section of it might be slurred over, and the red-
haired girl tossed and turned behind her.

Maisie put her chin in her hands and decided
that there could be no doubt whatever of the
villainy of Dick. To justify herself, she began,
unwomanly, to weigh the evidence. There was
a boy, and he had said he loved her. And he
kissed her—kissed her on the cheek—by a yellow
sea-poppy that nodded its head exactly like the
maddening dry rose in the garden. Then there
was an interval, and men had told her that they
loved her—just when she was busiest with her
work. Then the boy came back, and at their
very second meeting had told her that he loved
her. Then he had—— But there was no end
to the things he had done. He had given her
his time and his powers. He had spoken to
her of Art, housekeeping, technique, teacups, the
abuse of pickles as a stimulant,—that was rude,—
sable-hair brushes,—he had given her the best
in her stock,—she used them daily; he had
given her advice that she profited by, and now
and again—a look. Such a look! The look of
a beaten hound waiting for the word to crawl

to his mistress's feet. In return she had given him nothing whatever, except—here she brushed her mouth against the open-work sleeve of her nightgown—the privilege of kissing her once. And on the mouth, too. Disgraceful! Was that not enough, and more than enough? and if it was not, had he not cancelled the debt by not writing and—probably kissing other girls?

'Maisie, you'll catch a chill. Do go and lie down,' said the wearied voice of her companion. 'I can't sleep a wink with you at the window.'

Maisie shrugged her shoulders and did not answer. She was reflecting on the meannesses of Dick, and on other meannesses with which he had nothing to do. The remorseless moonlight would not let her sleep. It lay on the skylight of the studio across the road in cold silver; she stared at it intently, and her thoughts began to slide one into the other. The shadow of the big bell-handle in the wall grew short, lengthened again, and faded out as the moon went down behind the pasture and a hare came limping home across the road. Then the dawn-wind washed through the upturned grasses, and brought coolness with it, and the cattle lowed by the drought-shrunk river. Maisie's head fell forward on the window-sill, and the tangle of black hair covered her arms.

'Maisie, wake up. You'll catch a chill.'

'Yes, dear; yes, dear.' She staggered to her bed like a wearied child, and as she buried her face in the pillows she muttered, 'I think—I think. . . . But he ought to have written.'

Day brought the routine of the studio, the smell of paint and turpentine, and the monotonous wisdom of Kami, who was a leaden artist, but a golden teacher if the pupil were only in sympathy with him. Maisie was not in sympathy that day, and she waited impatiently for the end of the work. She knew when it was coming; for Kami would gather his black alpaca coat into a bunch behind him, and, with faded blue eyes that saw neither pupils nor canvas, look back into the past to recall the history of one Binat. 'You have all done not so badly,' he would say. 'But you shall remember that it is not enough to have the method, and the art, and the power, nor even that which is touch, but you shall have also the conviction that nails the work to the wall. Of the so many I have taught,'—here the students would begin to unfix drawing-pins or get their tubes together,—' the very so many that I have taught, the best was Binat. All that comes of the study and the work and the knowledge was to him even when he came. After he left me he should have done all that could be done with the colour, the form, and the knowledge. Only, he had not the conviction. So to-day I hear no more of Binat, —the best of my pupils,—and that is long ago. So to-day, too, you will be glad to hear no more of me. *Continuez, mesdemoiselles*, and, above all, with conviction.'

He went into the garden to smoke and mourn over the lost Binat as the pupils dispersed to their several cottages or loitered in the studio to make plans for the cool of the afternoon.

Maisie looked at her very unhappy Melancolia, restrained a desire to grimace before it, and was hurrying across the road to write a letter to Dick, when she was aware of a large man on a white troop-horse. How Torpenhow had managed in the course of twenty hours to find his way to the hearts of the cavalry officers in quarters at Vitry-sur-Marne, to discuss with them the certainty of a glorious revenge for France, to reduce the Colonel to tears of pure affability, and to borrow the best horse in the squadron for the journey to Kami's studio, is a mystery that only special correspondents can unravel.

'I beg your pardon,' said he. 'It seems an absurd question to ask, but the fact is that I don't know her by any other name: Is there any young lady here that is called Maisie?'

'I am Maisie,' was the answer from the depths of a great sun-hat.

'I ought to introduce myself,' he said, as the horse capered in the blinding white dust. 'My name is Torpenhow. Dick Heldar is my best friend, and—and—the fact is that he has gone blind.'

'Blind!' said Maisie stupidly. 'He can't be blind.'

'He has been stone-blind for nearly two months.'

Maisie lifted up her face, and it was pearly white. 'No! No! Not blind! I won't have him blind!'

'Would you care to see for yourself?' said Torpenhow.

'Now—at once?'

'Oh no! The Paris train doesn't go through this place till eight to-night. There will be ample time.'

'Did Mr. Heldar send you to me?'

'Certainly not. Dick wouldn't do that sort of thing. He's sitting in his studio, turning over some letters that he can't read because he's blind.'

There was a sound of choking from the sun-hat. Maisie bowed her head and went into the cottage, where the red-haired girl was on a sofa, complaining of a headache.

'Dick's blind!' said Maisie, taking her breath quickly as she steadied herself against a chair-back. 'My Dick's blind!'

'What?' The girl was on the sofa no longer.

'A man has come from England to tell me. He hasn't written to me for six weeks.'

'Are you going to him?'

'I must think.'

'Think! *I* should go back to London and see him, and I should kiss his eyes, and kiss them and kiss them until they got well again! If you don't go I shall. Oh, what am I talking about? You wicked little idiot! Go to him at once. Go!'

Torpenhow's neck was blistering, but he pre-served a smile of infinite patience as Maisie appeared bareheaded in the sunshine.

'I am coming,' said she, her eyes on the ground.

'You will be at Vitry Station, then, at seven this evening.' This was an order delivered by one who was used to being obeyed. Maisie said nothing, but she felt grateful that there was no

chance of disputing with this big man who took
everything for granted and managed a squealing horse with one hand. She returned to the
red-haired girl, who was weeping bitterly, and between tears, kisses,—very few of those,—menthol,
packing, and an interview with Kami, the sultry
afternoon wore away. Thought might come
afterwards. Her present duty was to go to Dick,
—Dick who owned the wondrous friend and sat
in the dark playing with her unopened letters.

'But what will you do?' she said to her
companion.

'I? Oh, I shall stay here and—finish your
Melancolia,' she said, smiling pitifully. 'Write
to me afterwards.'

That night there ran a legend through Vitry-
sur-Marne of a mad Englishman, doubtless suffering from sunstroke, who had drunk all the officers
of the garrison under the table, had borrowed a
horse from the lines, and had then and there
eloped, after the English custom, with one of
those more than mad English girls who drew
pictures down there under the care of that good
Monsieur Kami.

'They are very droll,' said Suzanne to the
conscript in the moonlight by the studio wall.
'She walked always with those big eyes that saw
nothing, and yet she kisses me on both cheeks as
though she were my sister, and gives me—see—
ten francs!'

The conscript levied a contribution on both
gifts; for he prided himself on being a good
soldier.

Torpenhow spoke very little to Maisie during the journey to Calais; but he was careful to attend to all her wants, to get her a compartment entirely to herself, and to leave her alone. He was amazed at the ease with which the matter had been accomplished.

'The safest thing would be to let her think things out. By Dick's showing,—when he was off his head,—she must have ordered him about very thoroughly. Wonder how she likes being under orders.'

Maisie never told. She sat in the empty compartment often with her eyes shut, that she might realise the sensation of blindness. It was an order that she should return to London swiftly, and she found herself at last almost beginning to enjoy the situation. This was better than looking after luggage and a red-haired friend who never took any interest in her surroundings. But there appeared to be a feeling in the air that she, Maisie, —of all people,—was in disgrace. Therefore she justified her conduct to herself with great success, till Torpenhow came up to her on the steamer, and without preface began to tell the story of Dick's blindness, suppressing a few details, but dwelling at length on the miseries of delirium. He stopped before he reached the end, as though he had lost interest in the subject, and went forward to smoke. Maisie was furious with him and with herself.

She was hurried on from Dover to London almost before she could ask for breakfast, and— she was past any feeling of indignation now—was bidden curtly to wait in a hall at the foot of some lead-covered stairs while Torpenhow went up to make inquiries. Again the knowledge that she was being treated like a naughty little girl made her pale cheeks flame. It was all Dick's fault for being so stupid as to go blind.

Torpenhow led her up to a shut door, which he opened very softly. Dick was sitting by the window, with his chin on his chest. There were three envelopes in his hand, and he turned them over and over. The big man who gave orders was no longer by her side, and the studio door snapped behind her.

Dick thrust the letters into his pocket as he heard the sound. ' Hullo, Torp ! Is that you? I've been so lonely.'

His voice had taken the peculiar flatness of the blind. Maisie pressed herself up into a corner of the room. Her heart was beating furiously, and she put one hand on her breast to keep it quiet. Dick was staring directly at her, and she realised for the first time that he was blind. Shutting her eyes in a railway-carriage to open them when she pleased was child's play. This man was blind though his eyes were wide open.

' Torp, is that you? They said you were coming.' Dick looked puzzled and a little irritated at the silence.

' No: it's only me,' was the answer, in a strained little whisper. Maisie could hardly move her lips.

' H'm ! ' said Dick composedly, without moving. ' This is a new phenomenon. Darkness I'm getting used to; but I object to hearing voices.'

Was he mad, then, as well as blind, that he talked to himself? Maisie's heart beat more wildly, and she breathed in gasps. Dick rose and began to feel his way across the room, touching each table and chair as he passed. Once he caught his foot on a rug, and swore, dropping on his knees to feel what the obstruction might be. Maisie remembered him walking in the Park as though all the earth belonged to him, tramping up and down her studio two months ago, and flying up the gangway of the Channel steamer. The beating of her heart was making her sick, and Dick was coming nearer, guided by the sound of her breathing. She put out a hand mechanically to ward him off or to draw him to herself, she did not know which. It touched his chest, and he stepped back as though he had been shot.

'It's Maisie!' said he, with a dry sob. 'What are you doing here?'

'I came—I came—to see you, please.'

Dick's lips closed firmly.

'Won't you sit down, then? You see, I've had some bother with my eyes, and——'

'I know. I know. Why didn't you tell me?'

'I couldn't write.'

'You might have told Mr. Torpenhow.'

'What has he to do with my affairs?'

'He—he brought me from Vitry-sur-Marne. He thought I ought to see you.'

'Why, what has happened? Can I do anything for you? No, I can't. I forgot.'

'Oh, Dick, I'm so sorry! I've come to tell

you, and—— Let me take you back to your chair.'

'Don't! I'm not a child. You only do that out of pity. I never meant to tell you anything about it. I'm no good now. I'm down and done for. Let me alone!'

He groped back to his chair, his chest labouring as he sat down.

Maisie watched him, and the fear went out of her heart, to be followed by a very bitter shame. He had spoken a truth that had been hidden from the girl through every step of the impetuous flight to London; for he was, indeed, down and done for—masterful no longer, but rather a little abject; neither an artist stronger than she, nor a man to be looked up to—only some blind one that sat in a chair and seemed on the point of crying. She was immensely and unfeignedly sorry for him— more sorry than she had ever been for any one in her life, but not sorry enough to deny his words. So she stood still and felt ashamed and a little hurt, because she had honestly intended that her journey should end triumphantly; and now she was only filled with pity most startlingly distinct from love.

'Well?' said Dick, his face steadily turned away. 'I never meant to worry you any more. What's the matter?'

He was conscious that Maisie was catching her breath, but was as unprepared as herself for the torrent of emotion that followed. People who cannot cry easily weep unrestrainedly when the fountains of the great deep are broken up. She had dropped into a chair and was sobbing with her face hidden in her hands.

' I can't—I can't!' she cried desperately. ' Indeed, I can't. It isn't my fault. I'm so sorry. Oh, Dickie, I'm so sorry.'

Dick's shoulders straightened again, for the words lashed like a whip. Still the sobbing continued. It is not good to realise that you have failed in the hour of trial or flinched before the mere possibility of making sacrifices.

' I do despise myself—indeed I do. But I can't. Oh, Dickie, you wouldn't ask me—would you?' wailed Maisie.

She looked up for a minute, and by chance it happened that Dick's eyes fell on hers. The unshaven face was very white and set, and the lips were trying to force themselves into a smile. But it was the worn-out eyes that Maisie feared. Her Dick had gone blind and left in his place some one that she could hardly recognise till he spoke.

' Who is asking you to do anything, Maisie? I told you how it would be. What's the use of worrying? For pity's sake don't cry like that. It isn't worth it.'

' You don't know how I hate myself. Oh, Dick, help me—help me!' The passion of tears had grown beyond her control and was beginning to alarm the man. He stumbled forward and put his arm round her, and her head fell on his shoulder.

' Hush, dear, hush! Don't cry. You're quite right, and you've nothing to reproach yourself with—you never had. You're only a little upset by the journey, and I don't suppose you've had any breakfast. What a brute Torp was to bring you over.'

' I wanted to come. I did indeed!' she protested.

' Very well. And now you've come and seen, and I'm—immensely grateful. When you're better you shall go away and get something to eat. What sort of a passage did you have coming over?'

Maisie was crying more subduedly, for the first time in her life glad that she had something to lean against. Dick patted her on the shoulder tenderly but clumsily, for he was not quite sure where her shoulder might be.

She drew herself out of his arms at last and waited, trembling and most unhappy. He had felt his way to the window to put the width of the room between them, and to quiet a little the tumult in his heart.

' Are you better now?' he said.

' Yes, but—don't you hate me?'

' I hate you? My God! I?'

' Isn't—isn't there anything I could do for you, then? I'll stay here in England to do it, if you like. Perhaps I could come and see you sometimes.'

' I think not, dear. It would be kindest not to see me any more, please. I don't want to seem rude, but—don't you think—perhaps you had almost better go now.'

He was conscious that he could not bear himself as a man if the strain continued much longer.

' I don't deserve anything else. I'll go, Dick. Oh, I'm so miserable.'

' Nonsense. You've nothing to worry about; I'd tell you if you had. Wait a moment, dear. I've got something to give you first. I meant it for you ever since this little trouble began. It's my Melancolia; she was a beauty when I last saw her. You can keep her for me, and if ever you're poor you can sell her. She's worth a few hundred in any state of the market.' He groped among his canvases. ' She's framed in black. Is this a black frame that I have my hand on? There she is. What do you think of her?'

He turned a scarred, formless muddle of paint towards Maisie, and the eyes strained as though they would catch her wonder and surprise. One thing and one thing only could she do for him.

' Well?'

The voice was fuller and more rounded, because the man knew he was speaking of his best work. Maisie looked at the blur, and a lunatic desire to laugh caught her by the throat. But for Dick's sake—whatever this mad blankness might mean—she must make no sign. Her voice was choked with hard-held tears as she answered, still gazing on the wreck:

' Oh, Dick, it *is* good!'

He heard the little hysterical gulp and took it for tribute. ' Won't you have it, then? I'll send it over to your house if you will.'

' I? Oh yes—thank you. Ha! ha!' If she did not fly at once the laughter that was worse than tears would kill her. She turned and ran, choking and blinded, down the staircases that were empty of life, to take refuge in a cab and go to her house across the Park. There she sat down in the almost dismantled drawing-room and thought of Dick in his blindness, useless till the end of life, and of herself in her own eyes. Behind the sorrow, the shame, and the humiliation, lay fear of the cold wrath of the red-haired girl when Maisie should return. Maisie had never feared her companion before. Not until she found herself saying, ' Well, he never asked me,' did she realise her scorn of herself.

And that is the end of Maisie.

For Dick was reserved more searching torment. He could not realise at first that Maisie, whom he had ordered to go, had left him without a word of farewell. He was savagely angry against Torpenhow, who had brought upon him this humiliation and troubled his miserable peace. Then his dark hour came, and he was alone with himself and his desires to get what help he could from the darkness. The Queen could do no wrong, but in following her right, so far as it served her work, she had wounded her one subject more than his own brain would let him know.

' It's all I had and I've lost it,' he said, as soon as the misery permitted clear thinking. ' And Torp will think that he has been so infernally clever that I shan't have the heart to tell him. I must think this out quietly.'

' Hullo ! ' said Torpenhow, entering the studio after Dick had enjoyed two hours of thought. ' I'm back. Are you feeling any better ? '

'Torp, I don't know what to say. Come here.'
Dick coughed huskily, wondering, indeed, what
he should say, and how to say it temperately.

'What's the need for saying anything? Get
up and tramp.' Torpenhow was perfectly satisfied.

They walked up and down as of custom,
Torpenhow's hand on Dick's shoulder, and Dick
buried in his own thoughts.

'How in the world did you find it all out?'
said Dick at last.

'You shouldn't go off your head if you want
to keep secrets, Dickie. It was absolutely impertinent on my part; but if you'd seen me rocketing
about on a half-trained French troop-horse under
a blazing sun you'd have laughed. There will be
a charivari in my rooms to-night. Seven other
devils——'

'I know—the row in the Southern Sudan.
I surprised their councils the other day, and it
made me unhappy. Have you fixed your flint
to go? Who d'you work for?'

'Haven't signed any contracts yet. I wanted
to see how your business would turn out.'

'Would you have stayed with me, then, if—
things had gone wrong?' He put his question
cautiously.

'Don't ask me too much. I'm only a man.'

'You've tried to be an angel very success-
fully.'

'Oh ye—es! . . . Well, do you attend the
function to-night? We shall be half screwed
before the morning. All the men believe the
war's a certainty.'

' I don't think I will, old man, if it's all the same to you. I'll stay quiet here.'

' And meditate? I don't blame you. You deserve a good time if ever a man did.'

That night there was tumult on the stairs. The correspondents poured in from theatre, dinner, and music-hall to Torpenhow's room that they might discuss their plan of campaign in the event of military operations being a certainty. Torpenhow, the Keneu, and the Nilghai had bidden all the men they had worked with to the orgy; and Mr. Beeton, the housekeeper, declared that never before in his checkered experience had he seen quite such a fancy lot of gentlemen. They waked the chambers with shoutings and song; and the elder men were quite as bad as the younger. For the chances of war were in front of them, and all knew what those meant.

Sitting in his own room a little perplexed by the noise across the landing, Dick suddenly began to laugh to himself.

' When one comes to think of it the situation is intensely comic. Maisie's quite right—poor little thing. I didn't know she could cry like that before; but now I know what Torp thinks, I'm sure he'd be quite fool enough to stay at home and try to console me—if he knew. Besides, it isn't nice to own that you've been thrown over like a broken chair. I must carry this business through alone—as usual. If there isn't a war, and Torp finds out, I shall look foolish, that's all. If there is a war I mustn't interfere with another man's chances. Business is business, and I want to be alone—I want to be alone.   What a row they're making ! '

Somebody hammered at the studio door.

' Come out and frolic, Dickie,' said the Nilghai.

' I should like to, but I can't.   I'm not feeling frolicsome.'

' Then I'll tell the boys and they'll draw you like a badger.'

' Please not, old man.   On my word, I'd sooner be left alone just now.'

' Very good.   Can we send anything in to you ? Fizz, for instance.   Cassavetti is beginning to sing songs of the Sunny South already.'

For one minute Dick considered the proposition seriously.

' No, thanks.   I've a headache already.'

' Virtuous child.   That's the effect of emotion on the young.   All my congratulations, Dick. I also was concerned in the conspiracy for your welfare.'

' Go to the devil and—oh, send Binkie in here.'

The little dog entered on elastic feet, riotous from having been made much of all the evening. He had helped to sing the choruses ; but scarcely inside the studio he realised that this was no place for tail-wagging, and settled himself on Dick's lap till it was bedtime.   Then he went to bed with Dick, who counted every hour as it struck, and rose in the morning with a painfully clear head to receive Torpenhow's more formal congratulations and a particular account of the last night's revels.

'You aren't looking very happy for a newly-accepted man,' said Torpenhow.

'Never mind that—it's my own affair, and I'm all right. Do you really go?'

'Yes. With the old Central Southern as usual. They wired and I accepted on better terms than before.'

'When do you start?'

'The day after to-morrow—for Brindisi.'

'Thank God.' Dick spoke from the bottom of his heart.

'Well, that's not a pretty way of saying you're glad to get rid of me. But men in your condition are allowed to be selfish.'

'I didn't mean that. Will you get a hundred pounds cashed for me before you leave?'

'That's a slender amount for housekeeping, isn't it?'

'Oh, it's only for—marriage expenses.'

Torpenhow brought him the money, counted it out in fives and tens, and carefully put it away in the writing-table.

'Now I suppose I shall have to listen to his ravings about his girl until I go. Heaven send us patience with a man in love!' said he to himself.

But never a word did Dick say of Maisie or marriage. He hung in the doorway of Torpenhow's room when the latter was packing, and asked innumerable questions about the coming campaign, till Torpenhow began to feel annoyed.

'You're a secretive animal, Dickie, and you consume your own smoke, don't you?' he said on the last evening.

' I—I suppose so. By the way, how long do you think this war will last?'

' Days, weeks, or months. One can never tell. It may go on for years.'

' I wish I were going.'

' Good heavens! You're the most unaccountable creature! Hasn't it occurred to you that you're going to be married—thanks to me?'

' Of course, yes. I'm going to be married— so I am. Going to be married. I'm awfully grateful to you. Haven't I told you that?'

' You might be going to be hanged by the look of you,' said Torpenhow.

And the next day Torpenhow bade him good-bye and left him to the loneliness he had so much desired.

CHAPTER XIV

Yet at the last, ere our spearmen had found him,
   Yet at the last, ere a sword-thrust could save,
Yet at the last, with his masters around him,
   He of the Faith spoke as master to slave;
Yet at the last, tho' the Kafirs had maimed him,
   Broken by bondage and wrecked by the reiver,—
Yet at the last, tho' the darkness had claimed him,
   He called upon Allah, and died a believer.

                      Kizilbashi.

'Beg your pardon, Mr. Heldar, but—but isn't nothin' going to happen?' said Mr. Beeton.

'No!' Dick had just waked to another morning of blank despair and his temper was of the shortest.

''Taint my regular business, o' course, sir; and what I say is, "Mind your own business and let other people mind theirs"; but just before Mr. Torpenhow went away he give me to understand, like, that you might be moving into a house of your own, so to speak—a sort of house with rooms upstairs and downstairs where you'd be better attended to, though I try to act just by all our tenants. Don't I?'

'Ah! That must have been a mad-house. I shan't trouble you to take me there yet. Get me my breakfast, please, and leave me alone.'

' I hope I haven't done anything wrong, sir, but you know, I hope, that as far as a man can I tries to do the proper thing by all the gentlemen in chambers—and more particular those whose lot is hard—such as you, for instance, Mr. Heldar. You likes soft-roe bloater, don't you? Soft-roe bloaters is scarcer than hard-roe, but what I say is, " Never mind a little extra trouble so long as you gives satisfaction to the tenants." '

Mr. Beeton withdrew and left Dick to himself. Torpenhow had been long away; there was no more rioting in the chambers, and Dick had settled down to his new life, which he was weak enough to consider nothing better than death.

It is hard to live alone in the dark, confusing the day and night; dropping to sleep through sheer weariness at mid-day, and rising restless in the chill of the dawn. At first Dick, on his awakenings, would grope along the corridors of the chambers till he heard some one snore. Then he would know that the day had not yet come, and return wearily to his bedroom. Later he learned not to stir till there was a noise and movement in the house and Mr. Beeton advised him to get up. Once dressed—and dressing, now that Torpenhow was away, was a lengthy business, because collars, ties, and the like, hid themselves in far corners of the room, and search meant head-beating against chairs and trunks—once dressed, there was nothing whatever to do except to sit still and brood till the three daily meals

came. Centuries separated breakfast from lunch,
and lunch from dinner, and though a man prayed
for hundreds of years that his mind might be
taken from him, God would never hear. Rather
the mind was quickened and the revolving
thoughts ground against each other as millstones
grind when there is no corn between ; and yet
the brain would not wear out and give him rest.
It continued to think, at length, with imagery
and all manner of reminiscences. It recalled
Maisie and past success, reckless travels by land
and sea, the glory of doing work and feeling that
it was good, and suggested all that might have
happened had his eyes only been faithful to their
duty. When thinking ceased through sheer
weariness, there poured into Dick's soul tide on
tide of overwhelming, purposeless fear—dread of
starvation always, terror lest the unseen ceiling
should crash down upon him, fear of fire in the
chambers and a louse's death in red flame, and
agonies of fiercer horror that had nothing to do
with any fear of death. Then Dick bowed his
head, and clutching the arms of his chair fought
with his sweating self till the tinkle of plates told
him that something to eat was being set before
him.

Mr. Beeton would bring the meal when he
had time to spare, and Dick learned to hang upon
his speech, which dealt with badly-fitted gas-
plugs, waste-pipes out of repair, little tricks for
driving picture-nails into walls, and the sins of
the charwoman or the housemaids. In the lack
of better things the small gossip of a servants'

hall becomes immensely interesting, and the screwing of a washer on a tap an event to be talked over for days.

Once or twice a week, too, Mr. Beeton would take Dick out with him when he went marketing in the morning to haggle with tradesmen over fish, lamp-wicks, mustard, tapioca, and so forth, while Dick rested his weight first on one foot and then on the other, and played aimlessly with the tins and string-ball on the counter. Then they would, perhaps, meet one of Mr. Beeton's friends, and Dick, standing aside a little, would hold his peace till Mr. Beeton was willing to go on again.

The life did not increase his self-respect. He abandoned shaving as a dangerous exercise, and being shaved in a barber's shop meant exposure of his infirmity. He could not see that his clothes were properly brushed, and since he had never taken any care of his personal appearance he became every known variety of sloven. A blind man cannot eat with cleanliness till he has been some months used to the darkness. If he demand attendance and grow angry at the want of it, he must assert himself and stand upright. Then the meanest menial can see that he is blind and, therefore, of no consequence. A wise man will keep his eyes on the floor and sit still. For amusement he may pick coal lump by lump out of the scuttle with the tongs, and pile it in a little heap in the fender, keeping count of the lumps, which must all be put back again, one by one and very carefully. He may set himself sums if he cares to work them out; he may talk to himself or to the cat if she chooses to visit him ; and if his trade has been that of an artist, he may sketch in the air with his forefinger ; but that is too much like drawing a pig with the eyes shut. He may go to his bookshelves and count his books, ranging them in order of their size ; or to his wardrobe and count his shirts, laying them in piles of two or three on the bed, as they suffer from frayed cuffs or lost buttons. Even this entertainment wearies after a time ; and all the times are very, very long.

Dick was allowed to sort a tool-chest where Mr. Beeton kept hammers, taps and nuts, lengths of gas-pipes, oil-bottles, and string.

' If I don't have everything just where I know where to look for it, why, then, I can't find anything when I do want it. You've no idea, sir, the amount of little things that these chambers uses up,' said Mr. Beeton. Fumbling at the handle of the door as he went out : ' It's hard on you, sir. I *do* think it's hard on you. Ain't you going to do anything, sir ? '

' I'll pay my rent and messing. Isn't that enough ? '

' I wasn't doubting for a moment that you couldn't pay your way, sir ; but I 'ave often said to my wife, " It's 'ard on 'im because it isn't as if he was an old man, nor yet a middle-aged one, but quite a young gentleman. *That*'s where it comes so 'ard." '

' I suppose so,' said Dick absently. This particular nerve through long battering had ceased to feel—much.

'I was thinking,' continued Mr. Beeton, still making as if to go, 'that you might like to hear my boy Alf read you the papers sometimes of an evening. He do read beautiful, seeing he's only nine.'

'I should be very grateful,' said Dick. 'Only let me make it worth his while.'

'We wasn't thinking of *that*, sir, but of course it's in your own 'ands; but only to 'ear Alf sing "A Boy's best Friend is 'is Mother!" Ah!'

'I'll hear him sing that too. Let him come in this evening with the newspapers.'

Alf was not a nice child, being puffed up with many school-board certificates for good conduct, and inordinately proud of his singing. Mr. Beeton remained, beaming, while the child wailed his way through a song of some eight eight-line verses in the usual whine of the young Cockney, and, after compliments, left him to read Dick the foreign telegrams. Ten minutes later Alf returned to his parents rather pale and scared.

''E said 'e couldn't stand it no more,' he explained.

'He never said you read badly, Alf?' Mrs. Beeton spoke.

'No. 'E said I read beautiful. Said 'e never 'eard any one read like that, but 'e said 'e couldn't abide the stuff in the papers.'

'P'raps he's lost some money in the Stocks. Were you readin' him about Stocks, Alf?'

'No. It was all about fightin' out there where the soldiers is gone—a great long piece with all the lines close together and very hard words in it.

'E give me 'arf a crown because I read so well. And 'e says the next time there's anything 'e wants read 'e'll send for me.'

' That's good hearing, but I do think for all the half-crown—put it into the kicking-donkey money-box, Alf, and let me see you do it—he might have kept you longer. Why, he couldn't have begun to understand how beautiful you read.'

' He's best left to hisself—gentlemen always are when they're downhearted,' said Mr. Beeton.

Alf's rigorously limited powers of comprehending Torpenhow's special correspondence had waked the devil of unrest in Dick. He could hear, through the boy's nasal chant, the camels grunting in the squares behind the soldiers outside Suakin; could hear the men swearing and chaffing across the cooking-pots, and could smell the acrid wood-smoke as it drifted over the camp before the wind of the desert.

That night he prayed to God that his mind might be taken from him, offering for proof that he was worthy of this favour the fact that he had not shot himself long ago. That prayer was not answered, and indeed Dick knew in his heart of hearts that only a lingering sense of humour and no special virtue had kept him alive. Suicide, he had persuaded himself, would be a ludicrous insult to the gravity of the situation as well as a weak-kneed confession of fear.

' Just for the fun of the thing,' he said to the cat, who had taken Binkie's place in his establishment, ' I should like to know how long this is going to last. I can live for a year on the hundred

pounds Torp cashed for me. I must have two
or three thousand at least at the Bank—twenty
or thirty years more provided for, that is to say.
Then I fall back on my hundred and twenty a
year, which will be more by that time. Let's
consider. Twenty-five—thirty-five—a man's in
his prime then, they say—forty-five—a middle-
aged man just entering politics—fifty-five—" died
at the comparatively early age of fifty-five,"
according to the newspapers. Bah! How these
Christians funk death! Sixty-five—we're only
getting on in years. Seventy-five is just possible
though. Great Hell, cat O! fifty years more of
solitary confinement in the dark! You'll die, and
Beeton will die, and Torp will die, and Mai—
everybody else will die, but I shall be alive and
kicking with nothing to do. I'm very sorry for
myself. I should like some one else to be sorry
for me. Evidently I'm not going mad before I
die, but the pain's just as bad as ever. Some day
when you're vivisected, cat O! they'll tie you down
on a little table and cut you open—but don't be
afraid; they'll take precious good care that you
don't die. You'll live, and you'll be very sorry
then that you weren't sorry for me. Perhaps
Torp will come back or . . . I wish I could go
to Torp and the Nilghai, even though I were in
their way.'

Pussy left the room before the speech was
ended, and Alf, as he entered, found Dick addressing the empty hearth-rug.

' There's a letter for you, sir,' he said. ' Perhaps
you'd like me to read it.'

' Lend it to me for a minute and I'll tell you.'

The outstretched hand shook just a little and the voice was not over-steady. It was within the limits of human possibility that—that was no letter from Maisie. He knew the heft of three closed envelopes only too well. It was a foolish hope that the girl should write to him, for he did not realise that there is a wrong which admits of no reparation though the evildoer may with tears and the heart's best love strive to mend all. It is best to forget that wrong whether it be caused or endured, since it is as remediless as bad work once put forward.

' Read it, then,' said Dick, and Alf began intoning according to the rules of the Board School :—

' " *I could have given you love, I could have given you loyalty, such as you never dreamed of. Do you suppose I cared what you were ? But you chose to whistle everything down the wind for nothing. My only excuse for you is that you are so young.*"

' That's all,' he said, returning the paper to be dropped into the fire.

' What was in the letter ? ' asked Mrs. Beeton when Alf returned.

' I don't know. I think it was a circular or a tract about not whistlin' at everything when you're young.'

' I must have stepped on something when I was alive and walking about, and it has bounced up and hit me. God help it, whatever it is——unless it was all a joke. But I don't know any one who'd take the trouble to play a joke on me.

. . . Love and loyalty for nothing. It sounds tempting enough. I wonder whether I have lost anything really?'

Dick considered for a long time, but could not remember when or how he had put himself in the way of winning these trifles at a woman's hands.

Still, the letter as touching on matters that he preferred not to think about stung him into a fit of frenzy that lasted for a day and night. When his heart was so full of despair that it would hold no more, body and soul together seemed to be dropping without check through the darkness. Then came fear of darkness and desperate attempts to reach the light again. But there was no light to be reached. When that agony had left him sweating and breathless, the downward flight would recommence till the gathering torture of it spurred him into another fight as hopeless as the first. Followed some few minutes of sleep in which he dreamed that he saw. Then the procession of events would repeat itself till he was utterly worn out, and the brain took up its everlasting consideration of Maisie and might-have-beens.

At the end of everything Mr. Beeton came to his room and volunteered to take him out. 'Not marketing this time, but we'll go into the Parks if you like.'

'Be damned if I do,' quoth Dick. 'Keep to the streets and walk up and down. I like to hear the people round me.'

This was not altogether true. The blind in the first stages of their infirmity dislike those who

can move with a free stride and unlifted arms—
but Dick had no earthly desire to go to the
Parks. Once and only once since Maisie had
shut the door he had gone there under Alf's
charge. Alf forgot him and fished for minnows
in the Serpentine with some companions. After
half an hour's waiting Dick, almost weeping with
rage and wrath, caught a passer-by who introduced
him to a friendly policeman, who led him to a
four-wheeler opposite the Albert Hall. He never
told Mr. Beeton of Alf's forgetfulness, but . . .
this was not the manner in which he was used to
walk the Parks aforetime.

'What streets would you like to walk down,
then?' said Mr. Beeton sympathetically. His
own ideas of a riotous holiday meant picnicking
on the grass of the Green Park with his family,
and half-a-dozen paper bags full of food.

'Keep to the river,' said Dick, and they kept
to the river, and the rush of it was in his ears till
they came to Blackfriars Bridge and struck thence
on to the Waterloo Road, Mr. Beeton explaining
the beauties of the scenery as he went on.

'And walking on the other side of the pavement,' said he, 'unless I'm much mistaken, is the
young woman that used to come to your rooms
to be drawed. I never forgets a face and I never
remembers a name, except paying tenants, o'
course!'

'Stop her,' said Dick. 'It's Bessie Broke.
Tell her I'd like to speak to her again. Quick,
man!'

Mr. Beeton crossed the road under the noses

of the omnibuses and arrested Bessie then on her way northward. She recognised him as the man in authority who used to glare at her when she passed up Dick's staircase, and her first impulse was to run.

'Wasn't you Mr. Heldar's model?' said Mr. Beeton, planting himself in front of her. 'You was. He's on the other side of the road and he'd like to see you.'

'Why?' said Bessie faintly. She remembered —indeed had never for long forgotten—an affair connected with a newly-finished picture.

'Because he has asked me to do so, and because he's most particular blind.'

'Drunk?'

'No. 'Orspital blind. He can't see. That's him over there.'

Dick was leaning against the parapet of the bridge as Mr. Beeton pointed him out—a stub-bearded bowed creature wearing a dirty magenta-coloured neckcloth outside an unbrushed coat. There was nothing to fear from such an one. Even if he chased her, Bessie thought, he could not follow far. She crossed over and Dick's face lighted up. It was long since a woman of any kind had taken the trouble to speak to him.

'I hope you're well, Mr. Heldar,' said Bessie, a little puzzled. Mr. Beeton stood by with the air of an ambassador and breathed responsibly.

'I'm very well indeed, and, by Jove! I'm glad to see—hear you, I mean, Bess. You never thought it worth while to turn up and see us again after you got your money. I don't know why you should. Are you going anywhere in particular just now?'

'I was going for a walk,' said Bessie.

'Not the old business?' Dick spoke under his breath.

'Lor', no! I've paid my premium'—Bessie was very proud of that word—'for a barmaid, sleeping in, and I'm at the bar now quite respectable. Indeed I am.'

Mr. Beeton had no special reason to believe in the loftiness of human nature. Therefore he dissolved himself like a mist and returned to his gas-plugs without a word of apology. Bessie watched the flight with a certain uneasiness; but so long as Dick appeared to be ignorant of the harm that had been done to him. . . .

'It's hard work pulling the beer-handles,' she went on, 'and they've got one of them penny-in-the-slot cash-machines, so if you get wrong by a penny at the end of the day—but then I don't believe the machinery is right. Do you?'

'I've only seen it work. Mr. Beeton?'

'He's gone.'

'I'm afraid I must ask you to help me home, then. I'll make it worth your while. You see?' The sightless eyes turned towards her and Bessie saw.

'It isn't taking you out of your way?' he said hesitatingly. 'I can ask a policeman if it is.'

'Not at all. I come on at seven and I'm off at four. That's easy hours.'

'Good God!—but I'm on all the time. I wish I had some work to do too. Let's go home, Bess.'

He turned and cannoned into a man on the
sidewalk, recoiling with an oath. Bessie took his
arm and said nothing—as she had said nothing
when he had ordered her to turn her face a little
more to the light. They walked for some time in
silence, the girl steering him deftly through the
crowd.

'And where's—where's Mr. Torpenhow?'
she inquired at last.

'He has gone away to the desert.'

'Where's that?'

Dick pointed to the right. 'East—out of the
mouth of the river,' said he. 'Then west, then
south, and then east again, all along the underside
of Europe. Then south again, God knows how
far.' The explanation did not enlighten Bessie in
the least, but she held her tongue and looked to
Dick's path till they came to the chambers.

'We'll have tea and muffins,' he said joyously.
'I can't tell you, Bessie, how glad I am to find
you again. What made you go away so suddenly?'

'I didn't think you'd want me any more,' she
said, emboldened by his ignorance.

'I didn't as a matter of fact—but afterwards—
At any rate I'm glad you've come. You know
the stairs.'

So Bessie led him home to his own place—
there was no one to hinder—and shut the door of
the studio.

'What a mess!' was her first word. 'All
these things haven't been looked after for months
and months.'

'No, only weeks, Bess. You can't expect them to care.'

'I don't know what you expect them to do. They ought to know what you've paid them for. The dust's just awful. It's all over the easel.'

'I don't use it much now.'

'All over the pictures and the floor, and all over your coat. I'd like to speak to them housemaids.'

'Ring for tea, then.' Dick felt his way to the one chair he used by custom.

Bessie saw the action and, as far as in her lay, was touched. But there remained always a keen sense of new-found superiority, and it was in her voice when she spoke.

'How long have you been like this?' she said wrathfully, as though the blindness were some fault of the housemaids.

'How?'

'As you are.'

'The day after you went away with the cheque, almost as soon as my picture was finished; I hardly saw her alive.'

'Then they've been cheating you ever since; that's all. I know their nice little ways.'

A woman may love one man and despise another, but on general feminine principles she will do her best to save the man she despises from being defrauded. Her loved one can look to himself, but the other man, being obviously an idiot, needs protection.

'I don't think Mr. Beeton cheats much,' said Dick. Bessie was flouncing up and down the

room, and he was conscious of a keen sense of
enjoyment as he heard the swish of her skirts and
the light step between.

'Tea *and* muffins,' she said shortly, when the
ring at the bell was answered ; 'two teaspoonfuls
and one over for the pot. I don't want the old
teapot that was here when I used to come. It
don't draw. Get another.'

The housemaid went away scandalised, and
Dick chuckled. Then he began to cough as
Bessie banged up and down the studio disturbing
the dust.

'What are you trying to do?'

'Put things straight. This is like unfurnished
lodgings. How could you let it go so?'

'How could I help it? Dust away.'

She dusted furiously, and in the midst of all
the pother entered Mrs. Beeton. Her husband
on his return had explained the situation, winding
up with the peculiarly felicitous proverb, 'Do
unto others as you would be done by.' She had
ascended to put into her place the person who
demanded muffins and an uncracked teapot as
though she had a right to both.

'Muffins ready yet?' said Bess, still dusting.
She was no longer a drab of the streets, but a
young lady who, thanks to Dick's cheque, had
paid her premium and was entitled to pull beer-
handles with the best. Being neatly dressed in
black she did not hesitate to face Mrs. Beeton,
and there passed between the two women certain
regards that Dick would have appreciated. The
situation adjusted itself by eye. Bessie had won,

and Mrs. Beeton returned to cook muffins and make scathing remarks about models, hussies, trollops, and the like, to her husband.

'There's nothing to be got of interfering with him, Liza,' he said. 'Alf, you go along into the street to play. When he isn't crossed he's as kindly as kind, but when he's crossed he's the devil and all. We took too many little things out of his rooms since he was blind to be that particular about what he does. They ain't no objects to a blind man, of course, but if it was to come into court we'd get the sack. Yes, I did introduce him to that girl because I'm a feelin' man myself.'

'Much too feelin'!' Mrs. Beeton slapped the muffins into the dish, and thought of comely housemaids long since dismissed on suspicion.

'I ain't ashamed of it, and it isn't for us to judge him hard so long as he pays quiet and regular as he do. I know how to manage young gentlemen; you know how to cook for them; and what I says is, let each stick to his own business and then there won't be any trouble. Take them muffins, Liza, and be sure you have no words with that young woman. His lot is cruel hard, and if he's crossed he do swear worse than any one I've ever served.'

'That's a little better,' said Bessie, sitting down to the tea. 'You needn't wait, thank you, Mrs. Beeton.'

'I had no intention of doing such, I do assure you.'

Bessie made no answer whatever. This, she

knew, was the way in which real ladies routed
their foes, and when one is a barmaid at a first-
class public-house one may become a real lady at
ten minutes' notice.

Her eyes fell on Dick opposite her and she
was both shocked and displeased. There were
droppings of food all down the front of his coat;
the mouth, under the ragged ill-grown beard,
drooped sullenly; the forehead was lined and
contracted; and on the lean temples the hair was
a dusty, indeterminate colour that might or might
not have been called grey. The utter misery and
self-abandonment of the man appealed to her, and
at the bottom of her heart lay the wicked feeling
that he was humbled and brought low who had
once humbled her.

' Oh ! it *is* good to hear you moving about,' said
Dick, rubbing his hands. ' Tell us all about your
bar successes, Bessie, and the way you live now.'

' Never mind that. I'm quite respectable, as
you'd see by looking at me. *You* don't seem to
live too well. What made you go blind that
sudden? Why isn't there any one to look after
you?'

Dick was too thankful for the sound of her
voice to resent the tone of it.

' I was cut across the head a long time ago,
and that ruined my eyes. I don't suppose anybody thinks it worth while to look after me any
more. Why should they ?—and Mr. Beeton
really does everything I want.'

' Didn't you know any gentlemen and ladies,
then, while you was—well?'

' A few, but I don't care to have them looking at me.'

' I suppose that's why you've growed a beard. Take it off, it don't become you.'

' Good gracious, child, do you imagine that I think of what becomes me these days?'

' You ought. Get that taken off before I come here again. I suppose I can come, can't I?'

' I'd be only too grateful if you did. I don't think I treated you very well in the old days. I used to make you angry.'

' Very angry, you did.'

' I'm sorry for it, then. Come and see me when you can and as often as you can. God knows, there isn't a soul in the world to take that trouble except you and Mr. Beeton.'

' A lot of trouble *he*'s taking and *she* too.' This with a toss of the head. ' They've let you do anyhow, and they haven't done anything for you. I've only to look to see that much. I'll come, and I'll be glad to come, but you must go and be shaved, and you must get some other clothes—those ones aren't fit to be seen.'

' I have heaps somewhere,' he said helplessly.

' I know you have. Tell Mr. Beeton to give you a new suit and I'll brush it and keep it clean. You may be as blind as a barn-door, Mr. Heldar, but it doesn't excuse you looking like a sweep.'

' Do I look like a sweep then?'

' Oh, I'm sorry for you. I'm that sorry for you!' she cried impulsively, and took Dick's hands. Mechanically, he lowered his head as if to kiss—she was the only woman who had taken pity on him, and he was not too proud for a little pity now. She stood up to go.

'Nothing o' that kind till you look more like a gentleman. It's quite easy when you get shaved, and some clothes.'

He could hear her drawing on her gloves and rose to say good-bye. She passed behind him, kissed him audaciously on the back of the neck, and ran away as swiftly as on the day when she had destroyed the Melancolia.

'To think of me kissing Mr. Heldar,' she said to herself, 'after all he's done to me and all! Well, I'm sorry for him, and if he was shaved he wouldn't be so bad to look at, but . . . Oh, them Beetons, how shameful they've treated him! I know Beeton's wearing his shirt on his back to-day just as well as if I'd aired it. To-morrow, I'll see . . . I wonder if he has much of his own. It might be worth more than the bar—I wouldn't have to do any work—and just as respectable if no one knew.'

Dick was not grateful to Bessie for her parting gift. He was acutely conscious of it in the nape of his neck throughout the night, but it seemed, among very many other things, to enforce the wisdom of getting shaved. He was shaved accordingly in the morning, and felt the better for it. A fresh suit of clothes, white linen, and the knowledge that some one in the world said that she took an interest in his personal appearance, made him carry himself almost upright; for the brain was relieved for a while from thinking of Maisie, who, under other circumstances, might have given that kiss and a million others.

'Let us consider,' said he after lunch. 'The girl can't care, and it's a toss-up whether she comes again or not, but if money can buy her to look after me she shall be bought. Nobody else in the world would take the trouble, and I can make it worth her while. She's a child of the gutter holding brevet rank as a barmaid; so she shall have everything she wants if she'll only come and talk and look after me.' He rubbed his newly-shorn chin and began to perplex himself with the thought of her not coming. 'I suppose I did look rather a sweep,' he went on. 'I had no reason to look otherwise. I knew things dropped on my clothes, but it didn't matter. It would be cruel if she didn't come. She must. Maisie came once, and that was enough for her. She was quite right. She had something to work for. This creature has only beer-handles to pull, unless she has deluded some young man into keeping company with her. Fancy being cheated for the sake of a counter-jumper! We're falling pretty low.'

Something cried aloud within him: This will hurt more than anything that has gone before. It will recall and remind and suggest and tantalise, and in the end drive you mad.

'I know it, I know it!' Dick cried, clenching his hands despairingly; 'but, good heavens, is a poor blind beggar never to get anything out of his life except three meals a day and a greasy waistcoat? I wish she'd come.'

Early in the afternoon time she came, because there was no young man in her life just then, and she thought of material advantages which would allow her to be idle for the rest of her days.

'I shouldn't have known you,' she said approvingly. 'You look as you used to look—a gentleman that was proud of himself.'

'Don't you think I deserve another kiss then?' said Dick, flushing a little.

'Maybe—but you won't get it yet. Sit down and let's see what I can do for you. I'm certain sure Mr. Beeton cheats you, now that you can't go through the housekeeping books every month. Isn't that true?'

'You'd better come and housekeep for me, then, Bessie.'

'Couldn't do it in these chambers—you know that as well as I do.'

'I know, but we might go somewhere else, if you thought it worth your while.'

'I'd try to look after you, anyhow; but I shouldn't care to have to work for both of us.' This was tentative.

Dick laughed.

'Do you remember where I used to keep my bank-book?' said he. 'Torp took it to be balanced just before he went away. Look and see.'

'It was generally under the tobacco-jar. Ah!'

'Well?'

'Oh! Four thousand two hundred and ten pounds nine shillings and a penny! Oh my!'

'You can have the penny. That's not bad for

one year's work. Is that and a hundred and twenty pounds a year good enough?'

The idleness and the pretty clothes were almost within her reach now, but she must, by being housewifely, show that she deserved them.

'Yes; but you'd have to move, and if we took an inventory, I think we'd find that Mr. Beeton has been prigging little things out of the rooms here and there. They don't look as full as they used.'

'Never mind, we'll let him have them. The only thing I'm particularly anxious to take away is that picture I used you for—when you used to swear at me. We'll pull out of this place, Bess, and get away as far as ever we can.'

'Oh yes,' she said uneasily.

'I don't know where I can go to get away from myself, but I'll try, and you shall have all the pretty frocks that you care for. You'll like that. Give me that kiss now, Bess. Ye gods! it's good to put one's arm round a woman's waist again.'

Then came the fulfilment of the prophecy within the brain. If his arm were thus round Maisie's waist and a kiss had just been given and taken between them,—why, then. . . . He pressed the girl more closely to himself because the pain whipped him. She was wondering how to explain a little accident to the Melancolia. At any rate, if this man really desired the solace of her company—and certainly he would relapse into his original slough if she withdrew it—he would not be more than just a little vexed. It would be delightful at least to see what would happen, and by her teachings it was good for a man to stand in a certain awe of his companion.

She laughed nervously, and slipped out of his reach.

'I shouldn't worrit about that picture if I was you,' she began, in the hope of turning his attention.

'It's at the back of all my canvases somewhere. Find it, Bess; you know it as well as I do.'

'I know—but——'

'But what? You've wit enough to manage the sale of it to a dealer. Women haggle much better than men. It might be a matter of eight or nine hundred pounds to—to us. I simply didn't like to think about it for a long time. It was mixed up with my life so.—But we'll cover up our tracks and get rid of everything, eh? Make a fresh start from the beginning, Bess.'

Then she began to repent very much indeed, because she knew the value of money. Still, it was probable that the blind man was overestimating the value of his work. Gentlemen, she knew, were absurdly particular about their things. She giggled as a nervous housemaid giggles when she tries to explain the breakage of a pipe.

'I'm very sorry, but you remember I was—I was angry with you before Mr. Torpenhow went away?'

'You were very angry, child; and on my word I think you had some right to be.'

'Then I—but aren't you sure Mr. Torpenhow didn't tell you?'

'Tell me what? Good gracious, what are you

making such a fuss about when you might just as well be giving me another kiss?'

He was beginning to learn, not for the first time in his experience, that kissing is a cumulative poison. The more you get of it, the more you want. Bessie gave the kiss promptly, whispering, as she did so, 'I was that angry I rubbed out that picture with the turpentine. You aren't angry, are you?'

'What? Say that again.' The man's hand had closed on her wrist.

'I rubbed it out with turps and the knife,' faltered Bessie. 'I thought you'd only have to do it over again. You did do it over again, didn't you? Oh, let go of my wrist; you're hurting me.'

'Isn't there anything left of the thing?'

'N'nothing that looks like anything. I'm sorry—I didn't know you'd take on about it; I only meant to do it in fun. You aren't going to hit me?'

'Hit you! No! Let's think.'

He did not relax his hold upon her wrist but stood staring toward the carpet. Then he shook his head as a young steer shakes it when the lash of the stock-whip across his nose warns him back to the path to the shambles that he would escape. For weeks he had forced himself not to think of the Melancolia, because she was a part of his dead life. With Bessie's return and certain new prospects that had developed themselves the Melancolia—lovelier in his imagination than she had ever been on canvas—reappeared. By her aid he might have procured more money wherewith to amuse Bess and to forget Maisie, as well as another taste of an almost forgotten success. Now, thanks to a vicious little wench's folly, there was nothing to look for—not even the hope that he might some day take an abiding interest in the wench. Worst of all, he had been made to appear ridiculous in Maisie's eyes. A woman will forgive the man who has ruined her life's work so long as he gives her love: a man may forgive those who ruin the love of his life, but he will never forgive the destruction of his work.

'Tck—tck—tck,' said Dick between his teeth, and then laughed softly. 'It's an omen, Bessie, and—a good many things considered, it serves me right for doing what I have done. By Jove! that accounts for Maisie's running away. She must have thought me perfectly mad—small blame to her! The whole picture ruined, isn't it so? What made you do it?'

'Because I was that angry. I'm not angry now—I'm awful sorry.'

'I wonder.—It doesn't matter, anyhow. I'm to blame for making the mistake.'

'What mistake?'

'Something you wouldn't understand, dear. Great heavens! to think that a little piece of dirt like you could throw me out of my stride!' Dick was talking to himself as Bessie tried to shake off his grip on her wrist.

'I ain't a piece of dirt, and you shouldn't call me so! I did it 'cause I hated you, and I'm only sorry now 'cause you're—'cause you're——'

'Exactly—because I'm blind. There's nothing like tact in little things.'

Bessie began to sob. She did not like being shackled against her will; she was afraid of the blind face and the look upon it, and was sorry too that her great revenge had only made Dick laugh.

'Don't cry,' he said, and took her into his arms. 'You only did what you thought right.'

'I—I ain't a little piece of dirt, and if you say that I'll never come to you again.'

'You don't know what you've done to me. I'm not angry—indeed, I am not. Be quiet for a minute.'

Bessie remained in his arms shrinking. Dick's first thought was connected with Maisie, and it hurt him as white-hot iron hurts an open sore.

Not for nothing is a man permitted to ally himself to the wrong woman. The first pang—the first sense of things lost is but the prelude to the play, for the very just Providence who delights in causing pain has decreed that the agony shall return, and that in the midst of keenest pleasure. They know this pain equally who have forsaken or been forsaken by the love of their life, and in their new wives' arms are compelled to realise it. It is better to remain alone and suffer only the misery of being alone, so long as it is possible to find distraction in daily work. When that resource goes the man is to be pitied and left alone.

These things and some others Dick considered while he was holding Bessie to his heart.

'Though you mayn't know it,' he said, raising his head, 'the Lord is a just and a terrible God,

Bess; with a very strong sense of humour. It serves me right—how it serves me right! Torp could understand it if he were here; he must have suffered something at your hands, child, but only for a minute or so. I saved him. Set that to my credit, some one.'

'Let me go,' said Bess, her face darkening. 'Let me go.'

'All in good time. Did you ever attend Sunday school?'

'Never. Let me go, I tell you; you're making fun of me.'

'Indeed, I'm not. I'm making fun of myself. . . . Thus. "He saved others, himself he cannot save." It isn't exactly a Board-School text.' He released her wrist, but since he was between her and the door she could not escape. 'What an enormous amount of mischief one little woman can do!'

'I'm sorry; I'm awfully sorry about the picture.'

'I'm not. I'm grateful to you for spoiling it. . . . What were we talking about before you mentioned the thing?'

'About getting away—and money. Me and you going away.'

'Of course. We will get away—that is to say, I will.'

'And me?'

'You shall have fifty whole pounds for spoiling a picture.'

'Then you won't——?'

'I'm afraid not, dear. Think of fifty pounds for pretty things all to yourself.'

'You said you couldn't do anything without me.'

'That was true a little while ago. I'm better now, thank you. Get me my hat.'

'S'pose I don't?'

'Beeton will, and you'll lose fifty pounds. That's all. Get it.'

Bessie cursed under her breath. She had pitied the man sincerely, had kissed him with almost equal sincerity, for he was not unhandsome. It pleased her to be in a way and for a time his protector, and above all there were four thousand pounds to be handled by some one. Now through a slip of the tongue and a little feminine desire to give a little, not too much, pain she had lost the money, the blessed idleness and the pretty things, the companionship, and the chance of looking outwardly as respectable as a real lady.

'Now fill me a pipe. Tobacco doesn't taste, but it doesn't matter, and I'll think things out. What's the day of the week, Bess?'

'Tuesday.'

'Then Thursday's mail-day. What a fool— what a blind fool I have been! Twenty-two pounds covers my passage home again. Allow ten for additional expenses. We must put up at Madame Binat's for old sake's sake. Thirty-two pounds altogether. Add a hundred for the cost of the last trip—Gad, won't Torp stare to see me!—a hundred and thirty-two leaves seventy-eight for *baksheesh*—I shall need it—and to play with. What are you crying for, Bess? It wasn't your fault, child; it was mine altogether. Oh, you funny little opossum, mop your eyes and take me out! I want the pass-book and the cheque-book. Stop a minute. Four thousand pounds at four per cent — that's safe interest — means a hundred and sixty pounds a year; one hundred and twenty pounds a year — also safe — is two eighty, and two hundred and eighty pounds added to three hundred a year means gilded luxury for a single woman. Bess, we'll go to the bank.'

Richer by two hundred and ten pounds stored in his money-belt, Dick caused Bessie, now thoroughly bewildered, to hurry from the bank to the P. & O. offices, where he explained things tersely.

' Port Said, single first; cabin as close to the baggage-hatch as possible. What ship's going? '

' The *Colgong*,' said the clerk.

' She's a wet little hooker. Is it Tilbury and a tender, or Gallions and the docks? '

' Gallions. Twelve-forty, Thursday.'

' Thanks. Change, please. I can't see very well—will you count it into my hand? '

' If they all took their passages like that instead of talking about their trunks, life would be worth something,' said the clerk to his neighbour, who was trying to explain to a harassed mother of many that condensed milk is just as good for babes at sea as daily dairy. Being nineteen and unmarried, he spoke with conviction.

' We are now,' quoth Dick, as they returned to the studio, patting the place where his money-

belt covered ticket and money, ' beyond the reach
of man, or devil, or woman—which is much more
important. I've three little affairs to carry through
before Thursday, but I needn't ask you to help,
Bess. Come here on Thursday morning at nine.
We'll breakfast, and you shall take me down to
Gallions Station.'

' What are you going to do? '

' Going away, of course. What should I stay
for? '

' But you can't look after yourself! '

' I can do anything. I didn't realise it before,
but I can. I've done a great deal already. Resolu-
tion shall be treated to one kiss if Bessie doesn't
object.' Strangely enough, Bessie objected and
Dick laughed. ' I suppose you're right. Well,
come at nine the day after to-morrow and you'll
get your money.'

' Shall I sure? '

' I don't bilk, and you won't know whether I
do or not unless you come. Oh, but it's long and
long to wait! Good-bye, Bessie,—send Beeton
here as you go out.'

The housekeeper came.

' What are all the fittings of my rooms worth? '
said Dick imperiously.

' 'Tisn't for me to say, sir. Some things is very
pretty and some is wore out dreadful.'

' I'm insured for two hundred and seventy.'

' Insurance policies is no criterion, though I
don't say——'

' Oh, damn your longwindedness! You've
made your pickings out of me and the other

tenants. Why, you talked of retiring and buying a public-house the other day. Give a straight answer to a straight question.'

' Fifty,' said Mr. Beeton, without a moment's hesitation.

' Double it ; or I'll break up half my sticks and burn the rest.'

He felt his way to a bookstand that supported a pile of sketch-books, and wrenched out one of the mahogany pillars.

' That's sinful, sir,' said the housekeeper, alarmed.

' It's my own. One hundred or——'

' One hundred it is. It'll cost me three and six to get that there pilaster mended.'

' I thought so. What an out-and-out swindler you must have been to spring that price at once ! '

' I hope I've done nothing to dissatisfy any of the tenants, least of all you, sir.'

' Never mind that. Get me the money to-morrow, and see that all my clothes are packed in the little brown bullock-trunk. I'm going.'

' But the quarter's notice? '

' I'll pay forfeit. Look after the packing and leave me alone.'

Mr. Beeton discussed this new departure with his wife, who decided that Bessie was at the bottom of it all. Her husband took a more charitable view.

' It's very sudden—but then he was always sudden in his ways. Listen to him now ! '

There was a sound of chanting from Dick's room.

We'll never come back any more, boys,
We'll never come back no more;
We'll go to the deuce on any excuse,
And never come back no more!

Oh, say we're afloat or ashore, boys,
Oh, say we're afloat or ashore;
But we'll never come back any more, boys,
We'll never come back no more!

' Mr. Beeton! Mr. Beeton! Where the
deuce is my pistol?'

' Quick, he's going to shoot himself—'avin'
gone mad!' said Mrs. Beeton.

Mr. Beeton addressed Dick soothingly, but it
was some time before the latter, threshing up and
down his bedroom, could realise the intention of
the promises to 'find everything to-morrow,
sir.'

' Oh, you copper-nosed old fool—you impotent
Academician!' he shouted at last. ' Do you
suppose I want to shoot myself? Take the pistol
in your silly shaking hand then. If *you* touch
it, it will go off, because it's loaded. It's among
my campaign-kit somewhere—in the parcel at
the bottom of the trunk.'

Long ago Dick had carefully possessed himself of a forty-pound-weight field-equipment constructed by the knowledge of his own experience.
It was this put-away treasure that he was trying
to find and rehandle. Mr. Beeton whipped the
revolver out of its place on the top of the package,
and Dick drove his hand among the khaki coat
and breeches, the blue cloth leg-bands, and the
heavy flannel shirts doubled over a pair of swan-

neck spurs. Under these and the water-bottle lay
a sketch-book and a pigskin case of stationery.

'These we don't want; you can have them,
Mr. Beeton. Everything else I'll keep. Pack
'em on the top right-hand side of my trunk.
When you've done that come into the studio with
your wife. I want you both. Wait a minute;
get me a pen and a sheet of notepaper.'

It is not an easy thing to write when you cannot
see, and Dick had particular reasons for wishing
that his work should be clear. So he began,
following his right hand with his left: ' " The
badness of this writing is because I am blind and
cannot see my pen." H'mph!—Even a lawyer
can't mistake that. It must be signed, I suppose,
but it needn't be witnessed. Now an inch lower—
why did I never learn to use a typewriter?—" This
is the last will and testament of me, Richard
Heldar. I am in sound bodily and mental health,
and there is no previous will to revoke."—That's
all right. Damn the pen! Whereabouts on the
paper was I?—" I leave everything that I possess
in the world, including four thousand pounds, and
two thousand seven hundred and twenty-eight
pounds held for me "—Oh, I can't get this
straight.' He tore off half the sheet and began
again with the caution about the handwriting.
Then: ' I leave all the money I possess in the
world to '—here followed Maisie's name, and the
names of the two banks that held his money.

' It mayn't be quite regular, but no one has a
shadow of a right to dispute it, and I've given
Maisie's address. Come in, Mr. Beeton. This

is my signature; you've seen it often enough to know it. I want you and your wife to witness it. Thanks. To-morrow you must take me to the landlord and I'll pay forfeit for leaving without notice, and I'll lodge this paper with him in case anything happens when I'm away. Now we're going to light up the studio stove. Stay with me, and give me my papers as I want 'em.'

No one knows until he has tried how fine a blaze a year's accumulation of bills, letters, and dockets can make. Dick stuffed into the stove every document in the studio—saving only three unopened letters: destroyed sketch-books, rough note-books, new and half-finished canvases alike.

'What a lot of rubbish a tenant gets about him if he stays long enough in one place, to be sure,' said Mr. Beeton at last.

'He does. Is there anything more left?' Dick felt round the walls.

'Not a thing, and the stove's nigh red-hot.'

'Excellent, and you've lost about a thousand pounds' worth of sketches. Ho! ho! Quite a thousand pounds' worth, if I can remember what I used to be.'

'Yes, sir,' politely. Mr. Beeton was quite sure that Dick had gone mad, otherwise he would have never parted with his excellent furniture for a song. The canvas things took up storage room and were much better out of the way.

There remained only to leave the little will in safe hands: that could not be accomplished till to-morrow. Dick groped about the floor picking up the last pieces of paper, assured himself again and again that there remained no written word or sign of his past life in drawer or desk, and sat down before the stove till the fire died out and the contracting iron cracked in the silence of the night.

CHAPTER XV

With a heart of furious fancies,
   Whereof I am commander;
With a burning spear and a horse of air
   To the wilderness I wander.
With a knight of ghosts and shadows
   I summoned am to tourney—
Ten leagues beyond the wide world's end,
   Methinks it is no journey.
Tom a' Bedlam's Song.

'Good-bye, Bess. I promised you fifty. Here's a hundred—all that I got for my furniture from Beeton. That will keep you in pretty frocks for some time. You've been a good little girl, all things considered, but you've given me and Torpenhow a fair amount of trouble.'

'Give Mr. Torpenhow my love if you see him, won't you?'

'Of course I will, dear. Now take me up the gang-plank and into the cabin. Once aboard the lugger and the maid is—and I am free, I mean.'

'Who'll look after you on the ship?'

'The head-steward, if there's any use in money. The doctor when we come to Port Said, if I know anything of P. & O. doctors. After that, the Lord will provide, as He used to do.'

Bess found Dick his cabin in the wild turmoil of a ship full of leavetakers and weeping relatives. Then he kissed her, and laid himself down in his bunk until the decks should be clear. He who had taken so long to move about his own darkened rooms well understood the geography of a ship, and the necessity of seeing to his own comforts was as wine to him. Before the screw began to thrash the ship along the Docks he had been introduced to the head-steward, had royally tipped him, secured a good place at table, opened out his baggage, and settled himself down with joy in the cabin. It was scarcely necessary to feel his way as he moved about, for he knew everything so well. Then God was very kind. A deep sleep of weariness came upon him just as he would have thought of Maisie, and he slept till the steamer had cleared the mouth of the Thames and was lifting to the pulse of the Channel.

The rattle of the engines, the reek of oil and paint, and a very familiar sound in the next cabin roused him to his new inheritance.

' Oh, it's good to be alive again ! ' He yawned, stretched himself vigorously, and went on deck to be told that they were almost abreast of the lights of Brighton. This is no more open water than Trafalgar Square is a common ; the free levels begin at Ushant ; but none the less Dick could feel the healing of the sea at work upon him already. A boisterous little cross-swell swung the steamer disrespectfully by the nose ; and one wave breaking far aft spattered the quarterdeck and the pile of new deck-chairs. He heard the foam fall with the clash of broken glass, was stung in the face by a cupful, and sniffing luxuriously, felt his way to the smoking-room by the wheel. There a strong breeze found him, blew his cap off and left him bareheaded in the doorway, and the smoking-room steward, understanding that he was a voyager of experience, said that the weather would be stiff in the chops of the Channel and more than half a gale in the Bay. These things fell as they were foretold, and Dick enjoyed himself to the utmost. It is allowable and even necessary at sea to lay firm hold upon tables, stanchions, and ropes in moving from place to place. On land the man who feels with his hands is patently blind. At sea even a blind man who is not sea-sick can jest with the doctor over the weakness of his fellows. Dick told the doctor many tales—and these are coin of more value than silver if properly handled—, smoked with him till unholy hours of the night, and so won his shortlived regard that he promised Dick a few hours of his time when they came to Port Said.

And the sea roared or was still as the winds blew, and the engines sang their song day and night, and the sun grew stronger day by day, and Tom the Lascar barber shaved Dick of a morning under the opened hatch-grating where the cool winds blew, and the awnings were spread and the passengers made merry, and at last they came to Port Said.

'Take me,' said Dick to the doctor, ' to Madame Binat's—if you know where that is.'

'Whew!' said the doctor, 'I do. There's not much to choose between 'em; but I suppose you're aware that that's one of the worst houses in the place. They'll rob you to begin with, and knife you later.'

'Not they. Take me there, and I can look after myself.'

So he was brought to Madame Binat's and filled his nostrils with the well-remembered smell of the East, that runs without a change from the Canal head to Hong-Kong, and his mouth with the villainous Lingua Franca of the Levant. The heat smote him between the shoulder-blades with the buffet of an old friend, his feet slipped on the sand, and his coat-sleeve was warm as new-baked bread when he lifted it to his nose.

Madame Binat smiled with the smile that knows no astonishment when Dick entered the drinking-shop which was one source of her gains. But for a little accident of complete darkness he could hardly realise that he had ever quitted the old life that hummed in his ears. Somebody opened a bottle of peculiarly strong Schiedam. The smell reminded Dick of Monsieur Binat, who, by the way, had spoken of Art and degradation. Binat was dead. Madame said as much when the doctor departed, scandalised, so far as a ship's doctor can be, at the warmth of Dick's reception. Dick was delighted at it. 'They remember me here after a year. They have forgotten me across the water by this time. Madame, I want a long talk with you when you're at liberty. It is good to be back again.'

In the evening she set an iron-topped café-table out on the sands, and Dick and she sat by it, while the house behind them filled with riot, merriment, oaths, and threats. The stars came out and the lights of the shipping in the harbour twinkled by the head of the Canal.

' Yes. The war is good for trade, my friend ; but what dost thou do here? We have not forgotten thee.'

' I was over there in England and I went blind.'

' But there was the glory first. We heard of it here, even here—I and Binat; and thou hast used the head of Yellow 'Tina—she is still alive— so often and so well that 'Tina laughed when the papers arrived by the mail-boats. It was always something that we here could recognise in the paintings. And then there was always the glory and the money for thee.'

' I am not poor—I shall pay you well.'

' Not to me. Thou hast paid for everything.' Under her breath, ' Mon Dieu, to be blind and so young ! What horror ! '

Dick could not see her face with the pity on it, or his own with the discoloured hair at the temples. He did not feel the need of pity ; he was too anxious to get to the Front once more, and explained his desire.

' And where? The Canal is full of the English ships. Sometimes they fire as they used to do when the war was here—ten years ago. Beyond Cairo there is fighting, but how canst thou go there without a correspondent's passport? And in the desert there is always fighting, but that is impossible also,' said she.

'I must go to Suakin.' He knew, thanks to Alf's readings, that Torpenhow was at work with the column that was protecting the construction of the Suakin-Berber line. P. & O. steamers do not touch at that port, and, besides, Madame Binat knew everybody whose help or advice was worth anything. They were not respectable folk, but they could cause things to be accomplished, which is much more important when there is work toward.

'But at Suakin they are always fighting. That desert breeds men always—and always more men. And they are so bold! Why to Suakin?'

'My friend is there.'

'Thy friend! Chtt! Thy friend is death, then.'

Madame Binat dropped a fat arm on the table-top, filled Dick's glass anew, and looked at him closely under the stars. There was no need that he should bow his head in assent and say:

'No. He is a man, but—if it should arrive . . . blamest thou?'

'I blame?' she laughed shrilly. 'Who am I that I should blame any one—except those who try to cheat me over their *consommations*. But it is very terrible.'

'I must go to Suakin. Think for me. A great deal has changed within the year, and the men I knew are not here. The Egyptian Light-house steamer goes down the Canal to Suakin— and the post-boats—But even then——'

'Do not think any longer. *I* know, and it is for me to think. Thou shalt go—thou shalt go and see thy friend. Be wise. Sit here until the house is a little quiet—I must attend to my guests—and afterwards go to bed. Thou shalt go, in truth, thou shalt go.'

'To-morrow?'

'As soon as may be.' She was talking as though he were a child.

He sat at the table listening to the voices in the harbour and the streets, and wondering how soon the end would come, till Madame Binat carried him off to bed and ordered him to sleep. The house shouted and sang and danced and revelled, Madame Binat moving through it with one eye on the liquor payments and the girls and the other on Dick's interests. To this latter end she smiled upon scowling and furtive Turkish officers of Fellaheen regiments, was gracious to Cypriote commissariat underlings, and more than kind to camel-agents of no nationality whatever.

In the early morning, being then appropriately dressed in a flaming red silk ball-dress, with a front of tarnished gold embroidery and a necklace of plate-glass diamonds, she made chocolate and carried it in to Dick.

'It is only I, and I am of discreet age, eh? Drink and eat the roll too. Thus in France mothers bring their sons, when those behave wisely, the morning chocolate.' She sat down on the side of the bed whispering:

'It is all arranged. Thou wilt go by the Light-house boat. That is a bribe of ten pounds

English. The captain is never paid by the Government. The boat comes to Suakin in four days. There will go with thee George, a Greek muleteer. Another bribe of ten pounds. I will pay. They must not know of thy money. George will go with thee as far as he goes with his mules. Then he comes back to me, for his well-beloved is here, and if I do not receive a telegram from Suakin saying that thou art well, the girl answers for George.'

' Thank you.' He felt out sleepily for the cup. ' You are much too kind, Madame.'

' If there were anything that I might do I would say, stay here and be wise; but I do not think that would be best for thee.' She looked at her liquor-stained dress with a sad smile. ' Nay, thou shalt go, in truth, thou shalt go. It is best so. My boy, it is best so.'

She stooped and kissed Dick between the eyes. ' That is for good-morning,' she said, going away. ' When thou art dressed we will speak to George and make everything ready. But first we must open the little trunk. Give me the keys.'

' The amount of kissing lately has been simply scandalous. I shall expect Torp to kiss me next. He is more likely to swear at me for getting in his way, though. Well, it won't last long—Ohé, Madame, help me to my toilette of the guillotine ! There will be no chance of dressing properly out yonder.'

He was rummaging among his new campaign-kit, and rowelling his hands with the spurs. There are two ways of wearing well-oiled ankle-jacks, spotless blue leg-bands, khaki coat and breeches, and a perfectly pipeclayed helmet. The right way is the way of the untired man, master of himself, setting out upon an expedition, well pleased.

'Everything must be very correct,' Dick explained. 'It will become dirty afterwards, but now it is good to feel well dressed. Is everything as it should be?'

He patted the revolver neatly hidden under the fullness of the blouse on the right hip and fingered his collar.

'I can do no more,' Madame said, between laughing and crying. 'Look at thyself—but I forgot.'

'I am very content.' He stroked the creaseless spirals of his leggings. 'Now let us go and see the captain and George and the Lighthouse boat. Be quick, Madame.'

'But thou canst not be seen by the harbour walking with *me* in the daylight. Figure to yourself if some English ladies——'

'There are no English ladies; and if there are, I have forgotten them. Take me there.'

In spite of his burning impatience it was nearly evening ere the Lighthouse boat began to move. Madame had said a great deal both to George and the Captain touching the arrangements that were to be made for Dick's benefit. Very few men who had the honour of her acquaintance cared to disregard Madame's advice. That sort of contempt might end in being knifed by a stranger in a gambling-hell upon surprisingly short provocation.

For six days—two of them were wasted in the

crowded Canal—the little steamer worked her way to Suakin, where she was to pick up the superintendent of Lighthouses; and Dick made it his business to propitiate George, who was distracted with fears for the safety of his light-of-love and half inclined to make Dick responsible for his own discomfort. When they arrived George took him under his wing, and together they entered the red-hot seaport, encumbered with the material and wastage of the Suakin-Berber line, from locomotives in disconsolate fragments to mounds of chairs and pot-sleepers.

'If you keep with me,' said George, 'nobody will ask for passports or what you do. They are all very busy.'

'Yes; but I should like to hear some of the Englishmen talk. They might remember me. I was known here a long time ago—when I was some one indeed.'

'A long time ago is a very long time ago here. The graveyards are full. Now listen. This new railway runs out so far as Tanai-el-Hassan—that is seven miles. Then there is a camp. They say that beyond Tanai-el-Hassan the English troops go forward, and everything that they require will be brought to them by this line.'

'Ah! Base camp. I see. That's a better business than fighting Fuzzies in the open.'

'For this reason even the mules go up in the iron-train.'

'Iron what?'

'It is all covered with iron, because it is still being shot at.'

' An armoured train. Better and better! Go on, faithful George.'

' And I go up with my mules to-night. Only those who particularly require to go to the camp go out with the train. They begin to shoot not far from the city.'

' The dears—they always used to!' Dick snuffed the smell of parched dust, heated iron, and flaking paint with delight. Certainly the old life was welcoming him back most generously.

' When I have got my mules together I go up to-night, but you must first send a telegram to Port Said, declaring that I have done you no harm.'

' Madame has you well in hand. Would you stick a knife into me if you had the chance?'

' I have no chance,' said the Greek. ' *She* is there with that woman.'

' I see. It's a bad thing to be divided between love of woman and the chance of loot. I sympathise with you, George.'

They went to the telegraph-office unquestioned, for all the world was desperately busy and had scarcely time to turn its head, and Suakin was the last place under sky that would be chosen for holiday-ground. On their return the voice of an English subaltern asked Dick what he was doing. The blue goggles were over his eyes and he walked with his hand on George's elbow as he replied :—

' Egyptian Government—mules. My orders are to give them over to the A. C. G. at Tanai-el-Hassan. Any occasion to show my papers?'

' Oh, certainly not. I beg your pardon. I'd

no right to ask, but not seeing your face before I——'

' I go out in the train to-night, I suppose,' said Dick boldly. ' There will be no difficulty in loading up the mules, will there? '

' You can see the horse-platforms from here. You must have them loaded up early.' The young man went away wondering what sort of broken-down waif this might be who talked like a gentleman and consorted with Greek muleteers. Dick felt unhappy. To outface an English officer is no small thing, but the bluff loses relish when one plays it from the utter dark, and stumbles up and down rough ways, thinking and eternally thinking of what might have been if things had fallen out otherwise, and all had been as it was not.

George shared his meal with Dick and went off to the mule-lines. His charge sat alone in a shed with his face in his hands. Before his tight-shut eyes danced the face of Maisie, laughing, with parted lips. There was a great bustle and clamour about him. He grew afraid and almost called for George.

' I say, have you got your mules ready? ' It was the voice of the subaltern over his shoulder.

' My man's looking after them. The—the fact is I've a touch of ophthalmia and I can't see very well.'

' By Jove! that's bad. You ought to lie up in hospital for a while. I've had a turn of it myself. It's as bad as being blind.'

' So I find it. When does this armoured train go? '

' At six o'clock.   It takes an hour and a half
to cover the seven miles.'

' Are the Fuzzies on the rampage—eh? '

' About three nights a week.   Fact is I'm in
acting command of the night-train.   It generally
runs back empty to Tanai for the night.'

' Big camp at Tanai, I suppose? '

' Pretty big.   It has to feed our desert-column
somehow.'

' Is that far off? '

' Between thirty and forty miles—in an infernal
thirsty country.'

' Is the country quiet between Tanai and our
men? '

' More or less.   I shouldn't care to cross it
alone, or with a subaltern's command for the
matter of that, but the scouts get through in some
extraordinary fashion.'

' They always did.'

' Have you been here before, then? '

' I was through most of the trouble when it
first broke out.'

' In the Service and cashiered ' was the subaltern's first thought, so he refrained from putting
any questions.

' There's your man coming up with the mules.
It seems rather queer—— '

' That I should be mule-leading? ' said Dick.

' I didn't mean to say so, but it is.   Forgive me
—it's beastly impertinence, I know, but you speak
like a man who has been at a public school.
There's no mistaking the tone.'

' I am a public-school man.'

' I thought so. I say, I don't want to hurt your feelings, but you're a little down on your luck, aren't you? I saw you sitting with your head in your hands, and that's why I spoke.'

' Thanks. I am about as thoroughly and completely broke as a man need be.'

' Suppose—I mean, I'm a public-school man myself. Couldn't I perhaps—take it as a loan, y'know, and——'

' You're much too good, but on my honour I've as much money as I want. . . . I tell you what you could do for me, though, and put me under an everlasting obligation. Let me come into the bogie truck of the train. There is a foretruck, isn't there? '

' Yes. How d'you know? '

' I've been in an armoured train before. Only let me see—hear some of the fun, I mean, and I'll be grateful. I go at my own risk as a noncombatant.'

The young man thought for a minute. ' All right,' he said. ' We're supposed to be an empty train, and there's no one to blow me up at the other end.'

George and a horde of yelling amateur assistants had loaded up the mules, and the narrow-gauge armoured train, plated with three-eighths-inch boiler-plate till it looked like one long coffin, stood ready to start.

Two bogie trucks running before the locomotive were completely covered in with plating, except that the leading one was pierced in front for the nozzle of a machine-gun, and the second

at either side for lateral fire. The trucks together
made one long iron-vaulted chamber in which a
score of artillerymen were rioting.

'Whitechapel—last train! Ah, I see yer
kissin' in the first class there!' somebody shouted,
just as Dick was clambering into the forward
truck.

'Lordy! 'Ere's a real live passenger for the
Kew, Tanai, Acton, and Ealin' train. *Echo*, sir.
Speshul edition! *Star*, sir.'—'Shall I get you a
foot-warmer?' said another.

'Thanks. I'll pay my footing,' said Dick, and
relations of the most amicable were established
ere silence came with the arrival of the subaltern,
and the train jolted out over the rough track.

'This is an immense improvement on shooting
the unimpressionable Fuzzy in the open,' said
Dick from his place in the corner.

'Oh, but he's still unimpressed. There he
goes!' said the subaltern, as a bullet struck the
outside of the truck. 'We always have at least one
demonstration against the night-train. Generally
they attack the rear-truck where my junior commands. He gets all the fun of the fair.'

'Not to-night, though! Listen!' said Dick.
A flight of heavy-handed bullets was succeeded
by yelling and shouts. The children of the desert
valued their nightly amusement, and the train was
an excellent mark.

'Is it worth while giving them half a hopper
full?' the subaltern asked of the engine, which
was driven by a Lieutenant of Sappers.

'I should just think so! This is my section of

the line. They'll be playing Old Harry with my permanent way if we don't stop 'em.'

' Right O ! '

' *Hrrmph !* ' said the machine-gun through all its five noses as the subaltern drew the lever home. The empty cartridges clashed on the floor and the smoke blew back through the truck. There was indiscriminate firing at the rear of the train, a return fire from the darkness without and unlimited howling. Dick stretched himself on the floor, wild with delight at the sounds and the smells.

' God is very good—I never thought I'd hear this again. Give 'em hell, men ! Oh, give 'em hell ! ' he cried.

The train stopped for some obstruction on the line ahead and a party went out to reconnoitre, but came back cursing, for spades. The children of the desert had piled sand and gravel on the rails, and twenty minutes were lost in clearing it away. Then the slow progress recommenced, to be varied with more shots, more shoutings, the steady clack and kick of the machine-guns, and a final difficulty with a half-lifted rail ere the train came under the protection of the roaring camp at Tanai-el-Hassan.

' Now you see why it takes an hour and a half to fetch her through,' said the subaltern, unshipping the cartridge-hopper above his pet gun.

' It was a lark, though. I only wish it had lasted twice as long. How superb it must have looked from outside ! ' said Dick, sighing regretfully.

' It palls after the first few nights. By the way, when you've settled about your mules, come and see what we can find to eat in my tent. I'm Bennil of the Gunners—in the Artillery lines—and mind you don't fall over my tent-ropes in the dark.'

But it was all dark to Dick. He could only smell the camels, the hay-bales, the cooking, the smoky fires, and the tanned canvas of the tents, as he stood where he had dropped from the train, shouting for George. There was a sound of light-hearted kicking on the iron skin of the rear trucks, with squealing and grunting. George was unloading the mules.

The engine was blowing off steam nearly in Dick's ear; a cold wind of the desert danced between his legs; he was hungry, and felt tired and dirty—so dirty that he tried to brush his coat with his hands. That was a hopeless job; so he thrust his hands into his pockets and began to count over the many times that he had waited in strange or remote places for trains or camels, mules or horses, to carry him to his business. In those days he could see—few men more clearly—and the spectacle of an armed camp at dinner under the stars was an ever fresh pleasure to the eye. There was colour, light, and motion, without which no man has much pleasure in living. This night there remained for him only one more journey through the darkness that never lifts to tell a man how far he has travelled. Then he would grip Torpenhow's hand again—Torpenhow, who was alive and strong, and lived in the midst of the action that had once made the reputation of a man called Dick Heldar: not in the least to be confused with the blind, bewildered vagabond who seemed to answer to the same name. Yes, he would find Torpenhow, and come as near to the old life as might be. Afterwards he would forget everything: Bessie, who had wrecked the Melancolia and so nearly wrecked his life; Beeton, who lived in a strange unreal city full of tin-tacks and gas-plugs, and matters that no men needed; that irrational being who had offered him love and loyalty for nothing, but had not signed her name; and most of all Maisie, who, from her own point of view, was undeniably right in all she did, but oh, at this distance, so tantalisingly fair.

George's hand on his arm pulled him back to the situation.

'And what now?' said George.

'Oh yes, of course. What now? Take me to the camel-men. Take me to where the scouts sit when they come in from the desert. They sit by their camels, and the camels eat grain out of a black blanket, held up at the corners, and the men eat by their side just like camels. Take me there!'

The camp was rough and rutty, and Dick stumbled many times over the stumps of scrub. The scouts were sitting by their beasts, as Dick knew they would. The light of the dung-fires flickered on their bearded faces, and the camels bubbled and mumbled beside them at rest. It was no part of Dick's policy to go into the desert with a convoy of supplies. That would lead to impertinent questions, and since a blind non-combatant is not needed at the Front, he would probably be forced to return to Suakin. He must go up alone, and go immediately.

'Now for one last bluff—the biggest of all,' he said. 'Peace be with you, brethren!' The watchful George steered him to the circle of the nearest fire. The heads of the camel-sheiks bowed gravely, and the camels, scenting a European, looked sideways curiously like brooding hens, half ready to get to their feet.

'A beast and a driver to go to the fighting-line to-night,' said Dick.

'A Mulaid?' said a voice, scornfully naming the best baggage-breed that he knew.

'A Bisharin,' returned Dick with perfect gravity. 'A Bisharin without saddle-galls. Therefore no charge of thine, shock-head.'

Two or three minutes passed. Then :—

'We be knee-haltered for the night. There is no going out from the camp.'

'Not for money?'

'H'm! Ah! English money?'

Another depressing interval of silence.

'How much?'

'Twenty-five pounds English paid into the hand of the driver at my journey's end, and as much more into the hand of the camel-sheik here, to be paid when the driver returns.'

This was royal payment, and the sheik, who knew that he would get his commission on the deposit, stirred in Dick's behalf.

'For scarcely one night's journey — fifty

pounds. Land and wells and good trees and wives to make a man content for the rest of his days. Who speaks?' said Dick.

'I,' said a voice. 'I will go—but there is no going from the camp.'

'Fool! I know that a camel can break his knee-halter, and the sentries do not fire if one goes in chase. Twenty-five pounds and another twenty-five pounds. But the beast must be a good Bisharin. I will take no baggage-camel.'

Then the bargaining began, and at the end of half an hour the first deposit was paid over to the sheik, who talked in low tones to the driver. Dick heard the latter say; 'A little way out only. Any baggage-beast will serve. Am I a fool to waste my cattle for a blind man?'

'And though I cannot see'—Dick lifted his voice a little—'yet I carry that which has six eyes, and the driver will sit before me. If we do not reach the English troops in the dawn he will be dead.'

'But where, in God's name, are the troops?'

'Unless thou knowest let another man ride. *Dost* thou know? Remember it will be life or death to thee.'

'I know,' said the driver sullenly. 'Stand back from my beast. I am going to slip him.'

'Not so swiftly. George, hold the camel's head a moment. I want to feel his cheek.' The hands wandered over the hide till they found the branded half-circle that is the mark of the Bisharin, the light-built riding-camel. 'That is well. Cut this one loose. Remember no blessing of God comes on those who try to cheat the blind.'

The men chuckled by the fires at the camel-driver's discomfiture. He had intended to substitute a slow, saddle-galled baggage-colt.

' Stand back!' one shouted, lashing the Bisharin under the belly with a quirt. Dick obeyed as soon as he felt the nose-string tighten in his hand,—and a cry went up, ' Illaha! Aho! He is loose.'

With a roar and a grunt the Bisharin rose to his feet and plunged forward towards the desert, his driver following with shouts and lamentation. George caught Dick's arm and hurried him stumbling and tripping past a disgusted sentry who was used to stampeding camels.

' What's the row now?' he cried.

' Every stitch of my kit on that blasted dromedary,' Dick answered, after the manner of a common soldier.

' Go on, and take care your throat's not cut outside—you and your dromedary's.'

The outcries ceased when the camel had disappeared behind a hillock, and his driver had called him back and made him kneel down.

' Mount first,' said Dick. Then climbing into the second seat and gently screwing the pistol muzzle into the small of his companion's back, ' Go on, in God's name, and swiftly. Good-bye, George. Remember me to Madame, and have a good time with your girl. Get forward, child of the Pit!'

A few minutes later he was shut up in a great silence, hardly broken by the creaking of the saddle and the soft pad of the tireless feet. Dick adjusted himself comfortably to the rock and pitch of the pace, girthed his belt tighter, and felt the darkness slide past. For an hour he was conscious only of the sense of rapid progress.

' A good camel,' he said at last.

' He has never been underfed. He is my own and clean bred,' the driver replied.

' Go on.'

His head dropped on his chest and he tried to think, but the tenor of his thoughts was broken because he was very sleepy. In the half-doze it seemed that he was learning a punishment hymn at Mrs. Jennett's. He had committed some crime as bad as Sabbath-breaking, and she had locked him up in his bedroom. But he could never repeat more than the first two lines of the hymn :—

> When Israel of the Lord beloved
> Out of the land of bondage came.

He said them over and over thousands of times. The driver turned in the saddle to see if there were any chance of capturing the revolver and ending the ride. Dick roused, struck him over the head with the butt, and stormed himself wide awake. Somebody hidden in a clump of camel-thorn shouted as the camel toiled up rising ground. A shot was fired, and the silence shut down again, bringing the desire to sleep. Dick could think no longer. He was too tired and stiff and cramped to do more than nod uneasily from time to time, waking with a start and punching the driver with the pistol.

' Is there a moon? ' he asked drowsily.

' She is near her setting.'

' I wish that I could see her. Halt the camel. At least let me hear the desert talk.'

The man obeyed. Out of the utter stillness came one breath of wind. It rattled the dead leaves of a shrub some distance away and ceased. A handful of dry earth detached itself from the edge of a rain-trench and crumbled softly to the bottom.

' Go on. The night is very cold.'

Those who have watched till the morning know how the last hour before the light lengthens itself into many eternities. It seemed to Dick that he had never since the beginning of original darkness done anything at all save jolt through the air. Once in a thousand years he would finger the nail-heads on the saddle-front and count them all carefully. Centuries later he would shift his revolver from his right hand to his left, and allow the eased arm to drop down at his side. From the safe distance of London he was watching himself thus employed,—watching critically. Yet whenever he put out his hand to the canvas that he might paint the tawny yellow desert under the glare of the sinking moon, the black shadow of the camel and the two bowed figures atop, that hand held a revolver and the arm was numbed from wrist to collar-bone. Moreover, he was in the dark, and could see no canvas of any kind whatever.

The driver grunted, and Dick was conscious of a change in the air.

' I smell the dawn,' he whispered.

' It is here, and yonder are the troops. Have I done well? '

The camel stretched out its neck and roared as there came down wind the pungent reek of camels in square.

' Go on. We must get there swiftly. Go on.'

' They are moving in their camp. There is so much dust that I cannot see what they do.'

' Am I in better case? Go forward.'

They could hear the hum of voices ahead, the howling and the bubbling of the beasts and the hoarse cries of the soldiers girthing up for the day. Two or three shots were fired.

' Is that at us? Surely they can see that I am English. Dick spoke angrily.

' Nay, it is from the desert,' the driver answered, cowering in his saddle. ' Go forward, my child ! Well it is that the dawn did not uncover us an hour ago.'

The camel headed straight for the column and the shots behind multiplied. The children of the desert had arranged that most uncomfortable of surprises, a dawn attack for the English troops, and were getting their distance by snap-shots at the only moving object without the square.

' What luck ! What stupendous and imperial luck ! ' said Dick. ' It's " just before the battle, mother." Oh, God has been most good to me ! Only '—the agony of the thought made him screw up his eyes for an instant—' Maisie . . .'

' Allahu ! We are in,' said the man, as he drove into the rearguard and the camel knelt.

'Who the deuce are you? Despatches or what? What's the strength of the enemy behind that ridge? How did you get through?' asked a dozen voices. For all answer Dick took a long breath, unbuckled his belt, and shouted from the saddle at the top of a wearied and dusty voice, 'Torpenhow! Ohé, Torp! Coo-ee, Tor-pen-how.'

A bearded man raking in the ashes of a fire for a light to his pipe moved very swiftly towards that cry, as the rearguard, facing about, began to fire at the puffs of smoke from the hillocks around. Gradually the scattered white cloudlets drew out into long lines of banked white that hung heavily in the stillness of the dawn before they turned over wave-like and glided into the valleys. The soldiers in the square were coughing and swearing as their own smoke obstructed their view, and they edged forward to get beyond it. A wounded camel leaped to its feet and roared aloud, the cry ending in a bubbling grunt. Some one had cut its throat to prevent confusion. Then came the thick sob of a man receiving his death-wound from a bullet; then a yell of agony and redoubled firing.

There was no time to ask any questions.

'Get down, man! Get down behind the camel!'

'No. Put me, I pray, in the forefront of the battle.' Dick turned his face to Torpenhow and raised his hand to set his helmet straight, but, miscalculating the distance, knocked it off. Torpenhow saw that his hair was grey on the temples, and that his face was the face of an old man.

'Come down, you damned fool! Dickie, come off!'

And Dick came obediently, but as a tree falls, pitching sideways from the Bisharin's saddle at Torpenhow's feet. His luck had held to the last, even to the crowning mercy of a kindly bullet through his head.

Torpenhow knelt under the lee of the camel, with Dick's body in his arms.

THE END

ℛ

£2.99

6B/22

THE LIGHT THAT FAILED

RUDYARD KIPLING

The Centenary Edition

THE LIGHT
THAT FAILED

BY

RUDYARD KIPLING

This book is copyright in all countries which
are signatories to the Berne Convention

ISBN (cased) 0 333 32803 5
ISBN (paper) 0 333 32804 3

MACMILLAN LONDON LIMITED
London and Basingstoke

Associated companies in Auckland, Dallas,
Delhi, Dublin, Hong Kong, Johannesburg,
Lagos, Manzini, Melbourne, Nairobi,
New York, Singapore, Tokyo, Washington
and Zaria

First edition March 1891
Reprinted April, July, December 1891, 1892, 1895, 1896, 1897,
1898, 1899, 1900, 1903, 1906, 1908, 1909, 1911, 1912, 1913,
1916, 1918, 1920, 1922, 1925, 1929, 1935, 1941, 1943
Library (Centenary) Edition 1951
Centenary Edition (n.s.) 1981
Paperback edition 1982

Printed in Great Britain by
St Edmundsbury Press
Bury St Edmunds, Suffolk